SMOKE SIGNAL

RACHEL HATCH BOOK FOUR

L.T. RYAN

with
BRIAN SHEA

LIQUID MIND MEDIA

Copyright © 2020 by L.T. Ryan, Liquid Mind Media, LLC, & Brian Christopher Shea. All rights reserved. No part of this publication may be copied, reproduced in any format, by any means, electronic or otherwise, without prior consent from the copyright owner and publisher of this book. This is a work of fiction. All characters, names, places and events are the product of the author's imagination or used fictitiously. For information contact:

contact@ltryan.com

http://LTRyan.com

https://www.facebook.com/JackNobleBooks

THE RACHEL HATCH SERIES

Drift

Downburst

Fever Burn

Smoke Signal

Firewalk

Whitewater

Aftershock

Whirlwind

Tsunami

Fastrope

Sidewinder (Coming Soon)

RACHEL HATCH SHORT STORIES

Fractured

Proving Ground

The Gauntlet

Join the LT Ryan reader family & receive a free copy of the Rachel Hatch story, Fractured. Click the link below to get started:

https://ltryan.com/rachel-hatch-newsletter-signup-1

Love Hatch? Noble? Maddie? Cassie? Get your very own Jack Noble merchandise today! Click the link below to find coffee mugs, t-shirts, and even signed copies of your favorite L.T. Ryan thrillers! https://ltryan.ink/EvG_

ONE

WAITING WAS THE HARDEST PART. *PATIENCE IS WHAT SEPARATES AVERAGE FROM greatness.* Billy Nighthawk's grandfather's wisdom came to mind as it always did during times like this. In his youth, the lessons had been hard fought. *Little Hawk, you're as thick as the fog,* he'd say. It had taken him until adulthood for it to make sense. But the fog of understanding had lifted. And those lessons learned had served him well.

He'd been lying under the spiny branches of a gray horsebush for several hours. The shrub looked like dried coral turned gray. The ground was damp, as morning thawed from the past night's dip in temperature. He had remained unmoving for the last several hours, even as the dampness soaked into his legs, through his thick, winter-lined jeans. His surroundings came into focus as the sky slowly brightened. Billy looked through the eyepiece of the binoculars, scanning the horizon for a sign of the two men.

In the distance, about three hundred meters away, he saw movement. The rubber eyecups pressed lightly against his leathery skin as he gently toggled the Bushnell's center focusing lever, bringing the enhanced image into clarity.

He blinked his eyes, trying to clear his vision. Maybe it was the cold start to the morning or the two days of tracking, and his mind was beginning to play tricks on him. Billy did a double take of a cluster of tightly woven chokecherry shrubs jutting out from behind a boulder of rock. The animal dipped its head low, skulking beneath a low hanging branch. Cheetah-like black spots dotted the fur lining the sleek muscular body of the big cat. At first glance, he thought it was a bobcat. With a flick of its tail, he realized, to his surprise, he was wrong. The end of his short tail was completely black, as if it had been dipped in tar. The lynx's subtle physical differences made it unique. Feathered tufts of hair protruding from the top of its ears and the Fu Manchu beard gave the majestic beast an air of wisdom.

In his culture, the lynx was believed to be the seer of secrets. And on the night of his passage into manhood, it had been his spirit animal.

Billy hadn't thought about that day in a long time. The return of the memory seemed fitting. It had been a day similar to this where the sky was gray and the ground was still cold from a late spring thaw. As was tradition, he'd spent the previous twenty-four hours in a fasted, detoxified state. He remembered the solemn look on his father's face when he was brought to the sweat lodge.

The lodge itself was not much to look at. It was set away from houses just beyond a slight rise in the land. A small hill blocked it from view of the other homes on the reservation, giving it a sense of isolation. Each family approached the use of the lodge in slightly different ways. In Billy's family, the tradition had been clearly laid out by prior generations. Only for the men. And the first time was when a Nighthawk turned sixteen.

The lodge was a place of transcendence and transformation. A connection to Mother Earth. Although, at the time, Billy hadn't taken the spiritual journey seriously, at least, in the beginning.

He remembered the stone lined pathway leading up to the lodge. The opening to the domed-shaped structure faced east, a purposeful connection to the rising of the sun, to new beginnings. Three paces from the opening was a wooden post with the cleaned skull of a bear affixed to the top, a marker set to warn of the danger.

Billy had entered the sweat lodge led by his grandfather and father. The withes of aspen were lashed together by rawhide to shape the deerskin dome. The opening was only a few feet high and each entrant needed to dip to a crawl when entering, forcing each to supplicate themselves in a gesture of humility.

The cramped space, only fifteen feet in diameter, was quickly filled by the three men. Billy's grandfather presided, beginning the ceremony with the passing of the chanupa, or peace pipe. The stones were heated, and each man's cheeks were then smudged with smoldering sage. The fire-heated stones glowed red as the flap dropped closed, shrouding them in relative darkness. The heat was intense, and Billy remembered sweating even before the stones were set in place.

Billy's grandfather, one of the reservation's esteemed elders, set the four large red-hot stones in a tight circle in the center of the lodge. He placed the first stone toward the west and worked in clockwork fashion until all four were in place.

Then came the water. As Billy's grandfather ladled the cool water onto the stones, an intense steam filled the confines of the space, swallowing the oxygen. Billy remembered the initial sense of panic. He'd never admitted it to anyone, but he was claustrophobic, and the experience had tested his resolve. Billy remembered fighting the urge to push his way out of the lodge. And then he remembered the moment when he relented and gave in to the power of the sweat. He breathed in the steam as his mind drifted.

The ceremony consisted of four rounds, or endurances. At the conclusion of each, Billy was given the opportunity to leave the sweat lodge and cool himself. He didn't. His grandfather and father didn't, and so neither did he.

At the onset of the third endurance, Billy remembered his frustration. He'd heard the stories from friends and relatives about the spirit walk. The connection made along the Red Road, the spiritual connection to the east, to wisdom. But Billy felt no sense of enlightenment. He'd found no spirit guide. And his sixteen years of buildup to this moment seemed a fanciful dream.

Then, as the fourth and final round began, something happened. Billy's grandfather's face shifted before his eyes. At first, the change was a flicker. Billy blinked hard. As the steam rose, his grandfather's long salt and pepper hair was now that of a lynx. His glowing eyes penetrated deep into

Billy's soul. Billy stared into the shimmering gold, and in that moment came a clarity unlike any other.

As the flap to the lodge opened and cool air washed over his bare chest, Billy Nighthawk knew his purpose in life, and he'd been following it ever since. It was what brought him here. In the thick cloud of the lodge, he had committed his life to protecting the people of his tribe. And that meant the animals of their land. Seeing the lynx, here and now, felt like a connection to his beginning.

Besides the flickering image of this majestic wildcat, Billy had only seen one other in his entire lifetime. It was a rare find, even rarer now in these parts. In the late '90s, due to the endangerment of the species and potential extinction, several of the rare cats were released into the San Juan Mountain Range, extending from southwestern Colorado into New Mexico. They'd been hunted and killed for sport previously, but since the humanitarian efforts, their population had been protected. Even with all of the efforts made to protect them, they were still rare, still endangered. There were believed to be less than two hundred and fifty left in the area. Seeing one now was like finding a diamond in the rough. He took a moment to absorb the majestic beauty of this rare beast.

Its head suddenly canted slightly and looked, not at him, but off to the left of him. The cat lowered itself slightly, as if ducking from view. Billy took one last look through the scoped lenses of the binoculars and silently said goodbye to the creature, knowing that it might not be there when he returned his gaze.

After making his silent goodbye, he slowly guided the binoculars over the rough and rugged terrain, looking for what spooked the lynx.

It took more time than he liked before he was able to pinpoint the target of the lynx's focused gaze. Off to the left, equidistant to him from the animal, was a heavyset man in a thick camouflaged jacket. A strange triangle of man and beast formed. Each in a different role, one as a protector, the other endangered, and the worst, the man who was preparing to break laws of both man and nature.

The large hunter was tucked neatly alongside a tree, his camouflage atypical for a hunter. Bright orange disregarded in lieu of military fatigues. He paid Billy no mind, focusing down the scope of his long-barreled rifle.

Before he could shout, the deafening crack of the rifle interrupted the silent peace, causing him to flinch. Gunshots rarely had that effect on him, having spent years around them and being an avid hunter himself. But this was different. This was something he had come to prevent. This was something he was supposed to stop from happening.

The world spun as his binoculars traced the direction of the shot back toward the lynx. He made a silent prayer that the cat had reacted to some noise prior to the pull of the trigger, that he had heard it, anticipated it, and in doing so escaped the impact of the high velocity round.

Billy scanned the area where the cat had once been, where he had locked eyes once again with his spirit guide, memorizing the detail and uniqueness of its face, but it wasn't there. A wave of relief crashed over him, and he exhaled loudly, suddenly aware he'd been holding his breath.

He'd finally caught up to the hunter he'd been tracking for over a day, and although he had gotten the shot off, it looked as though he had thankfully missed.

Billy began to rise up from his position when he heard the strangest sound. A wailing, pitchy, like a broken siren, echoed out of the distance ahead. Whatever calm he'd experienced in the split seconds following the shot after not seeing the animal was dashed completely.

He repositioned himself. The wail rose up again. The noise of it caused him to jump as much as the rifle shot had, maybe more so. Each pitched wail was like a knife in his heart. And then he saw it.

The lynx hobbled out from the other side of the rock. It took a few staggered steps and collapsed to the ground. Its hind legs kicked as if trying to run, like a dog in sleep, dreaming of a big open field. It kicked three times before all movement stopped. No more sounds, no more cries filled the air.

He set the binoculars down as the shock and fear and sadness gave way to anger, both at himself for not reacting quick enough, but more, at the man responsible.

Billy shifted again, this time scanning back across the uneven terrain to the camouflaged figure moving forward. The solitary hunter stalked closer, his weapon at the ready. He watched as he crossed the distance from where he'd taken the shot to the animal. *Where's his partner?* There had been two of them. That he was sure of.

Billy rose up from his hiding position and unholstered the revolver at his side. He stepped forward slowly, using the trees as cover and knowing that two men who had apparently broken the hunting laws might not be reasonable when confronted by law enforcement.

He moved carefully. Billy knew this land well. These men had desecrated the ground on which he walked.

About twenty feet away, he could hear the hunter clear his throat.

"Would you look at that?" the hunter said to himself.

Ten feet away now, he was close. He could smell him; a combination of day-old liquor circulated in the air around him. Not only did he just hunt and kill a protected animal, but he had done it drunk. Rage, a blinding red, the kind of anger that defies reason, took hold. The kind of anger that throws a person into action without thoughts of recourse.

Billy stepped out into view and leveled his gun at the thick-chested hunter.

"Drop your weapon," he said. His voice was steady, but he fought to control his nerves. It had been a long time since he'd pointed his gun at somebody, longer since he'd pulled the trigger. Although the thought of it now, seeing the dead animal down near their feet, seemed more reasonable, more appropriate and more just.

"Whoa now there, Sheriff," the large-framed hunter said. He raised his rifle up, but in a way that looked like he was yielding. Both hands went up around his chest area, and he took a few steps back.

"I said, drop your weapon. Do it now!"

The hunter lowered it but didn't drop it.

Billy looked down at the animal. Its patterned fur was matted with dark blood. He felt the tingle of adrenaline coursing through his veins, and even with all the willpower he mustered, the end of his gun trembled slightly.

"Why don't we just go on about our business here, chief, and we'll call it a day? You go your way, and we'll go ours."

"Not going to happen." His voice choked up a bit, his steely nerves beginning to disintegrate. The hunter still hadn't dropped his rifle. He was refusing to drop his weapon and was now bartering with him, as if he had some kind of leverage. "Don't make this any worse than it is."

"Like I said, boss, let's go our separate ways." The baritone of the larger man who reeked of whiskey seemed calm. "We were out here just hunting, minding our own business."

"You don't have permission to be here. Plus, you just shot an endangered species."

The hunter threw his hands up again, this time the rifle coming up a little higher. "Well, I don't right reckon I knew that when I pulled the trigger. Thought I was killing me a bobcat."

"You thought wrong. And you're hunting on reservation land." Billy eyed the man carefully and took in his pasty white complexion. "And from the looks of it, you two don't seem much like you belong on the reservation to begin with."

"Is that some type of racist comment?"

"Just an observation. Why don't you throw me your hunting permits?"

The hunter nodded and lowered the weapon to his side. He smiled.

It took Billy a second to realize that the hunter wasn't smiling at him. He was looking just past him.

Billy spun as the wooden buttstock crashed down on the base of his skull. The blow sent ice down his spine, and his legs buckled. Everything flickered dark as his face struck the cold dirt of the ground. He fought to remain conscious as his mind swirled. He felt a tugging of his arms, but he was incapable of mounting any resistance.

"Make sure it's tight," came the muffled voice of the big hunter.

Billy's vision cleared, but the searing pain pulsing from the back of his head increased. His arms were bound behind his back at the wrists. He looked up to see the skinny, shorter hunter standing above him. Billy felt sick when he saw his duty revolver in the hand of the man who'd just incapacitated him.

The skinnier man then walked the few feet over to the dead animal and knelt. "That's the strangest damn mountain lion I ever did see." His voice was like a bunch of rusty screws rattling around in a tin can, screechy and intolerable.

The larger hunter looked down at the dead animal, and then in a deep, baritone voice said, "That's because that ain't no mountain lion. That there is a lynx."

"You don't say?"

"It looks like we might've just made ourselves some extra money today."

"What do you think it will fetch?"

"Enough."

The answer seemed to satisfy the skinnier, screechy-voiced man. The smaller man's beady eyes seemed disproportionately larger than his face. It was almost cartoonish, as if he were a life size version of Gollum from *The Lord of the Rings*. He then turned his attention from the animal back to Billy, tapping the end of Billy's revolver on the rocky ground. "What do we do about him?"

"He's a problem," the bigger hunter said, rubbing his chin. "He's seen our faces. Not sure we have much choice."

Billy tried to speak out in his defense.

The Gollum stood and cocked back the revolver, putting it into single action. The sound caused Billy to lose his train of thought.

The bigger of the two then stepped in front, blocking him. "No. Not like that. I've got a better idea." He disappeared from view.

Billy tried to twist his head to follow the larger hunter, but any movement was met with a searing pain. There was a strange tingle over his extremities. Panic filled him. He worried the blow to his head might've done some damage to his spine. Hard to tell from his bound position.

The big man returned, filling Billy's field of vision.

"What's that?" Gollum squeaked.

"My momma used to make the most delicious jam from these berries."

A split second later, a thin branch with dark berries wafted in front of Billy's face. The big hunter teasingly tickled the end of his nose with one of the leaves.

"I don't get it," screeched the thinner hunter.

"The berries of the chokecherry are edible. The seeds are not. The seeds contain cyanide."

Gollum's eyes grew wider, which seemed an impossibility. And Billy did not like what he saw in them.

A moment later, berry after berry were forcibly being shoved into his mouth. Billy fought to keep his jaw locked but found he could offer little in the way of resistance to the large hunter's enormous hands. He was either going to suffocate or swallow the berries. Survival instinct overrode resistance, and he swallowed the berries, seeds and all. He lost count. Not that it would matter anyway. He had no idea how many he'd eaten or how many it would take to reach a lethal dose.

The force feeding stopped as abruptly as it began. Billy spat the tart remnants into the dirt. The two hunters left him and returned to their kill.

His gut twisted into a knot. A pain resonated from his stomach to his chest cavity. Each beat of his heart pounded like a war drum, the cadence increasing exponentially. A disorienting punch of pain knocked the wind out of him. His vision clouded as if he were back in the sweat lodge.

He couldn't breathe from the pain of it, surging, radiating outward from the center of his chest. He reached for the blade in his boot, trying to pull it free in a last-ditch effort. The end of the bone handle was just out of reach when the big man stepped in, pressing his dirty boot against the side of his face, pushing hard, turning his head to the right. The claustrophobia welled up inside him as he lay gasping.

Billy locked eyes with the dead lynx as he slipped into darkness.

TWO

This time, the bump and skip landing of the small aircraft as it touched down on the concrete tarmac of the Durango-La Plata Airport didn't come with the same sense of anxiety as it had the last time when returning after a fifteen-year absence. Although, that's not to say she was completely comfortable either.

Hatch was now nervous on a different front. It was initially hard connecting with her niece and nephew after having spent their entire childhood apart. Now, with their newfound relationship established, a different pressure mounted. Living up to their expectations unnerved her.

Up until this point in her life, Hatch only had to look out for herself or her teammates. She'd emotionally disconnected from others, particularly her family. All that had changed. And with change comes adaptation. Adapt and overcome. A mantra repeated throughout her time in the service. Resetting to an acceptable normal might prove to be the biggest obstacle for Hatch to overcome. That was saying a lot.

She'd taken Jabari's advice to heart, the African soldier who had proved himself every bit as worthy as any of her American counterparts. The saying he wished upon her, "When there is no enemy within, the enemies outside cannot hurt you." There was beauty in its simplicity. Hatch gave serious thought to the hope that in closing the chapter on her father's death, she would be capable of finding peace. A lifetime of war weighed heavily against her odds of achieving this, but it was worth a shot.

She set her sights on her family, on building a new sense of normal in the hometown she'd long since abandoned. Landing in Durango, she was again entering into uncharted territory. Her new role as an aunt would require her to take on a motherly figure for the children who had lost both mother and father within a few years of each other, both to tragedy. Motherhood frightened Hatch more than staring down the barrel of a loaded gun.

Beyond the children, Hatch was going to need to resume her role as a daughter herself. Mending the long-severed bond with her mother would be a daunting task. So many years stretched between them. Even though Hatch uncovered the truth about her father's death, the distance forged in its wake left their relationship in tattered shreds. Hatch wasn't totally certain she would be able to put to rest all of those feelings. The distance she'd put between her mother and herself over the years since leaving home and joining the Army was unfillable. It would be a true test of Hatch's strength, will power, and ultimately her humility. *Can I let go of the past in the hopes of a better future?* Hatch wondered, though she did not know the answer.

The pilot made the announcement of their arrival, updating gate and baggage claim information in a delivery akin to a weekend anchorman. Hatch listened on autopilot as she absentmindedly rubbed her fingers across the raised web of scars extending from beneath her short-sleeved shirt and down to her wrist. An acceptance of self was the other wisdom she took with her from her experience in Africa.

She'd learned it from the gregarious cafe owner, Khari, who'd been burned on half of his face, and yet seemed unfazed by it. His courage had given Hatch the strength to not hide her damaged right arm anymore. The looks she got and the questions asked no longer forced her into hiding. She exposed herself wholly and completely to the judging eyes of those around her.

In unveiling herself, and no longer hiding behind long-sleeve shirts, Hatch felt the burden lift. It was as if exposing the scar to the light of day had helped burn away some of the memory of what had caused it, the firefight that had left her maimed. The same battle had taken the lives of some of her dearest and closest friends. A moment in time that forever changed the course and direction of Hatch's life.

As she waited for the plane to taxi to a halt, she realized that all the roads of her life led here. Every step taken had been a long journey back home.

The passengers deplaned. Hatch headed down the metal stairwell that extended out of the fuselage to the white concrete below. She picked up her duffle bag from a line of carry-on suitcases and shouldered it. Hatch then proceeded with the shuffle of people into the airport's main space. It was small and didn't take her long to navigate her way past the baggage claim to the arrival area.

Up ahead, maybe forty feet in front of her, Hatch saw the ponytail flop in the air as Daphne leapt up and down, bobbing her head from side to side.

Catching sight of Hatch, Daphne squealed with delight. The excited fervor of the little girl drew the attention of a few nearby travelers. Daphne broke into a sprint, dashing toward Hatch at full speed.

Hatch, upon seeing this, began picking up her pace as well, taking up a slow jog. She accidently bumped shoulders with a thin man of almost equal height, nearly knocking him over. She caught him by the arm and kept him upright as she offered an apology. The man's stern face softened slightly at seeing the approaching child.

Her heart raced as she caught another glimpse of the girl zigzagging her way toward her. It hadn't been that long since the two had last seen each other, but much had changed, at least for Hatch.

And yet, even though the passage of time had been minimal, Daphne seemed to have aged. The trauma of her mother's death and the chaos that had followed undoubtedly left a mark no amount of time could completely heal. Nothing seemed to be able to diminish the light in the girl's eyes, however, and her infectious nature continued to shine brightly.

Hatch slowed to a walk as Daphne increased her speed, closing the distance rapidly. Only a few feet away, Hatch dropped to her knees, throwing aside the duffle to her left and outstretching her arms wide.

Daphne filled the void. Hatch absorbed her niece's delicate frame into hers with a swoop of her arms. Daphne's ponytail whipped wildly about as she peppered the cheek and neck of Hatch with a barrage of kisses. She giggled wildly, squealing in excitement.

"Auntie Rachel, Auntie Rachel, I cannot believe you're home," she said, loud enough for anyone inside the airport to hear.

"I missed you, too," Hatch said.

Daphne ratcheted down her hug even tighter around Hatch's neck.

"Where's Jacob?" Hatch asked.

"He's over there," Daphne said, releasing her death grip on Hatch's neck.

Hatch stood, taking the girl by the hand, almost forgetting her duffle in the excitement. The two nearly skipped back to where Hatch's mother and nephew stood side by side. This time, Jake didn't duck behind his grandmother and hide. He was different now.

Jake had shown a rare kind of bravery several months back, a bravery that enabled Hatch to get the upper hand in a dire situation. That act had christened the ten-year-old into early manhood. Although he was still just a boy, certain things in life cause you to grow up faster. He seemed to have grown from the experience during her absence and looked a bit taller than she remembered.

He broke free from his grandmother's gentle hand resting on his shoulders and ran to Hatch. A boy not accustomed to overt gestures of happiness and kindness, Hatch was caught off guard, but in a good way. The surprise was an amazing gift. She didn't have to bend as low to take his hug but did so anyway. Taking a knee brought her eye to eye with the boy. "You look good, Jake."

"Thanks. I've been practicing again, too."

He held up his arm in front of Hatch. The cast was off, and he proudly displayed his arm, the one broken in the car accident. He turned it as if showing off a new toy.

Hatch grabbed his arm and ran her finger across the bone. She could feel the slight bump where the bone had snapped. She then gave a playful squeeze of the boy's bicep. "You're getting strong." Hatch stood, kissed him on the forehead and bent down to grab her bag.

She walked over to her mother, who seemed overwhelmingly happy to see Hatch. It was such a difference from the last time they had met in this airport. That awkward arrival seemed like a lifetime ago. Those versions of Hatch and her mother, Jasmine, no longer existed. What this was, what their relationship had evolved into, was still in its infancy.

Hatch stood still for a moment. A new awkwardness presented itself as they entered this unfamiliar territory, a relationship still budding. *Do we hug? Shake hands? Just wave hello? What was the protocol for somebody trying to reconnect?*

She didn't know, nor did she care. Hatch dismissed her insecurity and put her arm around her mother, pulling her close. She felt her mom release a gasp. This impromptu hug dissolved whatever angst lay hidden, and she felt the tension in her mother's body ease with the droop of her shoulders.

"We're so glad you're home," Jasmine Hatch whispered. "We can talk later, but I hope you'll be staying for a while."

"I don't plan on going anywhere anytime soon," Hatch said.

THREE

Hatch had spent the last several hours reacclimating herself to her family. Each came with their own unique share time. Daphne got first dibs, taking Hatch by the hand and guiding her up to her room as soon as they arrived home. The chrysalis nestled inside a small terrarium on her bedroom dresser was the most important thing in the soon-to-be seven-year-old's life. On the wall behind the glass encasement were dozens of handmade drawings. The anticipation of the butterfly's pending transformation was captured in vibrant colors and designs.

Jake couldn't wait to show her some of the new moves he'd learned at his karate school during her absence. He had learned the way to swivel his hips to deliver a more devastating impact with his kicks. Hatch could tell he'd been practicing extra hard. The boy's movements were clean and precise. He demonstrated how a variety of different kicks were performed. Jake was able to chamber his knee and thrust out with surprising force for a boy his age. Hatch held her palm open as a target. She was confident the boy would develop into quite a fighter. The life and death incident that forced Jake to play the role of hero had forever changed him.

The last blow she'd absorbed with the palm of her hand struck with such ferocity that it still tingled minutes after his demonstration ended. It tingled now as she held onto the porcelain mug her mother had handed her. Even though it was midday, the piping hot coffee was refreshing.

Her mom's special brew. The one Dalton Savage had become addicted to during her short stint as a member of the Hawk's Landing Sheriff's Office. Thinking about Savage, she had told him she wouldn't be arriving until the following day. She didn't feel good about the lie, but she had needed some time to settle in before meeting up. In reality, she wasn't sure what she would say to the man. She wasn't sure about the status of their relationship. If there even was such a thing. *Were they more than friends?* Some things had been hinted at but never spoken aloud. Savage had pleaded with her to return to Hawk's Landing, telling her it might be her chance at a normal life. Did normal mean something more? Maybe the old adage was true, and her absence had made her heart grow fonder.

She had the answers to none of these questions, but after setting foot back in Hawk's Landing, Hatch couldn't imagine going a full day without seeing him. She had thought she would need time to settle in and collect herself before seeing the lawman's face again. After only a few hours, she'd given up any resistance to the idea. The thought of seeing him called to her like a lighthouse beacon.

She wasn't ready yet to speak to her mother about what she had been through in her absence. The things Hatch uncovered regarding the murder of her father and the closure she gained for her family was a conversation best left for when the children weren't around. Hatch wasn't completely sure how much she would share with her mother, but she planned to tell her enough to provide her closure. Hatch owed her that much.

After finishing her cup of coffee and enjoying some small talk with her mother, Hatch decided she would spend a little time visiting with Savage.

"Auntie Rachel, you just got here." Daphne's shoulders slumped as Hatch made her way to the door.

"I know, sweetheart, but I'll be right back. I've just got to stop over and see an old friend."

"You're going to see Dalton," she said in a sing-song way.

Hatch blushed slightly at the child's ability to read her so easily.

Dismissing the teasing, Hatch bent low and kissed her niece on the forehead. "I'll be back before you know it."

Hatch walked from the house out into the crisp clean Colorado air.

She surveyed her transportation options. There was only one. Hatch was forced to drive the raggedy old Chevy Astro van. She missed the beat-up F-150, but it had been totaled in the car crash that had left Jake's arm broken. The insurance claim had been quick and painless, but Hatch hadn't used the check for the total loss to purchase a replacement vehicle. At the time she didn't have any plans for sticking around on a long-term basis, but now things were different, and she put finding a new car on her mental list of things to do.

The van's engine whirred to a start. She drove down the winding dirt driveway to the main road. Hatch stopped at the bottom and stared for a moment at the boulder. The two identical handprints, faded with time, of her and Olivia. Like a phantom limb, Hatch still felt her sister as she drove away and headed into town.

ONCE ON THE MAIN ROAD, IT WASN'T LONG BEFORE HATCH WAS PULLING TO a stop in front of the sheriff's department. She sat in the van for a moment. Her heart rate increased. She took two quick breaths and loosened her death grip on the steering wheel, alleviating the white of her knuckles. *Why am I so nervous?* Hatch was angry at herself. Deep down she knew the answer but didn't allow herself to hear it.

She stepped out of the car and made her way into the main lobby where she saw a familiar face seated behind the bullet-resistant plexiglass. Receptionist, administrative assistant, and heart of the Hawk's Landing Sheriff's Office, Barbara Wright sat tending to her duties.

Wright looked up from a stack of paperwork. Seeing Hatch approach, a smile brightened her face as she set aside the papers. "Well, looky here, Rachel Hatch alive and in person!" Barbara's voice was sweet. Everything about the woman was kindness personified. Her eyes, her smile, the gentle way in which she spoke to every person who entered or left the building.

Hatch felt at home seeing her. This place, this town, it all felt right again. Like her world had been spun on its axle, righting itself.

"You look great Barbara."

She swatted at the compliment with her hand as if shooing a fly. "Oh, don't flatter me, sweetheart. I'm closer to the end than I am the start."

"Lies," Hatch said.

"And I know you're not here to see me."

"Sure, I am," Hatch said, a little more defensively than she intended.

"He's in back in the briefing room. Everybody is. Well—except for me. I'm guarding the fort," she said with a smile. Then she reached over and picked something up off her desk. Hatch laughed out loud at seeing the bronzed three-hole punch. At the base of it was a plaque that read, "The Cramer Club."

Barbara set it back on her desk as an enormous paperweight, patted it gently, and then smiled. "Best gift I've ever gotten in my forty years of working here."

The Cramer Club, the three-hole punch used to save the life of both Hatch and Savage when Donald Cramer, former deputy and now prison inmate, had held them at bay in an armed standoff. It had been Barbara who had rushed to their aid. Wielding the three-hole punch had rendered the man unconscious, saving their lives. Savage, or one of the others, had bronzed it and gifted it to her. A wonderful memento for a courageous act and a courageous woman.

The door to her left buzzed, which was followed by a metallic click, announcing its unlocking. Hatch walked over and pulled it open. She entered the short hallway, passing a bathroom on the left and the cubicle stations for the deputies' office space located to the right. Up ahead on the left was Savage's office. Around the corner, another hall led back to the holding cells and interview rooms and down into the sally port area. In the same corridor was a small conference room used for roll call briefings.

Hatch walked up to the conference door that was partially closed. The murmur of a solitary voice became clear as she moved closer. It was the familiar deep-throated voice of Dalton Savage. "This is going to be on an assistance only basis since it's technically out of our jurisdiction. We've been given approval by the Tribal Council to assist, but we are strictly operating in a support capacity. Do you guys understand?"

Hatch, not wanting to interrupt, stood in the hallway. Even though she was separated by the door, Hatch was convinced she caught a hint of Savage's distinct scent. Black licorice.

Through the gap in the door, she could see the slender frame of the rookie deputy, Kevin Littleton. He met her gaze and raised his eyebrows.

Littleton pointed toward the door where Hatch was standing. The distraction stopped Savage's speech dead in its tracks.

Hatch, figuring there was no point in delaying the inevitable, opened the door.

As it swung wide, Savage dropped a marker he was holding and then fumbled on the floor for a moment as he retrieved it. He came up red-faced, either from his sudden lurch forward or embarrassment. Impossible to tell. His blue eyes, salt and pepper hair and strong jawline hadn't changed a bit in her absence.

He wore the buttoned-down cream-colored shirt with the silver star badge above the pocket. A pair of neatly fitted blue jeans completed the rural lawman's uniform.

"Hatch?" Savage stammered, then looked at his watch. "I thought you weren't going to be here till tomorrow."

"Yeah, change of plans." Hatch figured at some point she'd explain, but didn't feel here and now was the time, or maybe there wouldn't come a time at all. She arrived early and that would be good enough for now. "I just got settled in back home. Sorry to interrupt."

"No need to apologize. I was just finishing up. We're helping out the Southern Ute Reservation. They've had an incident, and we're going to be assisting."

"An incident?" Hatch asked.

"A death."

"Murder?"

Savage shrugged. "I don't know yet. I have very little to go on."

"Then why are you being called in? Don't they have their own police?"

"They do," Savage said. "The victim is their police chief."

Hatch's eyes widened just a bit. Then she scanned the room.

Littleton and Becky Sinclair were present, but she didn't recognize the third man. There was a new face in a sheriff's uniform. He had jet black hair and tan skin along his taut jawline that pulsed with each clench of his teeth. His arms were tightly folded, the muscles of his exposed forearms were like coiled rope. Hatch guessed him to be in his early 20s, but the young deputy had a seriousness to him that made him seem much older.

"Hatch, meet our newest member. This is John Nighthawk."

Hatch nodded. "Like the lake?"

"My people," Nighthawk said quietly with a reserved confidence.

Nighthawk Lake held a different significance for Hatch. It was where her dead sister's body had been dumped. She pushed the thought from her mind.

"Nice to meet you, John."

"Likewise."

Hatch turned to Savage. "I'll leave you to it. I just wanted to let you know I was in town."

"No. Wait," Savage said. "Seriously—I was just finishing up. We're going to be heading out to the reservation shortly, but I've got a couple of minutes."

Savage then turned back to the trio of deputies. "Make sure you have plenty of gloves and bags for collecting evidence. We're going to assist in any way we can. Be prepared for anything that's asked of us."

The group started to clear the room, the three deputies and Savage making up the entire law enforcement contingent of Hawk's Landing.

Littleton, a little less sheepish than she'd remembered, passed by and gave her a pat on the back. Sinclair gave a quick hug. Nighthawk was the last to pass by. He gave Savage a solemn nod before moving out into the main space.

Once alone in the conference room, Savage whispered. "The other reason we're helping is that the dead tribesman is Nighthawk's father."

"I come back into town and things go all topsy-turvy."

"Well, hopefully it's not a homicide," Savage said. "There's no gunshot or stab wounds. We're going to be looking at other possible causes. Maybe it was a heart attack? They want to be thorough, and being that he's law enforcement, they wanted us to oversee it to make sure they didn't miss anything. I think they're just really kind of caught off guard by it and are looking for us to be a sounding board."

Savage made his way past her, brushing his arm against hers. The gentle warmth of his body reminded her of the time she'd fallen asleep next to him.

Hatch followed him, bathed in the sweet smell of licorice trailing him.

They sat down in his office, and before Hatch could say anything, Savage opened a drawer and pulled out a badge. The same badge he had given her on a temporary assignment when he had deputized her to assist in her sister's death investigation.

"I told you when you left, this badge would be here for you when you got back. Is this something you're still interested in? I know on the phone you didn't give me an answer. Do you have one now?"

Hatch looked at the badge and then at the man holding it.

"I don't. I wish I did, but it's not that simple."

"One thing I've come to accept is, with you, nothing's ever simple," Savage said, a smile creasing the corners of his eyes.

"I know you were hoping for one, but I—"

Savage held up a hand. "No need to apologize. I told you there's no expiration on my offer. As long as I'm Sheriff, it stands."

"Well, it looks like you filled Cramer's position."

He nodded. "Nighthawk's been a great addition. Smart kid. Probably, and don't repeat this, he's the best person I have on my team right now. He's got that natural talent for seeing details others miss. I've got high hopes for that one."

Hatch was silent. She heard Savage but was still in a mental deliberation about the offer. She had thought about it a lot since it was first made.

"I don't know about the badge. Let me get settled in, and then I'll have an answer for you."

"Fair enough. I don't want to push, but if you take this badge this time, it can't be on a temporary basis. You'd have to go through the academy, and when you finish, which I will have no doubt that you would pass with flying colors, then you'd be assigned here with me." He put the badge back in the drawer. "How about we talk more about it when you have some time? Let me get a feel for this situation over on the reservation, and then

I'll give you a call later. Maybe we can meet up tonight or sometime tomorrow."

Hatch stood. "I'd like that. I'd like that a lot."

As Hatch walked toward the front door, the deputies made their way out the back. She said goodbye to Barbara and left.

Hatch sat in the Astro van, lost in a moment of thought. As she pulled out, the caravan of Suburban police vehicles pulled out of the rear lot, heading off in the opposite direction.

Hatch watched them go, disappearing from her rearview mirror's view as Savage and his team headed off to fight crime and Hatch headed home to her new, normal life.

FOUR

Savage drove in relative silence for the nearly forty-minute commute from Hawk's Landing to the Ute Reservation. His passenger, Deputy Nighthawk, didn't seem to mind the quiet. The only indication they'd crossed over the invisible barrier into the Native American communal land was the four-foot wall with embossed lettering that read Southern Ute Tribal Reservation.

During the next few minutes after crossing into reservation land, Savage had noticed his newest deputy had tensed. There was a rigidity to his body, and he kept his eyes locked on the road ahead. If Savage hadn't come to know him better, Nighthawk would have appeared to be brooding.

Savage pulled the vehicle to a stop behind one of the nearby tribal police vehicles, an outdated light blue Bronco. The paint was faded. The bumper and undercarriage were heavily rusted with chunks of metal eaten away by years of corrosion. The vehicle looked like it had been commandeered from a junkyard. The only thing not falling apart on the SUV was the decal affixed to the driver's side door. The circular marker contained a bright orange sun, surrounded by the words Southern Ute Police.

Nighthawk rubbed his palms absentmindedly on his jeans and stared out the window.

"You want to talk about it?" Savage asked.

Nighthawk let out a long, slow hiss of an exhale. "Not really."

"I understand your desire to want to help with this. And God knows I could use your assistance, but I'm not sure this is going to do you any good. Working a case like this and seeing your father in whatever condition or state he's in isn't healthy. It may not be the best thing for you."

"I can handle it," Nighthawk said, still staring outside through the windshield, never making eye contact with Savage.

"Okay, fair enough. I had to say it. And if you need to walk away, there is no shame in that."

"So, that's the Rachel Hatch you spoke of?"

Savage nodded, understanding Nighthawk's need to change the topic. "The one and only."

"Sinclair said she is the toughest woman she's ever met."

"One and the same," Savage answered. "And if that's what Becky said, who am I to disagree?"

"Is she going to come work with us?"

"Not sure, I've tried barking up that tree quite a few times, but she hasn't bitten yet, except for the little time when she helped us with her sister's death investigation."

"Did you try to stop her from seeing her sister's body? Did you tell her to walk away?"

"There's no stopping Hatch once she's made her mind up on something." Savage laughed, recalling the moment when he'd first met Hatch, when she barged into the autopsy room where her twin sister lay dead.

He remembered being taken aback not only by the brash boldness of her actions, but also by her unique beauty. She was tall, fit and confident. But what truly set her apart was her mind, razor's edge sharp. "She was extremely helpful and did some pretty impressive things while she was here last time, saved some good folk and brought justice to her sister's death." Savage cut the engine. "You and she are a lot alike."

Nighthawk turned for the first time since they'd arrived on scene. "How so?"

"Well, for starters, you're both stubborn asses."

Nighthawk laughed. The sound of it seemed to ease some of the tension.

"But seriously, you both have a great eye for detail. It's like being an investigator was in your DNA, which is why I'm glad I have you here now."

Nighthawk gave a subtle bob of his head, which Savage took as the deputy's nod of approval.

Nighthawk's attention was then redirected back out the window to where a few tribal policemen in their powder blue buttoned down uniformed shirts stood in a loose cluster atop a low rise of ground.

"You ready to do this?" Savage asked.

"Ready as I'll ever be."

Both men exited the vehicle. Littleton and Sinclair, who'd been waiting for Savage's cue, got out of the SUV behind them.

"Grab the evidence bag, Becky," Savage called back to her.

His most senior deputy trotted to the back of the suburban to retrieve the duffle. She returned a moment later with a medium-sized duffle slung over her shoulder. The four then walked together toward the group of tribal officers.

There was no bright yellow police tape out here delineating the crime scene.

Savage announced themselves as they came near the front end of the closest tribal police vehicle. "How are we doing guys? Dalton Savage, Sheriff over at Hawk's Landing. I was asked to assist."

An older man wearing the powder blue of the tribal police walked over. He stuck out his hand. "I really appreciate you coming so quickly. I'm Darryl Clearwater. I'm the one who called you, I figured you were the closest agency, and I didn't want to involve the State."

"What about the BIA? Aren't they getting involved?" Savage asked.

"Bureau of Indian Affairs is going to be sending somebody, but they're always a day or two behind. Plus, I heard about all that stuff you did a few months back cracking that corrupt engineering company. Figured you're probably the right man to look at a case like this."

"What do you guys have so far?" Savage asked.

"We found our Police Chief over there just on the other side of this rise. A jogger came across his body while out on an early morning run."

"Any signs of foul play?"

"None that we can see. The jogger thought he was taking a nap by that rock. It wasn't until she came back down the trail that she realized he hadn't moved. She found him cold to the touch and without a pulse."

Savage scanned the scene. "Is the ME still on scene?"

"They called. They're running a bit late. Said they would have been here an hour ago, but apparently they were tied up on a murder/suicide in Durango."

"So, the body's still here?" Savage asked. With the gap in time between when the body was discovered until the time they were called to assist, he half-expected it to be a cold scene.

"We haven't moved him except to do a quick check for any wounds. We didn't find any. Just a bump on the back of his head and a small scrape on his forehead."

"Did he have any medical conditions, heart problems? Could it have been a heart attack, stroke, or something?"

Clearwater shrugged. "None that we know of, but that's not saying it isn't a possibility."

The younger Nighthawk folded his arms, the tension stretched across his body as if in rigor. He leaned slightly to the right, looking past Savage in the direction of where his dead father lay.

"It's up over the rise there, just beyond where those other officers are standing." Clearwater pointed. "I'll show you what we've got, and like I said, anything you can do to point us in the right direction would be greatly appreciated. We don't have much experience in murder here. We've got the occasional domestic or drinking related incident, a little bit of drugs, but who doesn't have that? But murder?" Clearwater paused. "No, I don't think anyone here on scene has ever worked one. We wouldn't know if something was amiss or not."

"Okay, well, I'll do my best. My team is here to support you in any way that we can." Savage turned and looked at Nighthawk, who was still gazing off into the distance. He didn't ask the young man again if he was ready to do this. He wouldn't do that to him in front of Clearwater and the other deputies.

Clearwater set off at a steady pace toward the rise in the ground, moving at a good clip for an older man. The two other patrolmen who'd been milling about stopped their conversation as the group approached. One looked to be about Deputy Nighthawk's age. He was a squat, heavyset officer with a double chin and dark circles under his eyes. The chubby officer folded his arms as the group approached. He had a look of disgust plainly displayed across his face. Savage initially figured it was out of some jurisdictional conflict, an annoyance at having Hawk's Landing deputies working a tribal case. But Savage quickly noted the glare in the portly officer's eyes was directed at one person in their group, Deputy John Nighthawk. Savage's newest deputy returned the glare with equal disdain.

They continued past them to the top of the rise. Below, they could see a boulder jutting out from the ground. Sitting against it and leaning sloppily to the right was a man in a button-down long sleeve khaki shirt. The badge on his chest caught the light and shimmered. Seeing him there, Savage understood why the jogger had initially thought he was resting. There was a peacefulness to the dead man that masked his current circumstance.

"Where does your scene begin?"

Clearwater kind of raised an eyebrow. "What do you mean?"

"Well, usually with any type of death investigation, until you know the causative factors or potential causative factors, you set a perimeter on the scene and work within it. As you look for evidence, you can expand or contract it depending. But the primary reason is to maintain its integrity by keeping people out of it."

"I know that," Clearwater said, slightly defensive, "We didn't set one up. Nobody's been through here since we arrived and took the statement from our jogger. The only time we went down there was to check the body and look around the immediate area a bit. We didn't find anything, and then that's when we decided to call you in."

"So, the body hasn't been moved? Who in this group has touched the body?"

"I did," Clearwater said. "The others didn't."

"And nobody besides the jogger came through here since you guys started the investigation?"

"Correct."

"And you have the information for the jogger who first came upon him and the time at which the body was found?"

"We do."

Savage felt himself shifting into the role as lead investigator even though he knew he was there to support the tribal police. The experience among the group was minimal at best, probably dating back to whenever they had attended an academy training course and the short period of time in which an instructor had taught them how to work a homicide, a skill that if left unpracticed would deteriorate. Savage had plenty of time and experience during his time with Denver Police, working many of those years within the homicide unit. Handling the volume of cases in a city as busy as Denver, he had definitely accumulated the amount of experience needed to handle most murder investigations that would come across his desk.

"All right, well, from this point forward, nobody moves past where we're standing, unless they've signed into the log."

"The log?" Clearwater asked.

"The crime scene log."

"Of course."

"Just have one of your guys grab a notepad. Note the name, rank, date and time that anybody enters this scene." Savage paused to momentarily survey the surroundings. "We should cordon off an area in a fifty-foot radial extension from the body. We can collapse in closer or expand it, but fifty feet would be a good start point for this terrain."

Clearwater called over to the heavyset deputy. "Ted, tape off the area in a fifty-foot radius from the Chief's body."

Ted did not seem pleased with his tasking but didn't verbalize his annoyance in any noticeable fashion. He walked away muttering something under his breath.

Savage was glad Clearwater didn't buck the assistance being offered. Even though it had been the tribal policeman who'd asked for it, Savage knew the challenge of giving up control. Most police were alphas by nature, and sharing the decision-making spotlight was always a delicate balance. It spoke to Clearwater's character that a) he'd asked for help and b) accepted it when given.

"All right, next step. I'm going to conduct a cursory walkthrough of the scene," Savage said. "Every investigator approaches their scenes slightly differently. Personally, I prefer to get a feel for the scene and the scope of the evidence before I begin recovery. Have you taken any photographs yet?"

Clearwater tapped the pocket of his windbreaker with a sense of accomplishment. "Yes. I took several."

"Good. I'm going to take some as well. I like to do overalls of the scene and then work in toward closeups. I know you said you moved the body, but I'll still photograph the current position before moving him again."

Clearwater's confidence diminished. Savage's explanation of what he meant by photographing the scene obviously differed from whatever Clearwater had done.

"When I get back to the office," Savage said, "I'll email them to you."

Clearwater looked relieved. "Thanks."

"I'm going to take John with me. The rest of you stay here. We're going to get our initial assessment and then we'll move on from there."

Nighthawk stepped forward, moving alongside Savage. They headed down the slight decline and made their way to the body. The ground still hadn't completely passed through spring's thaw and their steps crunched noisily.

Savage stopped a few feet away, taking a digital camera from his pocket and snapping a couple pictures. Nighthawk stopped and stood beside him. The two were about halfway between the rise and the body. Savage whispered so the others couldn't hear. "I'm going to stand here for a bit and look around. John, why don't you go ahead?"

Nighthawk looked at Savage out of the corner of his eye.

"Take however much time you need."

"Thanks," Nighthawk said, stepping forward toward his dead father.

Savage then squatted down and looked at the ground around him, scanning for evidence.

Nighthawk bent low near his father. There was a one-sided exchange between Nighthawk and his dad. Savage could only assume the words by context as Nighthawk paid his respects. Savage turned away, giving his deputy privacy.

Nighthawk stood a moment later, "I'm ready. Let's do this."

Savage didn't press and continued his role as lead in the investigation. "John, can you take two steps to your right?"

Nighthawk adjusted his position as Savage clicked several more photos, documenting his approach to the body. Closing the distance and now standing next to his bereaved deputy, Savage took several more pictures, capturing the body from multiple angles.

"Let's think about what we have right now. That will help focus our search for clues." Savage pocketed the camera. "We're not sure how long he's been here, but I'm going to assume he died early this morning. We'll wait for the official report from the medical examiner's office, but I'm not seeing much in the way of animal activity. If he'd been here all night, then we'd most likely see signs of disturbance."

Savage squatted down and balanced himself on the heels of his boots. "There's scraping to his face here. Clearwater said there was a lump on the back of his head. Thoughts?"

"Maybe he fell," Nighthawk said. "Maybe he did have a heart attack and collapsed out here and then crawled over to the rock. I don't know."

"What makes you say crawled?" Savage.

"There's disturbed earth." Nighthawk pointed to ground a few feet away. "It looks like drag marks in the dirt."

"Good eye." Savage was impressed. Nighthawk had been right. As he stared at the area around the chief's body, Savage saw the drag marks also. He pulled out his camera and snapped an additional series of photographs.

"What do you think?" Nighthawk asked.

"Why don't you tell me what you make of it?" Savage was interested in the young deputy's insight.

"Doesn't make sense. If he was having a heart attack, why wouldn't he call somebody? If my father was able to crawl over to this rock, then why couldn't he pick up his phone. And better question—where is his phone?"

Savage saw the phone was missing from a plastic belt clip attached to the dead police chief's belt but played devil's advocate. "Maybe he dropped it. We'll definitely have to check the area to see if he left it somewhere. But that's an excellent point. If your father had the ability to crawl, why wouldn't his first instinct be to call for medical assistance?"

Nighthawk stepped back and carefully maneuvered himself over to the area where the ground had been disturbed. He pressed himself close to the ground in a modified push up position as he looked down at the dirt. His eyes then shifted slowly away toward the wood line.

He then stood, carefully stepping around the disturbed dirt. Nighthawk moved as if possessed. He walked slowly in the direction of a thicket of shrubs. His eyes never left the ground and his head was on a swivel like a beachcomber looking for a lost treasure.

Ten feet from the body, Nighthawk stopped and bent down. "I've got something, over here."

"What is it?" Savage asked, following Nighthawk's footsteps, careful not to disturb the scene.

Seconds later, Savage stood behind Nighthawk, looking over his shoulder. He scanned the broken branches and leaves on the ground. His eyes came to rest on a dark brown imperfectly shaped circle on a wilted leaf. "Blood."

Nighthawk nodded. "Look at this." He focused his attention on the dirt around the blood-painted leaf.

"I'm not seeing anything."

"Exactly." Nighthawk remained in a low squat. "Makes no sense, right? There's no blood on the dirt around this leaf. But look carefully at the dirt itself and compare it to the rest of the ground."

Savage did. As if staring at a mind's eye image and finally seeing the hidden picture, the scene became clear. "Son of a bitch. You're right."

"Those markings in the loose dirt are man-made. Somebody covered their tracks." Nighthawk rose to face Savage.

"That's a hell of an eye you've got."

"My dad taught me to hunt, but he also taught me how to read the land."

"He taught you well." Savage looked back at the pattern in the dirt and wondered if he would've noticed had it not been for Nighthawk. He honestly didn't know the answer to that question. But what he did know was that this changed everything.

The two retreated to the others waiting at the top of the rise.

"I just got another update from the M.E.'s office," Clearwater said. "They should be here any minute now."

"Well, they're going to have to hold off for a bit," Savage said.

"Why is that?" Clearwater asked.

"Because this just became a homicide investigation."

FIVE

She had poured some concrete mix into the base of the hole she had dug. Hatch then sank three of the eight feet of the 2X4 oak beam into the ground. Centering the post, she held it in position, ensuring it would be straight when the quick drying concrete set.

After waiting for approximately twenty minutes, the concrete gripped the base well enough for Hatch to begin filling the remainder of the hole with the earth she had dug out. After spending several minutes packing it down firmly with the flat end of the shovel, Hatch was satisfied the three plus feet of dirt and concrete would provide enough support and balance to the plank when used for its intended purpose.

"Auntie Rachel, what are you doing?" Jake asked, standing behind her and looking at her sweat-covered face with the utmost curiosity.

She'd wiped her forehead with her dirty hands, smearing the earth across her face like an ancient warrior donning war paint. "This is for you," she said, looking at the erect oak plank. The top of the board fell just beneath her chin. The height at which she set the sponge would be set about head level for Jacob.

Content with the height and stability of her creation, Hatch then grabbed the thick yellow sponge. Lathering the back of the sponge in wood glue, she stuck the porous two-inch thick material to the board about a foot from the top. Hatch then began wrapping it tightly with a ¼-inch rope. Hatch worked the rope around until the sponge was completely covered, and then she did a second overlapping layer. She tied it off on the backside of the board and cut the excess off.

"I still don't know what it is?"

"It's a little bit of padding for your knuckles when you hit it."

Jake looked shocked. "When I hit it?"

"It's a makiwara board. My father had shown me this years ago when I was just a little bit older than you. And I figured with all your training, it'd be a perfect time for you to begin advancing your skills."

"But I'm getting better," he said. His voice held an air of defiance.

"I know, but you should never be satisfied with where you're at. Always push yourself to become better than the person you are. Never stay stagnant."

Jake acknowledged with a bob of his head, but Hatch wasn't wholly confident he understood what she meant.

"If two people are of equal skill, and one rests on their laurels and stops training because they feel that they have reached a certain level, and the other person continues—what happens?"

"The one who keeps training will be better," Jake said.

"Right. And if you're the one who continually challenges himself, then you'll grow in skill. In time, hard work pays off. With proper training, you'll surpass your peers."

Jake seemed to contemplate this but remained quiet for a moment. "So, what does it do?"

Hatch checked the knot she'd made binding the sponge to the board. She then squeezed it to ensure she'd created a thick enough padding for the strike pad so it would protect the boy's hand from the hard oak but leave enough rigidity that it would do its job.

She stepped back and aligned herself with the padded rectangle of rope and sponge. Hatch struck the board. A loud thwack rang out. The padding was good to go. The board remained rigid. Having sunk it three feet into the ground, it had a sturdy base. And then coupled with the now-drying concrete and the earth above it, it was well packed in and wouldn't budge much, which was the point and purpose of the board.

"It's critically important that when you strike this, you hit with these two knuckles and these two knuckles only when punching." Hatch held out her left fist and ran her two fingers over the big knuckles of the index and middle finger. She held them close enough to Jake's face that he could see the scar damage from the numerous times she'd used her hands in both training and real-world combat. Both knuckles were noticeably different in size, larger than the ring and pinky finger knuckles. "Those two knuckles here are going to be your weapons when you punch, but it's critically important when you're striking a makiwara board, your wrists are aligned with your forearm. Think of your fist as an extension of your whole body. Every strike needs to be focused when using the makiwara. It's important that your striking knuckles, wrist, and forearm are aligned when impact is made. That'll keep your wrist from flexing and keep from causing damage to the tendons when you hit something hard."

"My instructor has me wrap my wrists when I hit the punching bag."

"That's good," Hatch said. "Wrist wraps are great, and you need them when you're hitting a heavy bag, especially one that's much heavier than your own body weight. It's the same principle. But in the real world, you won't have wrist wraps or gloves when you fight. So, I want your body to work efficiently, safely, and effectively when delivering your blows to somebody on the street."

"My instructor says we're not supposed to use our karate outside of the dojo."

Hatch thought about this logic and understood why an instructor teaching younger martial artists would push that logic, but she also knew it was counterintuitive. The whole point and purpose of martial arts was to be able to effectively protect yourself and others if need be. And if you built in a mental block for the use of such skills, it could create hesitation. Hatch knew better than most the detriment hesitation caused.

She approached the subject delicately, not wanting to undo the wisdom and rules laid out by Jake's instructor.

"Listen, Jake, sometimes life puts us in a position where we have to use our skills either to protect ourselves or somebody else. You know this better than any kid your age."

Jake smiled.

"The things I'm going to show you and teach you aren't to go against the teachings of your instructor, but to provide an extra layer to your already impressive skill set that you're developing. And your teacher is right. You don't want to use your newfound skills to become the bully of the playground. I just want you to be able to take care of yourself and your sister. No matter your wish that you never have to use your karate, there will be people who challenge you. Most times you can turn the other cheek and walk away. And there are times when that is impossible. I want you to be ready for those times."

"Like you?"

"Yes." She thought about that statement. *Did she really want him to be like her?* "My father had told me a long time ago to take care of people who need help and to punish those responsible for their pain. You've already shown me that you're capable of doing it. Without you, I probably wouldn't be standing here now. You've already proven yourself to be the bravest boy I know. I hope the time never comes where you ever have to use your skills again. But I also want you to know that when and if you do use them, they will be effective."

And there was the truth of it, Hatch thought. It was great to pray for peace and hope that one would never have to resort to war. But the cold, hard reality was that sometimes war found its way into your life whether you wanted it or not.

And peace, well, that had come hard fought for Hatch in her life. That battle still raged on. She continued the search for the time when the past remained there. Even now, being back in Hawk's Landing and preparing to provide tutelage to her nephew, Hatch still felt a sense of disconnect. When your whole life was an endless string of battlefields between everywhere and nowhere, what does normal even feel like? When the hum of violence subsided and she was left with just the memories, would she be satisfied in her new role? The jury was still out on that, but she was determined to give it her all.

"So, what do I do, just punch it?" Jake asked, redirecting Hatch's train of thought back to the makiwara board and away from the bigger picture that was her ever-evolving life.

"Yes and no. You're not going to hit this board like you would a punching bag. You're going to align yourself directly in front of it, square your body to it, and strike at the padded area with those two knuckles that I showed you."

"And it's going to make my knuckles look like yours?"

The look on Jake's face was somewhere between disgust and interest, and Hatch couldn't discern which he had chosen.

"Some of these markings on my hands come from training. Some from my life in the military. To answer your question, yes, over time you'll condition the knuckles. You'll desensitize the nerves, but more importantly, your body will learn the mechanics of delivering an effective and proper strike. The board doesn't lie. If you hit it wrong with a loose wrist or awkward angle, then you'll feel it."

"Will it hurt?"

"Depends how hard you hit it."

Jake eyed the contraption warily.

"Listen, don't worry about how hard you hit right now. That will come with time. Eventually, you'll become proficient enough that you can strike as hard as you want without fear of damaging your hand."

Jake rubbed his knuckles and then made a fist.

"Let me see your fist."

Jake extended his arm. She took him by the wrist and then with her right hand checked his curled fingers, ensuring their tightness. Hatch flattened the palm of her hand and held it out facing him. She then guided his knuckles into her palm. "Do you feel that?"

"Yes."

"That's how you want to align your fist when you are striking without a glove. This will keep the bones aligned, strengthen the impact, and reduce any chance of injury to yourself while maximizing damage to your enemy."

"Enemy?" Jake looked up at her with childlike innocence.

"Enemies can take many forms. I think you understand that better than most. Don't you?"

His eyes seemed suddenly distant as he gave his affirmative in the form of a barely noticeable nod of his head.

"We're going to start slow, gently striking it, working on getting the alignment right before we worry about speed and power. Once you get comfortable with it, you can increase your level of intensity, but only hit it as hard as you can do comfortably. You don't want to damage your knuckle or hurt your wrist. If you feel any extreme pain, take a break. If your knuckles start to bleed, take a break. This type of conditioning takes place over a long period of time. You will not be able to condition your hands and knuckles in a matter of days or even weeks. This is a real commitment to the long haul. Eventually, you'll be able to strike it as hard as you want with little to no sensation in your knuckles. And as you progress, I'll show you other ways to use the makiwara board to condition other bits and pieces of your body, like the ridge of your hand." She mussed his hair playfully. "But for now, let's worry about your punches. Let me show you."

Hatch squared herself to the wood plank as Jake moved to the side. Hatch, being taller than the targeted area which was set for Jake's height, took a half squat into a modified horse stance, one of the basic stances she had learned years ago. Although she rarely used any formal stances in her actual combat, the principles taught in those deep-rooted martial arts forms had served her well. Hatch had effectively learned to use the power of her body to inflict devastation on her opponents.

She tucked both her fists back along her hip line. Then, leading with her left, Hatch struck out with her left hand. The two knuckles, her index and middle finger, struck hard into the dead center of the twine-wrapped sponge, christening the makiwara board.

The contact felt good. She struck out at the target again, snapping outward. Her knuckles slammed against the padding. Hatch's wrist, upon impact, made perfect alignment with her forearm. She then repeated the process with her right hand and then looked back over at Jake, who she saw was watching her carefully. He would be a good student to teach. She could see it in his eyes. He was absorbing everything, from her stance to the way her body moved to the impact, and then to its retraction back to its original preparatory stance.

"Just like that, Jake, but I want you to start off much lighter. And because you're a little shorter than me, you're going to stand a little more upright. I want you at a distance where your punch, when it makes contact with the board, is at full extension."

"Got it. Hit with the knuckles. Keep my wrist straight." Jake stood eagerly in front of the board.

"Remember, you're not looking to try to break the board."

Jake absently rubbed his knuckles.

"Are you ready to try?"

Jake nodded, but hesitantly approached the board. He seemed eager to want to apply what he had just seen, but also somewhat nervous, which was understandable.

"Learning anything new at any age carries with it a level of stress, especially for someone as driven as you, Jake."

Hatch too had been a perfectionist when she had trained, and it had come to serve her well later in life and still did. She wanted the same for her nephew.

He stepped in front of the board, squaring himself to it just as she had done. His stance was less of a squat as he lined himself up, extending his arm to get his spacing while touching his knuckles to the twine covering the sponge. The sponge was only thick enough to prevent the hardness of the oak wood from causing true damage to the hand. It was designed to give enough cushioning to aid in continual practice.

"All right, you look good," Hatch said, clapping a hand on his shoulder. "When you're ready, nice and easy, reach out, strike with the left, and then bring back and alternate with the right."

Jake did. He struck out but softly. The sound from the impact was barely audible.

"Good work," Hatch encouraged.

He stopped after delivering a few more blows with each hand. Jake was staring down at his knuckles. His soft, young skin was red along the index and middle finger knuckle of both hands. He rubbed at them and looked down. No blood, but they were bright red.

Hatch took both his hands in hers and looked down to examine.

"Well, how'd that feel?"

"It stung a bit," Jake said. "But not bad."

"Well, from what I saw, that was a great start. Your instructor is doing a great job with your punches. You turned your wrist at the last moment and aligned your arm. And do you see this?" Hatch ran her fingers gently across the knuckles of his left hand. "That redness is only on those first two knuckles, the ones I showed you to strike with. See, there's no redness down here by the pinky or ring finger. That means you were striking with the correct two knuckles."

Jake let a half smile crest his cheeks.

"This is a great start, Jake. I have high hopes for you. Now, remember, you're only to do this until you hit that point of uncomfortableness. You don't want pain. You don't want to injure yourself. You want to condition these knuckles. And like I said—"

Jake finished the sentence with a slight eye roll. "I know, it's going to take longer than weeks and months. It's okay, Auntie Rachel, I'm not going anywhere and neither are you."

It sounded strange to think that she wouldn't be leaving.

"I'll train as long as I have to in order to get myself just like you."

Hatch was taken back by the boy's comments. "Just like me." Did she want him to be like her? Did she want Jake to grow up to be her? Is that something she wanted? She didn't even know.

"Well, before you go about worrying about being like me, let's just get you where you want to be. And Jake, this is something you can practice every day. But I'm going to tell you, some days those knuckles are going to be a little bit sorer than others. So, feel free to take a break. And if it is bothering your hands, never hesitate to ice them when you're done. But know that in time you won't feel a thing."

And with that, Hatch snapped out with her right hand, the hand connected to the scar tissue that stretched up her arm toward her shoulder, now exposed by the short-sleeved shirt she wore. Her strike was fast. The impact against the makiwara board was hard, and it made a loud thwack. And in the stillness of the morning air, seemed louder still.

Jake's eyes widened.

"That'll be you soon enough," she said as she planted a kiss on his forehead. "I'll leave you to it. Get a little practice in and then head on in for lunch."

"Okay," he said as he turned back to square himself to the board.

Hatch walked around from the backyard to the front door, where she was greeted by Daphne, who was holding the phone.

"Auntie Rachel," she said sweetly.

"Yes, little Daffodil?" Hatch said.

"Phone call for you. And plus, I drew this picture of a unicorn just for you."

She held up both as if it was some test. What would Rachel choose? The mind of a six-year-old. She took both as she came up to the child. "Now, this is a gorgeous unicorn. Can I hang it in my room?"

Daphne squealed with pleasure and did a short jig-like dance as she handed off the phone and disappeared inside.

Hatch looked down at the brightly colored cartoon drawing of the fantastic beast and then held the phone to her ear. "Hello?"

"How about we catch up over dinner tonight?"

It was Savage. He seemed a little distant, but she was excited to hear his voice. And the prospect of sitting down to dinner with him made her equal parts excited and nervous. She tried to hide both.

"Sure. What time are you thinking?"

"I'll pick you up around 7:00 if that works."

"I've got nothing but time now, so 7:00 is just fine. Is it easier for me to meet you somewhere?" she said, opening up the idea that maybe this was just a casual encounter and nothing more.

"No, don't bother. I'll pick you up. Plus, you know you don't want to be seen driving around town in your mother's Astro van," he said with a laugh before hanging up.

SIX

SAVAGE HAD BEEN PROMPT. WELL, IN FACT, HE'D BEEN A FEW MINUTES early. It gave the family a little time to catch up with their favorite sheriff. Hatch's mother had grown fond of Savage in the months they'd spent together working the case of her sister's death.

Jasmine Hatch looked genuinely pleased to see him arrive at her doorstep to pick up her daughter tonight. The kids came to the door and greeted him cheerfully, too. There were a few minutes of verbal exchange before he walked Hatch out to his dusty old Chevy Suburban.

As the sheriff of a small town, he typically drove the police car. Hatch found it funny that his personal vehicle was a comparable make and model. Guess if you're comfortable, you're comfortable. Hatch climbed into the passenger seat and looked over at Savage.

He was clean-shaven, but the day had drawn on and the stubble had already begun to poke through along his rugged jawline. He was no longer in the attire of the Hawk's Landing Sheriff's uniform, but now wore a green and black flannel button down. Although he had thrown on some type of musky cologne or aftershave, she could still smell the faint scent of licorice, Dalton Savage's personal scent.

"Where are we heading?" Hatch asked.

"It's a great little spot. Opened up while you were gone. Place called Hal's Bistro."

"Oh, a bistro sounds kind of swanky," Hatch joked with the rugged lawman.

"It's got good food. I think you'll like it."

The town was spaced out with most of the houses separated by large swaths of land. The industrial and business area of the town consisted of a few blocks of tightly packed streets with locally run businesses. None of the big chains had made their way into Hawk's Landing. In a world constantly evolving and growing, Hatch was glad her small town had somehow remained untouched by much of the changes. At least on the surface. The town had gone through a major upheaval when Hatch and Savage had uncovered a deep-rooted conspiracy that had gripped the town. But now that the burn was lifted, it seemed as though things were back to normal.

Hatch saw people strolling down Main Street. The sun was quickly setting, and the temperatures were beginning to dip. Hatch had put on a lightweight sweater she'd taken from her sister's closet. Daphne helped pick it out.

Hatch looked at her long sleeves. She had learned to confidently wear the scars on her right arm without hiding them. Africa had taught her. The wise cafe owner, Khari, had enlightened her. She told herself she'd worn the shirt because of the cool night temperatures, but part of her wondered if she hadn't done it intentionally to mask her mangled right arm from Savage.

Savage had seen her arm before. He knew how she got it. Dalton Savage was one of the only civilians she'd ever shared the story with. Well, at least a sanitized version of the story. When Hatch had told him about her injury, she had left out the part about the little girl. Speaking about that piece held its own trauma, and she had tucked that deep. She'd thought about filling him in, letting this man into that space of her heart. But she hadn't. Maybe the time for that conversation had passed or maybe it was still to come. She wasn't quite sure what this dinner was all about. She knew one thing. In her absence, she had thought about Dalton Savage pretty much every day she had been away.

And now, seated next to him in the vehicle, her heart rate increased slightly. Not enough that she would feel flustered or worry that he'd notice a reddening of her cheeks, but enough that she noticed. She didn't like it. She didn't like the fact that this man and being around him had some type of electrical charge that messed with Hatch's wiring, that put her out of whack. The machine that was Rachel Hatch had a glitch. And that glitch was Dalton Savage.

She breathed slowly, trying to calm her nerves. It hadn't been that long since the two had been together, but long enough that there was a slight awkwardness in the silence. She was grateful for the engine's loud rumble. The roar made it difficult for much in the way of conversation. And she allowed herself to stare absently out the window as she tried to collect her thoughts on what they would talk about.

A lot had happened to Hatch in her absence. She'd been around the world. She'd found herself in New Mexico facing off against an outlaw motorcycle gang and then overseas in Africa. She wasn't sure how much, if any, she would tell Savage. She wasn't sure if he would understand. She didn't want him to look at her any differently, to judge her. Maybe he wouldn't understand the things she had done.

Her code was not everybody's code.

Although he was a man of the law, he sought justice. She did too, but in a different way. And her methodology clashed with the rules and regulations of law. She worried beyond the judgment about what she had done in both an effort to survive and to help those who couldn't help themselves. Would he see her for a monster? Would he worry that she brought more battle damage back with her? More scars? Invisible ones, the ugliest kind, the ones that sneak up and wake you in the middle of the night and shake you and take you to terrible places where terrible things have happened?

No. Savage wasn't ready for that. Although she knew he had his own demons, and if he had a few skeletons in his closet, Hatch had a graveyard full in hers. She would either keep most of what had happened a secret or slowly let it out in bite-sized chunks that he would be able to process better. More likely, she'd give him a sanitized, watered down version. Better for everybody, she thought.

Then she pushed the thoughts from her mind as she turned from the window and looked over at Savage. She saw him fumble with his shirt pocket and pull out a handful of licorice. His tell. His nerves were on edge, too. Something about seeing that made her happy. At least she wasn't the only one who had the jitters about their reconnection, their date. If this even was a date? Hatch fought making the mental leap on that line of thinking.

They'd never discussed their feelings for one another. And nothing had effectively ever happened besides the night she fell asleep in his arms. But in that moment, something had changed. Whether either of them was willing to talk about it was another thing.

Maybe that's what this dinner was about? To discuss that very thing. Hatch just hoped Savage would give her enough to show that he, too, had thought of her in her absence, as much as she did him.

They passed a small storefront that sold sporting goods. In Hatch's youth, it had been a tuxedo rental called Dream Maker's Formalwear. She remembered when her high school sweetheart Cole Jensen tried to return his prom tux with a giant red stain on the shirt and ended up having to buy it. It was a funny memory to call up. The man Jensen had become was not the carefree teen. And his death sent a ripple back in time tainting any memory of him. This town was filled with them.

She realized in that split-second instant that the Hawk's Landing of her youth would never be the same again for her. That although it looked the same, it smelled the same and much of the same people that she'd grown up with and knew were still here, it was wholly different now. She didn't know if that was good or bad. She just knew it was different.

Maybe change didn't necessarily equal a good or bad. Maybe it was just a deviation on the same narrow path. She hoped that life came with an evolution of self, a growth. Like the caterpillar's transformation into a butterfly, the ones of Daphne's drawings.

Hatch had hoped her interim experiences since leaving Hawk's Landing did just that. She felt she emerged from Africa a new person, a better person, somebody who could connect with others, somebody who could open herself to the idea of normal, somebody who could find peace in a place she had left long ago. More importantly, somebody who could find happiness.

As he pulled to the stop in front of the bistro and the engine cut, Hatch could hear light music carried on the evening breeze. There was a live jazz band playing in the front window. It wasn't loud, but loud enough that the strumming could be heard from outside.

She looked at him and gave a nod of approval. "Live band. Nice touch."

"I told you, it's a pretty neat place."

She looked at the sign. Hal's Bistro. They walked into the restaurant with Savage taking a slight lead over Hatch. Although they were similar in height, he had an edge on her in stride and seemed to move quick enough to beat her to the door. He smiled, pulling the door open and gave a bow of his head.

"Chivalry isn't dead," she said.

"Not that you're looking for it," he retorted.

They went inside. A hum of the stringed instruments vibrated the room, giving it a nice buzz of energy. The smell of fresh coffee filled the air.

They were greeted by a young girl at the hostess station. She smiled, welcoming them both in and then guided them to a seat in the back, a little further from the makeshift stage where the jazz band played quietly on. Hatch was enjoying the music but was grateful she could focus on the conversation without having to shout over the ensemble. A waiter arrived moments later and went through the list of items on the specials' menu.

As Hatch was absently listening, she heard a voice call out, shaking her from her momentary daze. "Rachel Hatch?"

She spun to see a well-dressed and clean-cut man come out from the back area of the restaurant where the kitchen was open so that the diners could see the work being put into their food. It took a second for Hatch to recognize the man.

"Hal Rigsby," Hatch stammered.

He was the first openly gay person Hatch had ever met in her life. His father had walked out on him and his mother the summer before high school. Hatch and Hal had bonded over the fact that they both were fatherless. He was brave before Hatch ever found her strength.

He walked right over, and as she stood, he gave her a larger than life hug. Rigsby had been an extrovert when they'd been in high school. He used to say, "If I'm going to stand out, then I might as well stand up." Hatch had always liked Rigsby's code. She learned a lot about standing up for one's self from him. Hatch had also learned to stand up for others. And she had a code, too.

"Hal, I never would have figured you for a restaurateur," Hatch said.

"Well, to be honest, it's always been a passion of mine, and growing up in small town Hawk's Landing, it wasn't like there were a lot of culinary schools. So, I kind of kept my interest to myself. But after high school, that's what I did. I traveled abroad, went to several culinary schools and cooked at fancy restaurants. But I began to miss home, and I came back. I opened here, figuring I could be closer to my mother."

"That's great to hear. It's actually why I'm back."

"Make every second count. My mother's been sick. So, the timing of my arrival has been a blessing in disguise. Being able to be there for her when she needs me most." He cleared his throat and lowered his voice. "I'm sorry to hear about your sister. I was out of town when it happened and wish I had been there for you."

Hatch thought about the words, the natural kindness in them, and the way he presented his worldly experience without flaunting it.

She remembered liking Hal Rigsby, but seeing he remained true to himself, to his code, after all these years made her respect him even further.

"This is a fantastic place you got here. You've even got live music."

He smiled broadly.

"Yeah. It's actually a high school group. I volunteer over there in the music department, and I like to bring them in here to practice in front of a live audience. They get free coffee and lattes while they're performing. My way of paying them."

"I'm happy to see things worked out so well for you Hal," Hatch said. "Any recommendations?" Hatch almost forgot the waiter was standing idly by and had just finished his memorized dissertation of all of the specials for the night.

"I'd try the swordfish. I basted it in this sauce that I came up with, and we cook it to perfection. You'd almost think you were eating a steak. If you don't like it, I'll get you something else. I'll tell you what. It's so great seeing you, dinner is on the house."

"Oh, I can't," Hatch said.

"Think nothing of it. It was great seeing you, Rachel. I'm glad you've come back. This town needs more good people. And I heard about what you did a while back."

Rigsby was already moving on to greet another table with a wave and a smile. He glided around the small restaurant as if floating.

Hatch, having heard her sister's name and Hal's kind comment, softened a bit. She offered no further resistance and took her seat. She looked at the waiter, who was still waiting for the official nod.

Hatch looked over at Savage. "What do you think?"

"Sounds like swordfish it is."

The waiter nodded, smiled. "Can I get you anything to drink with that? Might I recommend the Kendall-Jackson Sauvignon Blanc. It's a perfect match for this fish."

"Who are we to argue?" Hatch said.

Savage smiled and the waiter disappeared into the kitchen.

"Well, you can't seem to go anywhere without your past creeping up," Savage said with a laugh.

"There's more truth in that than you know," Hatch offered as she took a sip from the water glass. She decided to change topics and shift the focus from her back to Savage. "How did it go today?"

"I really could have used you out there," he said.

"You have me right now. I'm all ears."

SEVEN

"Why don't you fill me in on what's going on with the case, unless this isn't some subtle attempt at wining and dining me in an effort to bring me in?"

Savage subconsciously reached for the licorice in his pocket but stopped himself and picked up a glass of wine instead. He drank a couple sips as his face reddened. She wasn't sure if it was from the dry aromatic white, or the pressure she just put on him to define the reason for their dinner.

Savage set the glass down on the table and cleared his throat. "I was hoping this dinner would be a little bit of both, but I know no matter what I do and as stubborn as you are, Hatch, you'll make your own decision."

Hatch smiled and took a sip of her wine.

"It seemed simple enough at first glance. When the body of Nighthawk's father was found, it was originally assumed that maybe he had a heart attack, or something of the sort. The tribal police figured it was due to an unknown pre-existing medical condition, a natural cause."

Savage was slow in his delivery. He was dragging it out. Hatch could tell there was more to it and prodded. "But?"

"But we found some blood not too far away. Well, when I said 'we,' I mean Nighthawk did. He's good."

"You said that," Hatch said.

Savage continued. "The blood was a distance away, maybe ten feet or so from where the body had been found. I'm going to be honest with you. Not sure I would've found it. I'd like to think I would, but it was a needle in a haystack kind of a find. Nighthawk also discovered that the area where the blood had been found was cleaned."

"You mean as in somebody covering their tracks?"

"As far as we can tell, yes."

"I assume you took a sample of the blood?"

"We did. It's at the lab now, and I was told by Clearwater that they were working on expediting the results. He'll contact me as soon as they come in."

"Were there any wounds on the chief that would have explained the blood?"

"No, nothing apparent. There was a slight scrape on his face and a lump at the base of his skull, but nothing that would've led to the blood we found. If he'd had a heart attack while walking and collapsed, it might've explained the injuries. The initial conjecture was that he collapsed and then managed to crawl himself over to the boulder where he was later found. But too many things didn't add up."

"Like what?"

"For starters, his cell phone was missing. Also, the area where the blood had been found was brushed over. No tracks or footprints. But later, once we began processing the scene, we carefully cleared away some of the dirt and found a deep stain of blood underneath where the ground had been covered."

"So, what are your thoughts?" Hatch asked.

"Well, I have some ideas, but I'd like to hear yours."

Just then, the waiter returned. He had a basket of fresh bread and a plate with oil and fresh ground pepper for dipping. "Your meal will be out shortly. This focaccia bread is made from scratch every day. I think you'll love it."

Hatch smiled but stopped listening as the waiter went into a description, brief as it was, on how the bread was baked and prepared each day. Her mind was elsewhere, processing the scene Savage had just described.

A few seconds later, the waiter was scurrying off to tend to another table closer to the jazz band that continued to play in the background.

The interruption hadn't broken her train of thought. She now knew their dinner date was not just one in which they would reminisce and look at the potential of where things may or may not go as far as personal relationships went. Savage was all business right now, although in a nice setting. And Hatch, if she were truly honest with herself, had to admit that the information Savage had just shared with her piqued her investigative senses. She felt the itch, the yearning for understanding. The desire to solve the ultimate puzzle. Murder.

In her time with the military police, before she had been brought into Taskforce Banshee, which had redirected the course of her military life for years after, she had been an investigator. Hatch climbed the ranks within the Military Police, working her way up from the patrol side of things into investigations. Upon attaining the rank of warrant officer, she'd entered into the Criminal Investigations Division, or CID. And she found that each case, regardless of the crime, had puzzle-like qualities. She'd become addicted to the mental chess match and found she couldn't rest until she found the solution.

As an investigator, she had a high clearance rate, closing cases that for others would have been left as unsolvable. It was her tenacity in the interrogation room that had later made her an asset to her special operations counterparts in Taskforce Banshee. But before that, she'd cut her teeth working murder investigations between everywhere and nowhere.

Nothing proved her desire for the truth more than her last adventure that took her halfway across the world. And here she was trying to start over, to find herself anew in her hometown, rebuild the relationships, become a new version of herself. But less than a day back in Hawk's Landing, she was being drawn into another murder investigation.

As much as she wanted to push back and tell Savage that's not why she was here, that she was looking at a second chance at starting anew, and that maybe, just maybe, he was the man she could start that new path with. She couldn't help herself. All those things Savage had just described now circled her mind like flurries in a squall.

Savage had laid out a tantalizing teaser. Whether he'd done so by design to lure her in, she wasn't sure. But the case now had her undivided attention. A body with no external injuries consistent with the blood on scene and the effort made to cover the evidence made for one hell of a puzzle. That's without adding in the fact that the decedent was the Southern Ute Reservation's chief of police.

She was now vested in the solution of the case, whether she wanted to be or not. Making it worse was the fact that she knew that the dead man was the father to the young deputy she'd met earlier in the day. Hatch had experienced the death of a father, although at an earlier age, and knew the hole that it left. Although she didn't personally know John Nighthawk, she knew that razor sharp pain he must be feeling. From what Savage said, Johnny Nighthawk, the newest member of the Hawk's Landing Sheriff's Office, was a good man, a good person, and an up-and-coming deputy with promise. With his father dead, she didn't want to see tragedy derail somebody else as it had done her nearly two decades before.

Her code of ethics began to bubble like a kettle on a stove just before it started to whistle. *Help good people and punish those who hurt others.* Who better to fit the bill than somebody who had just lost their father?

Hatch felt herself being drawn in. Even so, she was certain about one thing. She didn't want to do this as a full-time gig. This would be a one-and-done: help Savage get justice for Nighthawk and his family. She would also use this time to reconnect with Savage, realizing it was an area of common ground. Maybe this case would work to help Hatch ease herself back into life here in Hawk's Landing. It would give her a sense of purpose while she figured out her new role. But she was firmly committed that she would not become a full-fledged deputy.

"All right," she said. "I'll help. I'll give you my two cents, and maybe I'll be able to make myself available to assist in some way, if you need."

Savage seemed to lean forward at this. She could see the excitement in his eyes.

"But," she said, "I would do this solely on a consultant basis. I don't want a badge. I don't want a gun. I'll look at what you have evidence-wise, maybe even assist in digging some things up, but I do not want to go back into the world of law enforcement. I've hung up my guns for good this time."

His eyes did little in the way of hiding his surprise.

"You understand that, right, Dalton? I'm coming back here for a new start, a fresh start, and not to be thrown back into the life that I've sought to avoid."

"I don't want you to do anything you don't want to."

"If you're good with those terms, then I will give you my two cents and see where it measures up with what you've got so far. After that, everything you ask me to do will be measured with how far I'm willing to go."

"Sounds like you've been through a bit of some self-actualization in the time since you've been gone."

Hatch nodded. She didn't want to go into the details of New Mexico or Africa. Those would be complicated stories, better left unspoken. She didn't want to scare him off, but she also wanted to lay down her guns for good. She had hoped that maybe this would be the time in her life to find that peace Khari had spoken to her about in that cafe halfway across the world. She hoped the licorice-scented man across from her would be the person to share that peace with. Tonight left her with more questions than answers on that front.

"I met some interesting people, and I got some closure on my father," Hatch said, finishing her sentence.

"Do you want to talk about it?"

Hatch reached out and grabbed a piece of the squared focaccia bread. It was soft and warm, and there was a little bit of seasoning on the top of the bread that came away on her fingers as she tore it and dipped it into the oil. "I don't think so," Hatch said before taking a bite. The waiter had been right to sing the praises of the bread.

She could see Savage was somewhat hurt by her dismissive comment and tried to soften it a bit. "It was just a lot, and I think I'm still processing much of it, kind of a whirlwind. I'm sure you understand. Maybe when I get a little time and distance between it, I'll share it with you."

"Well, if you found closure and that brings you some peace, then I'm happy for you. And if and when you ever want to talk about it, I'm here." And like that, Savage let it rest.

At that moment, she didn't know if she loved him, but she loved the way he let her keep her secrets and didn't press. He would open the door to discussion, and leave it open, just as he had done with the badge. But Savage never forced his need for answers on her. The pressure she felt came from her and her alone.

"Thank you."

"For what?" he said.

"For understanding."

Savage now took some of the bread. Sopping up some of the oil, he shoved the whole thing in his mouth and swallowed it down, washing it with a swig of the Kendall Jackson.

"You want my opinion on the Nighthawk matter?"

"I do." Savage looked intently into her eyes.

"Well, what is that land used for typically? On the reservation, where Chief Nighthawk's body was found?"

"It's a non-residential section, and the portion of land where he was found is designated as the reservation's hunting grounds."

"What are their rules for hunting?"

"How do you mean?"

"I mean, aren't they required to operate with a hunting permit? Is it open to the general public?"

"That's the thing about tribal lands. The only people authorized to hunt on those lands have to be Native American. They have to be a member of the Southern Ute Tribe or a visiting member from another reservation with authorization to use the land from somebody at the council. There is a registry of hunters."

"Maybe the chief had a problem with one of them. Maybe there's some issue. Did any of his patrolmen know why he was out there?"

"There was a report of some poachers in the area. He had told one of his guys that he was going to look into it. They didn't think much of it at the time. I guess it's a pretty regular call they look into on the reservation."

"Maybe you've got your solution staring you in the face. Sometimes the simplest explanation is the right one. There was somebody hunting illegally, and he confronted them. Could've broke bad."

"That's kind of where we're leaning."

"It sounds like they just need to go through the list of hunters in the area and see if anybody's seen something. Anybody who has been authorized by the reservation to hunt on the land should be called into question."

"The tribal police have already begun that process. There's not a large list, but large enough that going through and interviewing each one will take a bit of time. Clearwater looked at the list of names and said the reservation has had no issue with any of the locals but will call in each hunter to verify their whereabouts at the time Chief Nighthawk died. Their initial look into the hunting angle doesn't raise any red flags, at least internal to the reservation."

"But if they weren't from the reservation?"

"Exactly. If the chief was looking into hunters not privy to access the reservation, it's going to be a little more difficult for them to track. Their name wouldn't be on any list." Savage washed down the bread with a swig of his wine.

"So, you're thinking that this is most likely somebody from outside the reservation?"

Savage nodded.

"You have the bruising but no injuries. Do you have a cause of death established yet?"

"We didn't determine the cause of death yet. We're waiting for the official determination from the medical examiners' office. There was some bruising and swelling around the head area, which could have been from a fall."

"Or," Hatch interrupted, "a strike."

Savage nodded.

"We're keeping our minds open to all possibilities at this point, and like I said, when we spoke earlier today, I'm acting in more of an advisory capacity. This is still a tribal investigation."

"It's also a personal one," Hatch said.

"I know. There are some concerning aspects. If poachers were involved, they very likely would've skipped town by now."

"Unless they're local."

"It's a possibility," Savage said.

"You know, there's somebody that might be able to help, at least at this point in the investigation, more so than me."

Savage cocked an eyebrow, shocked at her statement. "Who?"

"Ole Jed Russell," Hatch said, thinking of the man who had saved her life, the man who took up arms against the people trying to kill her and nearly cost his own. The tough former 101st Screaming Eagle, turned mountain recluse, Jedediah Russell. "He's from these parts. He's a bit of an outcast, but I know he does his own hunting and trapping. He probably moves in circles of other hunters and might have some information. Small town and all. Maybe he can help point us in the right direction."

"Then I guess we know where we're stopping after dinner."

Hatch put up her hands in a ready defense. "Whoa, whoa. I said I would consult. I would help as best I can, but I don't want to go getting involved. I'm not an investigator. I'm not one of your deputies."

Savage looked hurt by the comment. "I just figured you have a much better relationship with Jed, and his natural disdain for law enforcement would obviously be a barrier to any conversation I would have with him. Even with our history, I think he'd be more agreeable if you were with me. It would make things a lot easier."

Hatch gave up the resistance and then thought fondly of the idea of seeing Jed again. There were times in both New Mexico and Africa that she thought she wouldn't see anybody again, and the thought of seeing the man who had stood shoulder-to-shoulder with her pleased her. She had departed for New Mexico before he'd fully recovered from his wounds, and she'd meant to stop by and see him regardless.

"All right, I'll go with you, but let's not make this a habitual thing."

Savage gave a coy smile.

"I know what you're thinking, Dalton, but I am not getting involved beyond this. Do you understand?"

"Whatever you say, Hatch."

The food arrived and not a moment too soon. Hal Rigsby was right. The swordfish was amazing.

With full stomachs and two glasses of Sauvignon Blanc to wash it down, Hatch felt refreshed.

As she ate, she thought of the prospect of seeing Jed Russell again, and looked forward to the impromptu visit.

EIGHT

THEY MADE THE LAST BEND IN THE ROAD THROUGH THE THICK WOOD LINE of high pines that secluded Jed Russell's place. The gated entrance to the recluse's home, which Hatch had driven through during a desperate escape a few months ago, had been repaired in her absence.

Savage pulled to a stop in front of the gate with an oversized "No Trespassing" sign affixed to its center just as his cell phone rang. He answered it before the second ring concluded its rhythmic beat.

"What do you got?" he said into the phone.

Hatch could only hear the garbled response of another male's voice coming through the receiver but couldn't make out the words. She allowed their conversation to continue uninterrupted as she sat silently in the passenger seat.

She was only able to pick up Savage's half, but it didn't take long for her to realize it was in relation to the crime scene from earlier in the day.

"The serology report gave you what again?" He paused, listening for the answer. "Non-human blood type? If it's non-human, then what type of blood was it? Okay," he said, rubbing at the gray hair along his temple. "Can you fax that over to me? Email's even better. I'll take a closer look at the report when I get back to the office. Thanks, Dale. I appreciate it."

Savage clicked the phone off and slipped it back into his pants pocket, then looked over at Hatch.

"That was Dale Tyrell over at the ME's office. They haven't gotten into the body, but they did a quick analysis of the blood."

Hatch nodded and waited for his explanation.

"Feline. Some type of cat."

"Could be a bobcat. They're pretty prevalent in these parts."

"Well, that would go to prove our theory on him stumbling across some poachers or confronting them."

"I guess it makes our visit with Jed all that more important," Hatch said.

"Seems so, and like I said, I trust your judgment. You called it while we were at the bistro."

"I didn't call anything. The case is still wide open, and I'm pretty sure you were leaning in that direction as well. It sounded like the tribal police were already beginning to look into the hunter angle."

The good thing about working the reservation is that it was a small community and the tribal police officers knew most of the hunters by first name and could personally vouch for them as people and any connection they would have had to Nighthawk. It was the unknown that bothered Hatch, not knowing who could have been there and without putting feet on the ground at the crime scene herself, she felt that she was playing an unending game of catch up.

Although she trusted Savage's judgment in his eye for detail when it came to a scene, she wished she'd been able to be physically present at the scene. Seeing things with her own two eyes would've helped. Now she was conflicted because she offered her assistance as a consultant, as an outsider looking in. Deep down she knew there was only one way to truly work a case. To be involved. It was the real reason she hadn't put up much of an argument against coming along for the ride tonight. It was what brought her here to the mended gate entrance to Russell's mountain hideaway. As much as she wanted to stay out of it, Hatch found herself getting sucked in and could do little in the way of stopping it.

"Hopefully Jed can shed us a little light on the subject."

As if on cue, giant flood lights beamed out from posts on either side of the gate.

"That's a new addition," Hatch said looking over at Savage, who was just as surprised by the blinding light.

Shielding his eyes, he said. "Well, I guess it's safe to say Jed knows we're here."

A PA system squelched, piercing the stillness of the night. Hatch heard Russell's distinct voice echo out of its amplified command.

"I don't know what y'all are doing here, but unless you want my shotgun to pepper the front of your vehicle, I suggest you best turn that beast of an SUV around and head on back to wherever you came from."

Savage rolled his shielded eyes as if to say, here we go again.

Hatch put down the passenger side window. "Jed! It's Rachel Hatch," she said, loud enough for her voice to carry, hopefully to wherever the old Army vet was undoubtedly eyeing down at them through a long barrel of his shotgun.

The first time they'd met, the old man had gotten the drop on her.

A second later, the bright flood lights went out, and now with their night vision gone, they blinked rapidly to regain their ability to make out anything in the dark stillness around them. A second later, the gate lifted, and standing not too far off in the distance, just before the rise that led up to Jedidiah's custom-built home, was the man himself.

"Well, I never thought I'd see that face again." Russell walked over to her side of the Suburban.

She exited the car and the two gave a quick embrace, his long-barreled shotgun now lowered down by his side.

"How's the shoulder?" Hatch asked.

"Still hurts. But the upside is I can tell when it's going to rain," he gave a slap to where the bullet had passed through when he had taken a stand with her against the men trying to kill her several months back.

"You look good, and I'm happy to see you're doing well. Floodlights were a nice touch, as was the PA system. Getting a little more sophisticated, I see."

He smirked, and although she still hadn't fully adjusted her eyes back to the darkness, she could see well enough to notice the recluse's gaunt cheeks reddened a bit.

"I had to up my game after you barreled through that last time. Realized if you could crash through, then anybody could. The lights really help. Nothing like taking away someone's night vision."

Savage exited the vehicle, rubbing his eyes as he walked around the front to the passenger side. "Yeah, thanks for that, Jed. Once again our meetings are always so pleasurable."

Jed eyed the law man, and then outstretched his hand. "Sheriff."

"Good to see you're taking a kinder view of law enforcement these days," Hatch joked.

"Well, they did help me out of that jam after those bastards shot up my place. Savage seems like a decent enough fellow."

"Don't go gettin' all mushy on me Jed," Savage offered in jest.

"Did y'all just pop in to visit? Or should I be worried?"

"We wanted to pick your brain a bit," Savage said.

Russel eyed the lawman warily. "I've got a kettle on. I was preparing to make myself a cup of tea, and then I was going to sit on my porch for a little bit. One of my nightly routines. I love to watch the fireflies at night." He then focused his attention on Hatch. "And when, may I ask, did you get back into town, soldier?"

"Today."

"Well, at least you came to see me on your first day back. Makes me feel kind of special."

"I would have come and seen you either way, although things spiraled a bit, brought me here tonight, and I apologize for interrupting your evening routine."

"Likewise," said Savage, "but, you know, sometimes things can't wait."

"There's a truth in that statement," Russell said. "Can I assume y'all will be joining me for that cup of tea?"

"Just point the way," Hatch said. The armed recluse led the way up the hill toward his house.

"Anything I can help you with?" Hatch offered.

"No, just relax and find yourself a spot on the porch. I'll be out in just a moment with the tea." Russell disappeared inside, resting his shotgun against the inside of the door as he entered.

Savage took up a rocker, and Hatch took a seat on a bench swing.

"Hell of a different greeting than the first time you met," Savage said.

"A lot's changed since then."

She thought about herself and the truth behind those words. Sitting here on Jedidiah Russell's porch less than ten feet from where the former paratrooper had got the drop on her when they'd first met felt a bit surreal. Everything was spun on its axis.

A few moments later, the screen door opened and Russell appeared holding a folding tray. It looked funny to see the ironclad, tough old coot carrying a tray with three mugs and a hot kettle in the center.

"I hope you like Earl Grey. It's all I have. It's the only tea I drink. I'm particular 'bout these things."

"Anything is fine by me," Savage said.

"Likewise." Hatch then thought of the tea she'd had in Africa at Khari's cafe. A shipment of his wife's homemade tea blend was on its way to her. Now that she'd learned Jed was a tea drinker, she made a mental note to bring some over to him when it arrived.

Russell plopped his thin frame into the seat next to Hatch. The Screaming Eagle tattoo's faded ink was visible from his rolled-up sleeve. He blew at the top of the tea after steeping the bag and took a sip. Apparently, it needed more time for the flavor to steep because he set it back down on the tray.

"So do tell—what brought you here tonight?"

"I don't know if you heard, but Billy Nighthawk, the chief of police on the Southern Ute Reservation, was found dead this morning."

Russell curled his brow forward and looked at both Savage and then Hatch. "Murder?"

"We're not sure, but something doesn't feel right," Savage said.

"Well, like my father told me, if something doesn't feel right, it isn't, and you've got to dig until you find out what is right."

"Sound logic," Hatch said. Pretty much everything in her life was summed up by Jed's simple statement.

"So, what can I do to help or facilitate your understanding of the situation?"

"We're looking at it from all angles right now but leaning heavily toward his death being a murder."

Russell looked suddenly edgier than he had moments before. "You thinkin' I had somethin' to do with it?"

"Not at all." Savage held up his hands in surrender. "The chief might've crossed paths with some hunters recently."

"You're saying you think a couple hunters might've killed the chief?"

"We're not sure of anything at this point. Until we have the autopsy and the ME gives us some type of indication of what the cause of death was, I don't want to give in to conjecture. It could have been a natural cause, but the hunter theory seems viable. We found blood on the scene not too far away that comes back to an animal, a feline. I'm guessing in that area, most likely a bobcat."

Russell rubbed at the stubble on his chin.

"It may be something as simple as hunters seeing him out earlier," Savage said. "But the placement of his body and its proximity to the blood of an animal causes some concern."

"Well, me just being me, that should cause concern in anybody's books, as long as they've got a right head on their shoulders. Wouldn't you agree, Hatch?"

Hatch nodded. "And that's why we're here. All of the people that hunt on the Ute reservation are supposed to be Native American."

Jed nodded.

"And we also know you're a hunter, Jed. You know this area about as good as anyone. You've been hunting and fishing it for years. Maybe there's a chance you know of some people we should be talking to."

"You mean people like me, recluses, people who follow their own path and maybe don't go by the rules?"

Hatch smiled. "You said it, not me."

"I'm flattered, Hatch, that you think I run with a tough crowd."

"I'm not saying you know these people personally. I'm just saying that maybe there's a chance you know of them and can point us in the right direction."

Jed was quiet and he picked up his mug again, this time wrapping the teabag's string around the spoon and squeezing the last bit of flavor from the pouch into the pool of dark steaming liquid. He then took a long, slow sip.

"I was at Weaver's gun shop the other day." Jed took another sip as steam rose up in front of his face. "I've seen the guy before. He's a wiry shell of a man. Never had much of a conversation with him, but I've seen him in the store a couple of times. Looks like he's been bitten by the bug."

Savage looked at Hatch and shrugged. "Drugs?" he asked.

"That boy looks like he got an itch he can't scratch," Jed said. "He's a skittish, jittery type. And the way he reacted when he was accusing Hank Weaver of shortin' him on price showed just that. He's unstable. I wouldn't trust him as far as I could throw him, and mind you, I've got a bum shoulder. He was alone every time I saw him."

"Do you have a name?" Savage asked.

"No. Never been formally acquainted with the man."

"Anybody else you can think of?" Savage asked. "Who might be worth our time?"

"None that I can think of." Russell seemed to be lost in thought. "I'd say your best bet is to find the guy from Weaver's."

"At least now we've got our person of interest," Savage said, looking at Hatch.

Hatch nodded. She wanted to get excited at the prospect of hunting down this potential killer but was immediately stung by the reality that she would be watching this one unfold from the sidelines.

"I don't know the guy by name, but I do by reputation. It's all hearsay, of course." Jed set the cup down and leveled a gaze at them, making sure he had their full attention.

Neither spoke.

"I move in different circles, and I hear things. I was at Miller's Walk not too long ago and overheard a conversation with him. He was pretty drunk as far as I could tell." Russell paused.

Hatch watched Jed. He was thinking. She noticed he had a tell. Earlier when he'd mentioned the incident at the gun shop, Jed had pressed his tongue against his left incisor just before speaking. He was doing it again now.

"Wait a minute! I'm not sure it will assist you in any way, but I recall him saying something to the bartender that night about partnering up. He kept shouting about coming up in the world. The way he looked, the way he talked, and the way he was flashing his cash every time he purchased a beer made me think it had something to do with drugs. I don't associate with people like that myself."

"Never thought you did," Hatch said.

"But knowing the people in these parts and those who keep to themselves, I would warn you of this. If he's into the drug trade, then I'm guessing he's probably well-armed and probably pretty damn dangerous, too. If you plan on paying him a visit, keep an eye on booby traps. A guy like him is bound to protect himself. I could have sworn I heard him pounding his chest about being one of the CFAs."

Hatch had never heard the term. "CFAs?" She looked at Savage, who seemed to recognize the acronym, but Jed answered first.

"Colorado Free Americans."

"Never heard of it," Hatch said.

"Probably a good thing," Savage offered. "They don't believe that laws apply to them. It's a spin-off group from the sovereign citizen movement. They've got a small contingent around here in the hill country. Some change their given names for a fresh start. I don't have many run-ins with them. They mostly keep to themselves, live off the grid, but they have a strong disdain for law enforcement and are willing to take up arms in their resistance."

Savage finished his tea and immediately popped a couple bite-sized rectangles of licorice into his mouth.

Jed gave a wire-thin smile. "Now, Sheriff, I don't want you putting me in a category with those crazies, you hear me? Just 'cause I keep to myself doesn't mean I'm part of that."

"I never thought you were, Jed."

"I can't imagine a Screaming Eagle from the 101st would turn their back on their country and its laws." Hatch patted him on his shoulder.

Jed's mood lightened slightly. His smile remained and he reached down and grabbed his cup. "I'd be happy to make a trek out there with you if you need me to. I'm good with that kind of stuff. Hell, I might be able to just walk up on the man's property, might not see me as much of a threat as you all."

"Don't lump me in here with the sheriff. I'm a civilian now, Jed," Hatch said. "I've got no dog in this fight. I'm just here as a consultant."

Jed laughed and almost spit his tea out. "Consultant, my ass. Rachel Hatch, you're about as far from a sideliner as any person I've ever met in my entire life. I can't see you sitting idly by and letting everyone else get out there and mix it up."

Hatch took a sip of her tea, still piping hot, but delicious. She added a bit of honey to sweeten it, stirring it in, and took another sip before answering. That's the thing about sitting on a porch in the middle of nowhere. Conversation wasn't done at a sprinter's pace. Hatch liked the pace of things right now. She hoped her future could hold such a pace, and she reminded herself to be cognizant and not to let it grow into tedium, to appreciate the calm now that her stormy life was over.

"I'm out of the game, Jed. I'm just a plain old civilian, just trying to get my life back in order and reconnect with my family."

Jed's paper-thin smile widened into a toothy grin. Seeing him in such a state gave the crusty old timer an almost childlike quality. "Well, that's about the best damn present your homecoming could ever give. You deserve it!" Then he turned his attention to Savage. "Now, you listen here, Sheriff, don't go draggin' Hatch here into any of your troubles."

He held his hands up defensively. "Never thought of it."

Jed didn't seem to buy it, and neither did Hatch.

"Do me a favor, if you pay Hank Weaver a visit at his gun store, don't tell him that I'm the one that talked about this. I'd prefer not to get involved in anything, especially if this becomes a murder investigation. Might ruin my reputation around these parts. I don't want to be put out as some kind of gossip."

"Fair enough." Hatch raised her mug and clinked it gently against Jed's.

The three sat quietly for a moment, embracing the stillness, each in their own way as they drank their tea. Hatch's eyes had adjusted to the night, and he was right, the way the lightning bugs danced in the darkness was beautiful. Ironically, it reminded Hatch of a time when she'd been struck in the head and saw stars. At least the ones she saw tonight didn't come with the accompanying pain.

Jed Russell had found peace, and Hatch hoped she was close to finding hers.

NINE

Hatch was still soaked with the sweat from her morning run as she sat at the kitchen table drinking her second cup of her mother's delicious coffee. Jake was silently eating a waffle while staring at his iPad. Daphne was still asleep. It was quiet except for the occasional fork full of waffle that Jake was noisily devouring between gaming sessions. He was intense, immersed wholly in the screen in front of him, oblivious to Hatch's presence. It's like the electrons in the screen were sucking out the animation of his very soul. Watching her nephew dissolve into the screen saddened her for some reason. Maybe it was because it was foreign to her. She hadn't had such things when she was a child, so seeing the hold it had on him was something she couldn't completely understand. The thought of it made her feel old, and maybe that's what bothered her most.

She was in her mid-thirties and had spent most of her adulthood in relative isolation. She felt the clock ticking even though she would never admit it to anyone.

Hatch nearly jumped when she heard the floorboard creak. She hadn't even noticed her mother sneak up from behind. Before she instinctively spun, her mother gently patted her shoulder with ice cold hands.

Maybe these past few days of easy life and finding peace had already started to dull her awareness. She pushed the thought from her mind as foolishness, but it lingered. Too much free time, idle hands, and her mind was already beginning to play tricks on her.

Although she had only been back in Hawk's Landing for a minute, Hatch felt a shift in her life as if time had begun to slow down, as if the things that used to matter no longer held the same weight.

"How's the coffee?" Hatch's mother asked, interrupting her thought.

Hatch was actually grateful for the interruption. "It's fantastic. I'm already on my second cup."

The compliment brought a smile to her mother's face.

Smiles used to come in heaping doses in Hatch's life before her father's death. It had been hard for Hatch to remember those times, to remember her mother before the devastation. But Hatch now recalled the mother of her youth. And she had been, by all accounts, one of the happiest people she had ever seen. That was until the death of her husband had dimmed the light in her eyes to barely a flicker.

Hatch just caught her first glimmer of it, the first in almost twenty years. It made Hatch truly happy to see her mother's smile return again. Although it only lasted a moment before it dissipated. Her mother walked back to the kitchen to grab her own cup. She returned less than a minute later, taking a seat next to Hatch.

"I see you're up early as always."

Hatch breathed in the aromatic scent created by the freshly ground beans and nodded. "Hard to break old habits."

"Your father never could. That's for sure," she said. And again, the smile returned.

Maybe in Hatch's return, her mother knew she could finally close the door to the pain of the last two decades.

"We're glad you're back. I'm glad." Her mother struggled with the words.

Their relationship was still askew. Not everything hard in life tidied up in neat, easy packages. The most important things took time. The healing process needed to mend their relationship would be a tedious one. The distance between Hatch and her mother would need time to close the gap.

Hatch could see her mother was eagerly awaiting an explanation on what Hatch had found since leaving to find the truth about her father's death. She could see it in her teal eyes that caught the morning's light in dazzling fashion. They asked the question her mouth could not verbalize. Hatch pretended not to see it. She feigned distraction every time they were alone. Hatch still wasn't ready to talk about it. She wasn't sure what kind of closure her mother needed. Plus, the way in which Hatch had come about seeking those answers was vastly different from her mother's peaceful ways. The ultimate outcome had been more dead bodies laid at the feet of a criminal organization responsible for the murder of her father. She wasn't sure how, if ever, she could share that particular piece of her journey for truth with her mom. Hatch had been working on a sanitized explanation, one that would ultimately keep her mother safe.

If Talent Executive Services, formerly the Gibson Consortium, the black ops private contractor group that had killed her father, ever came for Hatch, she wanted it to stop with her. And she didn't want to expose her mother to anything that might make her a risk or a perceived risk. The less she knew, the better. Hatch understood this, even if her mother didn't, and she was trying to come up with a way of delivering the message.

"So, what'd you find out?" her mother asked after taking a sip from her coffee.

And there it was…the question. Out in the open. Hatch wasn't ready for this. She fiddled and reached for her mug, looking to delay her response.

Hatch held the cup to her lips, and her phone rang. She looked down at it, grateful for the interruption. She didn't care if it was a bill collector or telemarketer. At this point, she would answer any caller, but was relieved when she saw that it was Savage. She grabbed onto the phone like it was a lifeline. In effect it was, saving her from the conversation with her mother.

"Hey, Dalton, hold on one second." Hatch covered the phone and raised a finger as she stood from the table and made her way outside to the back porch overlooking the entrance to her running trail.

"Thanks for the call."

"Thanks for answering," Savage said.

"Sorry, you just saved me from a conversation I've been putting off with my mom."

"The one about your dad?" Savage asked.

"Yeah." He seemed to understand and didn't press.

"So, what's up? Find anything out about that guy Jed mentioned last night, the one from the gun store?"

"Yeah, Sinclair stopped in this morning. Clint Wesson. He's actually a local. His place is here in Hawk's Landing. On the outskirts of town. We're going to pay him a visit if you want to come for the ride."

"Like I said, I'll consult, but I'm not going to be hands on."

"Well, what was Jed's place about then?"

"Jed's visit was about seeing Jed. The guy took a bullet for me. If I didn't go and see him when I first got back, I'd be in big trouble. If you hadn't driven me, I had planned to see him after our dinner anyway. But as for going with you on a manhunt? No thanks. That puts me back at square one, and as far as I recall, I'm not a deputy."

"You could be."

"Not really feeling the idea of a sixteen-week Academy."

"You'd fly through it."

"Not happening. I think I'm good here." Hatch looked through the window at her mother, who was still sitting at the table. "I've got some stuff to figure out."

"Sorry, I don't mean to push. I just like having your eyes on things."

For a split-second, Hatch blushed. She thought he had said, "I like having your eyes on me." Her subconscious had temporarily overridden her active listening. She was so glad he was not there to see her face now as it brightened three shades of red.

"I'll call you when I get back," Dalton said.

"Sounds good."

"Hope this guy's not as crazy as Jed. You remember that first time we met?"

Hatch smiled.

"You saved us that day from what could have been an ugly confrontation."

"Well, sometimes things have a way of working themselves out," she said.

"All right, well I've got to run. Let me know if you change your mind."

He ended the phone call, and Hatch felt alone as she stared out at the high mountain rise behind the tall pines that littered her backyard.

She could look in every single direction from any point outside of her house and not see a single solitary other house or person. Her dad had picked this house for that very reason. Even with that, no matter how hard he tried to run from his past, it still found him here in total and complete isolation.

Savage was asking her to return to the life she'd struggled to leave behind. She could feel her past sneaking up, following her. Maybe it always would.

Daphne appeared. She plopped down at the table across from where Jake was seated. He didn't seem to notice. Hatch put her phone away and walked back inside.

Hatch crept up behind Daphne, who was head down, already scribbling furiously on the paper she'd brought with her. She was lost in her art, going from color to color in her open marker kit sprawled out across the table. Papers were strewn everywhere, and she seemed to be caught up in whatever images or thoughts were dancing in her imagination.

Hatch bent low and kissed her on the back of her head. Her hair smelled of the bubble gum shampoo she'd used the night before during her bath.

Daphne turned and looked up at her. "Auntie Rachel, are you joining me?"

Hatch had no excuse not to, although the thought of attempting to draw terrified her. But less so than returning to the conversation with her mother.

"Sure, hun," Hatch said, taking a seat next to the child who immediately slid over a stack of papers, further spreading her markers. Hatch caught a red one before it rolled off the end of the table. Hatch's lifesaving, cat-like reflexes were now being utilized to catch washable markers.

"I'm going to be honest with you, Daphne. I haven't drawn anything since grade school," she said, holding the marker in her hand.

"It's easy. You just draw what's in your head."

Hatch leaned close and whispered in her young niece's ear. "What if there's nothing in my head?"

"You're so silly," Daphne said in between bursts of laughter, and then went back to her drawing.

Hatch looked at the drawing Daphne was creating. Nearly three decades younger than Hatch and the six-year-old was drawing at a level lightyears beyond hers.

It was a butterfly with its wings wide, each segment of the wing a bright and dazzling color. There was no rhyme or reason or pattern, but what she had created was absolutely beautiful.

"You can copy me," Daphne said.

"I'll do my best." Hatch uncapped the marker and began trying to simulate the movements of the girl beside her.

The two drew in relative silence for the next fifteen minutes. Daphne's butterfly now had a flower to sit on and a rainbow in the background with clouds and a sun. Hatch was still working on forming the wings and shape of the creature on her page. She began adding several different colors, but quickly saw that the image on her paper was nowhere close to the one her six-year-old niece had just created.

Daphne was lost in her own thoughts. She would pause momentarily and shoot a glance at Hatch's artwork and smile encouragingly, even though Hatch knew deep down her niece must be holding back her true opinion of the catastrophe appearing on the page in front of her. Daphne chewed on a pen cap while she worked diligently, and then reached a point where nearly all of the white of the 8x11 sheet of computer paper was filled.

Daphne held up her picture and shifted the page in her hand, angling it to look at her artwork with a critical eye. Then, she smiled and capped her final marker with a click.

"All done," she said, proud of herself.

The confidence of a child. As much tragedy as the little girl had faced, life had yet to kick those confidences out from under her. When did childlike wonder give way to realistic expectations? When did the dreams fade into oblivion? Hatch thought about her own childhood and wondered if she had ever had this creative energy to see the world in bright and happy colors. She honestly couldn't remember.

Sure, there were fleeting moments of happiness from her childhood, but being catapulted into adulthood at the age of twelve under such tragedy had shattered those good times. Bearing witness to the murdered body of her father had nearly erased all memories of happiness that had come before. It was like that one moment in time had dissolved the twelve years of good leading up to it. She was happy to see Daphne was stronger than her, that even though she had lost both her mother and father to tragedy, she had been resolute and committed to her happiness. Here it was, displayed in full color on the page before Hatch.

Hatch thought she was strong because she had channeled her anger and her rage and forged ahead. In hindsight, that life carried a different burden. She still held the weight of it to this very day. Daphne had a different strength and one that burned much brighter than Rachel's. The light of it made Hatch happy.

"I don't think I quite nailed it," Hatch said, holding her picture up just as Daphne had done, extending her arms out in front of her as if looking at it from a different angle would make the hideous design any better.

Daphne broke into laughter, and so did Hatch.

"What were you drawing?" she asked with genuine curiosity.

Hatch looked at her drawing and then back at Daphne's. "I was drawing a butterfly like yours." Making the verbal comparison didn't match what she was seeing when holding up the two sheets next to each other.

"It looks like a pterodactyl," she said, giggling even harder.

Hatch took a second, looked at her picture, and burst into laughter when she realized that her niece was right. Somehow Hatch, in her attempts to draw a simple butterfly, had created a prehistoric dinosaur. Hatch hadn't laughed that hard in a very long time.

She wanted to stay in this moment for as long as she could, taking it in completely and embracing the simple purity of it.

Hatch then thought of Savage. He was heading out to find a potential murderer while she was drawing butterflies. The dichotomy of her past and present life had never been clearer.

TEN

Savage looked at his ragtag group and couldn't get over the fact that his newest addition and youngest member of the team, John Nighthawk, seemed to be the most prepared for what was coming. Becky Sinclair and Littleton looked more scared than ready.

Littleton's hand shook as he tried to stick the police patch onto the center of his raid vest.

Savage made a mental note to put Littleton in the rear security position or perimeter if things escalated. He hoped none of these mental precautions would prove necessary and that their contact with Clint Wesson would be civil. But life and experience had taught him the simple lesson that being prepared was the single greatest way to level the playing field. And going to find a person who may or may not have been responsible for the death of a chief of police warranted a fair amount of preparation. Savage just hoped his group of relatively green deputies were up for the task.

"All right guys, listen up. We're going to meet up with Clearwater on the main road outside the path leading to where Wesson lives. It's a one way in, one way out driveway to our target location. We're going to approach in marked vehicles. I want to make sure we are clearly identifiable as police when we move in."

"How many cars are we taking?" Littleton asked.

"We're going to all ride together in my Suburban. I don't want this to look like a raid. Remember, this is just a meet and greet as of right now. Clint Wesson's just a person of interest. We just want to know what he may or may not have seen. We're not sure of his level of involvement at this point. Showing up in a caravan of police vehicles might spook him."

"Why the raid vests then?" Littleton asked nervously.

"Because based on the circumstances surrounding Chief Nighthawk's death, we have to take him very seriously and treat him as a potential threat. Plus, he's a hunter, which means he has access to weapons and ammunition. And furthermore, being that he's a hunter, he's trained to use them. We don't want him picking us out as potential prey, is that clear?"

"Great," Littleton mumbled.

They loaded into the Suburban and headed out, driving south toward the town line. The drive took less than twenty minutes. They met with Clearwater where the road forked. The black and white Crown Victoria driven by Clearwater followed their Suburban up the long driveway.

Savage noted several pole cameras staggered amongst the trees along the dirt path. If the overhead map imagery he'd pulled up before leaving was correct, the road leading in was approximately a quarter mile long and dead-ended into the couple acre swath of private property owned by Wesson.

They pulled to a stop at a ten-foot-tall gate. Posted along the chain links of the gate were various signs threatening the life of any person who dared enter without permission. One caught Savage by particular surprise, a triangulated yellow sign with a bright red explosion. He understood the inferred threat. The thought of someone protecting their property with explosives definitely gave him pause as he looked over at the faces of his deputies.

Sinclair was in the front passenger seat. She looked steady, but her eyes told him she was fighting to remain calm.

Littleton, seated behind her, was as skittish as a squirrel. Every movement in a tree, every gust of wind, seemed to cause him to twist and turn. He was terrified and wore the colors of that for everyone to see.

In the rear-view mirror, Savage caught the eye of Nighthawk. His gaze was steely calm. For a young man, he had the look of someone who had experienced a full life and seemed unphased by whatever potential threat lay in wait.

"Guys, give me a second. I'm going to step out and talk to Clearwater."

The three remained in the vehicle. Savage walked up to the Crown Vic.

"Hey, Sheriff," Clearwater said. "I know this is your turf, but not sure how we're going to get this guy's attention unless you're planning to ram your Suburban into his gate."

"Give me a second, and I'll double check to see if I can find a phone number in the system. Maybe I can get a hold of Wesson and have him come to the gate." Savage pulled out his cellphone.

"Looks like you can hold off on that," Clearwater said.

Savage pocketed the phone. "Why is that?"

"Because I think he's coming our way now."

Savage suddenly understood as he heard the sound of a Kawasaki dirt bike's engine buzzing in the distance. A lanky man, matching the description given by Russell, rode toward them on the loud motorcycle. He skidded to a stop, sending a sandstorm of dust their way.

Savage shielded his eyes and swatted at the remaining dust as it settled. The man on the bike took off his helmet. He had close-cropped hair, cut tight on the sides. The strands on top of his head were matted with sweat. The uneven lengths of slicked hair looked as if his barber had given up halfway through the cut. He was greasy and unwashed. His sunburnt face had a band of red starting at the midway point of his forehead. In the cool morning air, sweat dripped down his face.

"Bitten by the bug" was the phrase Jed had used. Seeing Wesson now, Savage knew it was right. Methamphetamines played a large part in this man's life.

Wesson spit on the ground in front of him as if some sign of defiance.

"Clint Wesson?" Savage asked.

"Who's asking?" He stuffed tobacco into his lower lip and wiped the excess off on his dirty jeans while staring hard at Savage. "What business do you got to do with me? You ain't got no jurisdiction here."

"I'm not trying to get into a pissing contest with you. I'm just following up on an investigation in Hawk's Landing, and your name came up. I'd like to talk to you about it."

"What investigation?"

"I would prefer we speak privately about that."

"Well, how about I tell you to go piss off?"

"You are well within your rights to do that," Savage said. "But I'll tell you this, if I walk away from here without talking to you, then there's probably going to be a whole heap of trouble coming down on you that you'll never see coming."

"Don't try to come here and intimidate me!" He spat, and a dribble of brown spit remained in the corner of his mouth.

"Not my intention," Savage offered calmly.

The skinny, sunburnt hunter rubbed at his forehead. Even though it was relatively cool out, he was sweating profusely, more now since Savage identified his purpose for the unannounced visit. It registered on Savage's radar that this man might know something, but he knew his leverage was limited. He couldn't force the man to talk with him.

"It's up to you," Savage said, intentionally avoiding tipping his hand as to the nature of the investigation. He turned, tapped his forehead as if tipping an imaginary hat and began walking back to his vehicle.

Just as his hand touched the door handle to his Suburban, he heard Wesson say, "You said Hawk's Landing?"

Savage turned and took a few steps closer. "I did."

Wesson was scared. Savage could see it. The hunter wanted to know what Savage was working on. The need to know sometimes outweighed reason. Wesson would be better off not talking to him at all. But Savage was glad the man didn't realize this.

"You going to put me in the back of that police car? This some type of trick?"

Savage gave a slow shake of his head. "Like I said, Mr. Wesson, this is completely on you. If you want to come and talk to me? Good, maybe you can help me out. If you don't, then I don't know how this is going to turn out for you."

Wesson was quiet.

"If you decide to come and talk with me, it has to be your decision. It's got to be one-hundred percent voluntary."

Wesson spit again. "I ain't shook. You don't intimidate me!"

"I didn't say you were," Savage said. "Or that I did. Tell you what, I'm going to head back to the station. You know where it is?"

Wesson nodded with his arms folded in defiance as he straddled the motorcycle.

"Okay, well how about this? How about you go and do whatever you need to do and meet us there?"

"You telling me I come talk to you, and you ain't going to put no trick on me and put me in jail tonight?"

"That's not the plan."

Wesson wiped his nose on his forearm, leaving a glisten of snot. "Fine. See you there, Sheriff."

Before Savage could say anything, Wesson revved the engine of the motorcycle. It sounded like a buzz saw on steroids. A second later, the thin-framed hunter disappeared into a cloud of dust as he drove away.

Savage hopped back into the driver's seat of the Suburban.

Sinclair looked at him wide-eyed and said, "What was that all about?"

"Just a friendly conversation."

"I thought that was going to turn into a standoff," Nighthawk said from the backseat.

Savage smiled. "Not everything's a gun fight. This isn't the movies."

"What's next?" Nighthawk asked.

"I'm guessing he's probably going to go clean himself up and then head to our department to be interviewed."

Littleton let out a long sigh much louder than he obviously intended as evident by the redness of his cheeks. His most terrified deputy must've been holding his breath for the majority of that confrontation.

What he would give to have Hatch along instead. But you play the hand you're dealt.

ELEVEN

CLINT WESSON KEPT HIS WORD. HE ONLY LAGGED BEHIND SAVAGE'S ARRIVAL at the Hawk's Landing Sheriff's Office by twenty minutes or so. Savage used the interim time to research through federal and local databases to see what he could find on the man who would soon be sitting across from him in the interview room. Savage was a seasoned investigator, having cut his teeth in Denver's homicide unit, but he liked the idea of approaching the hunter with an equally seasoned backup detective to observe from a distance. It had served him well in the past.

The interviews he had conducted in Denver were typically done with one interviewer in the room, not the good cop bad cop rendition played out in television dramas. His partners typically watched the interviews through a live feed from the room's cameras. None of the deputies, not even Nighthawk, had proven themselves worthy enough to sit second chair to the keen-eyed lawman. Investigative experience was critical when it came to the delicate chess game of interview and interrogation. And two minds were better than one.

There was one person who he did trust to observe and assist, somebody whose skill undoubtedly bested his. Somebody who would be capable of picking up on the subtleties of deception that Savage might miss while facing off with Wesson.

The observing detective, or investigator, would be watching for nonverbal clues, listening to the flow of conversation. Sometimes the interviewer in the room got caught up in the moment and would miss something subtle. But being outside of the limelight made it easier to pick up on these nuances. Savage, in his past life as a city homicide detective, used to keep his phone on silent, but on his thigh so when his partner was observing the interview from the other room, he could text him questions, remind him of things, point out discrepancies in facts.

It also enabled Savage to minimize note taking, transferring some of that responsibility to his partner in the other room. It gave Savage an advantage, making him a more engaged listener. Working in tandem evened the odds when going against a criminal on the defensive. Plus, it gave extra time for research. When some new information was given, the detective watching from the other room could quickly do a search, either database or Google-wise to find out the veracity of the information being provided. References to people and places could be fact checked while the interview was taking place, expediting and streamlining the interviewer's ability to call out any lies or missteps. He wanted that support at his disposal for this interview and knew his deputies didn't have the experience to provide it. But he knew the right person for the job.

Sinclair had just escorted Wesson to the interview room. She'd provided him a Sprite from the vending machine along with a bag of corn chips.

From the monitor in his office, Savage watched the thin man with the two-toned forehead tear open the bag of chips. He fidgeted anxiously as he sipped from the soda can. He knew he was being recorded. As per policy, Sinclair had advised him of it when he was brought inside. Every few seconds Wesson would peer up at the camera in the corner.

Savage picked up his phone and called the one person he felt could help level the playing field. She answered on the first ring.

"Hey." Her voice sounded different. The edge that he'd heard when he had first met her months ago seemed to have dissipated. It wasn't completely gone, but it had definitely softened. Savage loved to hear the sound of it, although he would never openly admit this.

"As a consultant," Savage began with a touch of mockery in his voice, "would you be willing to come down to the station and assist me on an interview?"

"That sounds pretty hands on to me, Dalton," she said playfully.

"I'm not asking you to do the interview, Hatch. I'm just asking if you would be willing to sit in my office, act as a consultant and watch the interview take place."

"You want an extra set of eyes."

"Never hurts to have them."

Hatch's voice was muffled for a moment, and Savage could make out some of what she was saying. She was talking to Daphne, telling her she would get back with her in just a second, after she got off the phone.

"Look, Hatch, I know you're busy, and I know you're trying to settle back in. It's a lot to ask."

"No, I'd be happy to do it. And to be honest, the more I've been thinking about this case, the more I want to help you as best I can."

Savage had expected more resistance from her but was happy he didn't have to push it upon her. He was also happy to hear that she was thinking about the case. He had hoped her investigative fire had started to burn a little brighter upon learning some of the details. Hard to let go of her prior life as a CID investigator. Savage, wisely, had played to that fact, knowing it would be hard for her to resist.

He felt guilty, also knowing she was working hard at resetting and restarting her life without this piece in it, and here he was tugging at her to come back into the fold. But maybe he could just keep her on as a consultant, use her in odds and ends like this until the case was done, and then he'd see where things went from there.

"When do you think you want me down there?"

Savage laughed a bit. "He's already here."

"Give me ten minutes then," she said.

"Works for me. I'll get in and get started, do a little rapport building to get things moving along. He's pretty anxious. I don't want him to get cold feet and bolt. Text me when you check-in. I'll let Barbara know you're going to be coming through, and she can get you set up in my office. I'll leave my computer open with the live feed to the interview room."

"What do you need from me?" Hatch asked.

"Just see if you notice anything I don't. It's always good to have a second pair of eyes on a case like this, and I trust you."

"Do my best," Hatch said, hanging up.

Savage looked at the screen in front of him. Clint Wesson's life in the form of a criminal resume, everything from minor drug charges to drunk and disorderly, plus a few DUIs, but nothing of the felony nature. Although, in one of the police reports he had come across, it appeared that Wesson had claimed to be a sovereign citizen and did not need to adhere to laws outside of his own beliefs. Savage wasn't overly thrilled about confronting someone that believed laws didn't apply to him, but it wasn't the first time, and undoubtedly in this part of the world, would not be the last.

Regardless of what Wesson thought about the laws of this country, they still applied to him. And if he was somehow criminally involved in the Ute Reservation Chief of Police's death, then he would face the repercussions.

TWELVE

Nighthawk interrupted Savage's thoughts as he knocked on the frame of the open door. "Sheriff, he's ready to go. Do you want me to come in there and help?"

There was a glint in his eye. Savage had seen it before. He had been there himself. This case was personal. Savage wanted to keep Nighthawk close enough to the case that he'd feel involved, but he didn't want him directly interacting with a man who may or may not have had a hand in his father's death. Any emotional response inside of a recorded interview room could be extremely detrimental to the long-term effectiveness of the case, and Savage had to temper his responsibility to the dead chief with his son's desire for justice.

The best justice was served without emotion, with clear-headed vision. Hatch had it when dealing with her sister's death. He could see that Nighthawk was not ready for that. The intensity in Nighthawk's eyes spoke of vengeance. Savage could see that the young deputy wanted nothing more than to beat the information out of Wesson.

A case is only as good as the evidence presented, and as of right now, they were lacking in that area. Wesson might be the best shot at gathering some usable information, and Savage didn't want Nighthawk's anger to be what got in the way.

Savage could almost read Nighthawk's mind. The newest addition to his small department would be of no use with respect to the upcoming interview. But that didn't mean he couldn't use it as a teachable moment to demonstrate some interview and interrogation tactics.

"I think I'm going to be good for the interview. It's probably best if you don't go in there right now. I want to keep things on an even keel while I work him. Hatch is coming by. She should be here in about ten minutes. You can sit with her in my office and watch the interview. She's got a real depth of experience when it comes to interrogation, and I want her eyes on this one. She's going to forward me information that she sees, and maybe you can learn something from her."

Nighthawk nodded, the muscles in his jaw flexed and rippled along the rigid jawline of the young Native American deputy. He exhaled slowly and agreed.

SAVAGE HAD SPENT THE LAST HALF HOUR TALKING WITH CLINT WESSON. Savage hadn't discussed anything about the case, except for the early conversation about when Wesson asked him, "Why the hell am I here?" to which Savage had nonchalantly responded he was looking into a case on the Ute Reservation. Upon hearing that, Wesson's body went rigid. Savage could see right off the bat that was a topic they weren't ready to discuss, so he eased back out and began talking to Wesson about his life here in Colorado. Simple questions designed to establish a connection to how long he had lived in the area, and where he was from. It was interview small talk to build up a mental list of things he could use when resistance was offered.

Savage had planned to confront him on several issues as the interview went on, but in the early stages, the conversation had to be as amiable as possible so he could establish a relationship with the suspect, build trust and minimize any perceived threat he saw in Savage. As they talked, Savage found hooks, positives that Wesson responded favorably to. These were topics of conversation where he could redirect him if things went south. And ultimately, because this was a voluntary interview, Savage wanted to keep the man comfortable enough that he stayed in the room long enough to give him whatever information he had with regard to Chief Nighthawk's death.

There were no clocks on the wall. Savage intentionally did not wear a wristwatch while in the room. Time was the ultimate tool. Without a reference, the time spent in the room became impossible to track. He recalled a murder interview in Denver. The suspect thought he'd confessed after only an hour. Savage remembered the shock on his face when he learned he'd spent nearly six hours in the interview box. The longer they sat, the more likely the interviewee was to slip up.

He had received a text message eighteen minutes ago from Hatch letting him know she was in his office and watching. She hadn't texted again since that point and he hadn't replied. Savage knew she'd understand. It wasn't a conversational text and anything she would say while Savage was in the interview would be for the sole purpose of assisting in the case.

With the fundamentals of rapport somewhat established with Wesson, Savage began to turn up the heat.

"So, Mr. Wesson—"

"I told you before," he interrupted. "Call me Clint! Mister sounds stupid."

"Clint. Sure. And you can call me Dalton if you like."

The man folded his arms, apparently not wanting to get on a first-name basis with the law.

"Clint, you've been in this area for several years. Is that right?"

"Moved here from Wyoming, back when I was twenty."

"And why was it you left Wyoming?"

"None of your damn business."

Savage already knew, having pulled his record, that Wesson had several run-ins with local police in his hometown in Wyoming. They were misdemeanor cases, but once you became known to law enforcement, it was a hard thing to shake. Maybe Wesson felt he could get a better deal if he started anew somewhere else, or maybe the drug trade had drifted him down into the Rockies. Either way, one thing was for certain, he had left when he was twenty and now, only four years later, he was sitting in another police department. Apparently, trouble followed Clint Wesson no matter where he went.

"How long we got to talk?"

"Like I said, Clint, this here is a conversation."

"Well, all you've done is asked me about my life and where I'm from. Did I do something wrong or not?"

"I don't know. Did you?"

The man sipped at his can of Sprite, but it had been empty for nearly ten minutes. Savage knew this. Wesson was nervous, and Savage knew he'd touched on something that bothered him.

"You're free to go, Clint. I told you that. The door's unlocked. You're here voluntarily. But I think you and I both know why you're here."

"I don't know what the hell you're talking about, Sheriff."

"You're an avid hunter, right?"

"What the hell's an avid?"

Savage fought the laugh swelling inside his chest. "Let me rephrase. You hunt a lot, right?"

"Yeah."

"When's the last time you were out on a hunt?"

"Not too long ago."

"Clint, I hope we're going to get a little more open and honest with each other. You keep talking in circles, and I'm going to assume there's more to this conversation." Savage leaned in slightly, closing the physical space between him and his suspect.

"I hunt a lot...so...I don't know. Couldn't tell you exactly. What's it to you anyway?" He played with the aluminum can in front of him.

"When's the last time you hunted on the Southern Ute Reservation?"

"I ain't never been on no Ute Reservation."

Wesson broke eye contact. Savage caught it. A second later, he received a text from Hatch. *Lying* was all the message said. Hatch immediately followed with another text, *Push*.

Savage knew what it meant. Wesson was quickly becoming unraveled.

Pushing confrontation was the interrogation phase of the interview, and he was entering it now.

"I saw at your house when we rolled up that you had some pole cameras leading up to your property."

Wesson looked up and stared back into the eyes of Savage. The redirect confused the man, and Savage could see it.

"Yeah. That's my property, and I have every right to protect it."

"Of course you do. It was just an observation. You like to keep an eye on your property to keep an eye out for trespassers. Is that right?"

"Ain't nothin' wrong with that. You got a camera up there in the corner of this room right now."

"You're right."

"What of it?"

"Well, the reservation is very small in terms of population, but the land is pretty expansive. So, how do you think they keep an eye on all that property with such a small police department and a limited manpower?"

"Beats me." The man shrugged, breaking eye contact again.

Text from Hatch, *He's nervous.*

"They use pole cameras."

If Clint Wesson had drunk a gallon of spoiled milk, he couldn't have looked worse than he did right now. It was as if all the blood and color from his half-sunburnt face drained completely. In the climate-controlled interview room, sweat poured out of his poorly cut hairline, and his left index finger began to tremble. All subtle clues, taken out of context, might mean nothing. But in direct reaction to the ruse Savage had just used, it meant Wesson was afraid they'd seen something.

"So, what about some cameras." His effort at being dismissive was half-hearted.

Savage had seen the man's full rage and wrath early on. This was a feigned attempt at saving face.

"Well, what do you think? What are your pole cameras able to show you when someone's driving on that road leading to your place?" Savage could see Clinton thinking, "Can you make out a truck? Can you make out a face?"

Wesson eyed the door behind Savage.

"You ever wonder how we knew to come all the way out to your place? We saw you on camera." Savage knew this was a risk for a couple of reasons. If, at this point, Clint Wesson wasn't involved and had never been on the Ute Reservation, the interview would be pretty much over. If they hadn't traveled into the Ute Reservation by vehicle and had moved in by foot from somewhere else, then it too could have been over. That's why Savage left out anything regarding how they got there because he had no idea.

The fact that Clint Wesson hadn't stood up and walked out, meant he was now invested in protecting the outcome of this interview.

"What do you want to know?" Wesson's voice was softer. He was defeated.

Savage's gamble had paid off. "Why were you on the Ute Reservation?"

"Denny said it was good hunting." Wesson bit his lip. "Shit!"

"Who's Denny?"

Wesson looked madly around the room as if some type of answer was written on the plain beige walls.

Savage caught the slip. Wesson was scrambling. He tried not to let his excitement show, but by mentioning Denny, whoever that was, Wesson had given him his first potential break in the case.

He waited patiently. Wesson's finger began to twitch as sweat flowed down the forehead of his gaunt face. Savage wondered if the hunter's methamphetamine problem was adding to his jitters. It was hard to tell, but whatever biochemical imbalance Wesson had definitely wasn't helping his case. He was slipping and rapidly.

"Shit, shit, shit," he said. The gap between his two front teeth giving a whistling sound to his words.

"I'm listening, Clint. You're the first person I've talked to about this, so you get the first shot of coming clean and telling me everything that happened. And then I can determine how involved you are and how best I can help you."

His eyes watered as the shaking extended from his index finger to his hand. Wesson grabbed it with his other in an attempt to control the shake. "We were just out hunting. There was supposed to be a lot of big cats out there. Better to hunt out there because it's not as, you know, populated and such. We ain't mean nothin' by it."

"You know it's illegal to hunt on the Ute Reservation if you're not a member of the tribe, right?"

"Their laws don't mean nothing to me. Hunting is hunting. I have just as much right to hunt there as they do."

"That's not up for debate right now." Savage calmly held firm without being argumentative.

"Well, it should be."

Wesson trying to make this a political statement about what he believed were his rights was a poor choice, but Savage understood why. Deflection, another technique used by the guilty. Typically, it was done when deflecting to another person, but trying to steer Savage away from the main point was done so for the same purpose. Savage didn't take the bait. He waited in the silence that followed Wesson's last comment.

"So ain't no crime that you're going to charge me with, for hunting on the land?"

"No. That piece of the puzzle will be handled by the Ute Reservation police. I can't enforce their tribal laws. I'd have to check with them after we finish our conversation. But I think there's something much more important we need to discuss."

No amount of restraint was stopping the shaking in his hand. Wesson made his nervousness more obvious by picking up the empty Sprite. In his shaking hand, the empty can rattled loosely on the tabletop, undoubtedly mirroring the rapid heart rate of the guilty-eyed man.

"What happened while you were there?" Savage adjusted his seat to the corner of the table near Wesson, never breaking eye contact as he moved closer. Their knees were almost touching.

"I told you it was Denny. It was all Denny."

"Denny who?" Savage's voice was calm, softer than normal.

"Denny Paulson."

"How old is Denny Paulson?"

"I don't know. Thirty-five or somethin'. He's smart. He's a good hunter. He knows the land."

"So, you and Denny Paulson were hunting on the Ute land? Illegally."

"C'mon, man. Don't do this to me," Wesson pleaded desperately. His gaze bounced from Savage to the door.

"I told you we had to have a conversation, and I told you that the fallout from it, whether we talked or didn't talk, might be pretty bad for you. If you choose to end the conversation now, which is still well within your right to do, you've led me to believe that there is much more to this, and your involvement is definitely in question."

"I told you already it was Denny's idea."

"Tell me about what happened," Savage said calmly, but delivering each word of his message very effectively. He then let the four bland walls encroach as silence followed.

Wait for it, Hatch texted.

Savage knew this was the break point, the time in an interrogation when silence intertwined with the timeless interview room. The void worked against the anxiety of the man seated across from him, adding to the incredible pressure he was under. Silence was one of the best investigative tools and was not utilized nearly as often as needed.

Without a watch himself, Savage also had no idea exactly how long he waited. The silence felt long for him as well. It was a different kind of pressure, but one that he felt all the same. It stemmed from the burning desire to push for the truth, and it was bubbling up inside Savage. He fought to keep it in check, holding his ground amid the silence as seconds passed to minutes.

They neared what Savage guessed to be the 10-minute mark of dead air between them. The only noise was the rattle of the can in Wesson's hand.

Wesson made a sigh that sounded more like a whimper before breaking the silence. "You got to help me out, man. It was never supposed to go down like that. Do you understand me? It was all Denny. He's crazy!"

"Why don't you explain it to me. Help me understand what happened. And in turn, I will tell you honestly what will happen next."

"We were hunting a bobcat, a big one. Been tracking it for about a day. They're real hard to find. But it turned out it wasn't no bobcat."

"I'm not sure I understand."

"It was a damn Lynx. You ever seen a Lynx?"

Savage had not. He knew of the animal, knew it was endangered. And knew, without checking any hunting laws, that it could not be hunted in Colorado or anywhere else for that matter. "You know you were hunting an endangered animal, right?"

Wesson's face collapsed into his hands, and he whimpered softly. He rubbed at his bloodshot beady eyes. "Don't you think I know that," he hissed, the whistle of his teeth punctuating his desperation. "That cop crept up on us while we were getting our kill."

"I'm sorry, what?" Savage was caught off-guard by the admission.

"That old coot popped up on us."

"What did you do?"

"I told you, it was Denny."

"What happened?" Savage increased the pressure through the tone in his voice.

"He got knocked to the ground."

"How did he get knocked to the ground?"

"Ugh," the man grunted, rubbing furiously on the sides of his head, and then he began slapping the back of his neck. "You idiot! Idiot!"

"It's too late now. The only thing you can do is try to make it right by telling the truth."

"I hit him, dammit. I hit him, but I didn't kill him."

"Who said anything about killing?"

Wesson looked shook to the core. "I just... It was Denny. He's the one that came up with the plan. He made that cop eat those crushed up berries, chokeberry, chokecherry, or something like that. He said they were poisonous. I thought it would just make him sick. Knock him out, ya know. I didn't think it'd kill him."

"And what happened? After the berries?"

"The guy started frothing, making some wild-eyed looks, and then he just stopped breathing."

"What did Denny do?"

"Denny? Denny just grabbed the damn lynx and told us to cut out and go."

"What did you do, Clint?"

"I just tried to give him some respect. I put him up against a boulder and sat him there. Thought maybe someone would come find him or something."

"He was found. In fact, his son's in the other room, watching this interview right now."

Wesson looked up at the camera, as tears welled in his eyes.

THIRTEEN

Savage entered his office. Hatch and Nighthawk were still seated behind his desk, where they had watched the interview take place. Hatch had been impressed with Nighthawk's ability to remain calm. He didn't utter a word during the entire interview process. Never interrupted, never asked a question, never swore even after hearing the description of the events that led up to the murder of his father.

Savage looked a little bit depleted. Hatch recognized the look immediately.

After the mental challenge of delivering a well-orchestrated, well-planned interview, the mental exertion took a physical toll. Hatch had remembered a time overseas where she had been interrogating someone for eight, nearly nine hours straight. When she had walked out of the room with the confession in hand, she nearly collapsed.

Hatch watched on the monitor as Deputy Littleton took a seat in the interview room, taking Savage's recently vacated seat. At Savage's direction, he was in the process of taking the sworn written statement from Wesson.

"Did you get anything on the name he gave?" Savage asked.

Nighthawk shook his head, "Nothing. No history, at least not locally with a name like that. Denny Paulson hasn't received a ticket or minor offense arrest anywhere in the state that I can see. I ran him through the federal database as well, but I'm not seeing anything."

Savage nodded.

Hatch could tell from the look on Savage's face that he was impressed not only with the deputy's diligence in checking the multiple sources for information on their suspect before being asked, but in the concise, clear, and articulate manner in which he relayed the information.

"Well, Clint in there has told us that he's been staying at his place, but he warned it's going to be a bit tricky getting in."

"I don't think a guy like him is going to roll out the red-carpet treatment when you arrive. I'd imagine Wesson might be holding back a little bit of information, like maybe where some of his booby traps are set. I don't like the idea of his partner getting the drop on you." Hatch wished she could protect Savage and his deputies from this potential threat. But she was an outsider looking in now.

"Well, there's not much else we can do. Sometimes we have to just play the cards we're dealt."

"I'm in," Nighthawk said. His gaze held steady on Savage as if he was ready to confront any argument to the contrary.

"I'd expect you would be. We're going to need all hands on deck for this one. I want everybody's eyes and wits about them. I already put a call in to Clearwater. He and one of his patrol officers are going to be meeting us. Hopefully if this Denny guy sees us coming and with enough troops in support, he'll make the right decision. Like his friend did. Hoping this guy's more bark than bite."

"You've got another disadvantage," Hatch said.

"What's that?" Savage asked.

"He's likely to know you're coming. I'd assume he knows Wesson is here now. Who knows, maybe Denny was at the house when you went to see Wesson. Assuming he knows you'll be coming for him next means he has time to prepare. And based on what that runt in there had to say, this guy's dangerous."

"I agree," Savage said. "That's why I'm going to contact Durango. A good friend of mine who spent years on Denver's SWAT now commands Durango's Emergency Response Team."

"Good idea."

"We've got a little bit of time. I'm going to get started on drafting an arrest warrant based on the details from Wesson. I'll forward it to Clearwater and then we'll go find a judge. The toxicology report will confirm Wesson's claim."

Hatch agreed. Savage had a good plan in place. She suddenly felt like a third wheel, as though she wasn't needed.

She looked down at the monitor. Littleton, who appeared to be frightened of most things police related, would definitely not do well in a high stress tactical situation. Apparently, Savage was also cognizant of this. Instead of putting the lanky, inexperienced deputy in harm's way, Savage had utilized him in the administrative function of completing the paperwork aspect of Wesson's interview statement. This gave Littleton a pass, whether he knew it or not.

"I'll call you after. Okay?" Savage said, turning his attention to Hatch.

Nighthawk walked out into the main space of the Sheriff's Office to gather his gear, leaving the two of them alone.

"Why bother?" she said.

Savage looked hurt and she immediately regretted the attempt of humor.

"I meant *why bother* because I'm coming with you."

Savage's lips curled up in a grin. "As a consultant?"

"Yes," she said, not taking the bait and not returning his playful smile. "Look, it sounds like you're going up against a guy that has, if not a military background, at least a definite interest in the paramilitary lifestyle. If what Wesson said in there was true, then you've got a real problem."

In the last bit of the interview before Savage had turned the room over to Littleton, Wesson had described a series of rigged explosives and countermeasures lining his property.

"And you have some experience in this?" Savage asked.

"I do," Hatch said without going into any further detail. "But if nothing else, you can use me as an overwatch while you make your approach on the house."

"I'm not arguing. I'll take you any way I can get you."

Hatch made a wide-eyed face as Savage burst into laughter and offered, "I am so sorry. That came out wrong."

Hatch laughed, but deep down she knew she wished it were true. For the split-second after he said it, she caught something in his face that made her think he meant it. But then he had hidden it again. It was back to business as usual for Hatch too as she quickly mentally reset and prepared herself for the task ahead.

Savage walked around his desk as Hatch crossed the other side toward the main area. He opened the drawer and held up the badge, "Might need this again."

"You can't keep making me a deputy every time it's convenient. Listen, keep me as a consultant, and I'll do everything I can to assist. But I'm not taking the badge, and you can keep the gun that comes with it."

He closed the drawer.

"I've hung up my guns for good," she said. "But I'll do anything I can to keep you safe. And your deputies."

"Like I said, I'm happy to have you along for the ride."

"Well, that's not exactly what you said." Hatch winked as she walked out of the office.

FOURTEEN

"Littleton's taking the statement in the other room," Savage said. "We're going to need a little bit of time to get some corroborating information if we're going to have enough for an arrest warrant or, at the very least, a search warrant. I've got a call in to the ME's office, and they've already begun to run blood toxicology for Chief Nighthawk. They put his death as a top priority, seeing as he was the chief of police and the unusual circumstances surrounding his death.

"In the interim, while we're waiting for those little bits and pieces of evidentiary support, I'm going to need somebody to head out to Wesson's ranch and keep an eye on things, make sure Denny Paulson doesn't take off. If he hasn't already. I'd rather contain this before it becomes a nationwide manhunt."

"If he doesn't trust Wesson to keep his mouth shut, he may already be gone," Sinclair offered.

"I'll stand post," Nighthawk said.

Hatch saw the eagerness in his eyes, but just behind it, there was something else, something she recognized. She'd seen it in herself. Seeing it in Nighthawk concerned her. Since it wasn't technically her place to speak up, she decided to table it for now and speak with Savage when no one else was around.

Savage must have caught it too, the fact that Nighthawk would be on his own to keep an eye on the killer who had ended his father's life.

"John, I know you want to be a big part of this, but I don't want you going off half-cocked and doing something stupid that you'll regret later." Savage delivered the sentiment with a gentle firmness.

"Trust me, Sheriff. I won't." His eyes were steely hard, but his facial expression was flat. He looked to have a numbness to him. Hatch also recognized that. She had walked around at various levels of numbness in the years since her father had died, a constant ping pong between anger and vengeance that dipped at times into total apathy.

"I do trust you." Savage was pensive for a moment as he surveyed everybody present. He didn't have a lot of options. Savage sighed. "That's why I'm going to have you go and hold the perimeter of Wesson's property."

Nighthawk looked as surprised as Hatch at the decision.

"Park at the end of the road where their driveway meets the main street. It's a one-way in, one-way out path into the property. If you position yourself there, you should be in a good enough position to get eyes on him should he move."

"And if he does?"

"Give a loose follow. Don't move until we're with you. Do not engage. I want this thing to go as smoothly as possible. It needs to be by the numbers if it's going to hold up in court. I want to have that arrest warrant in hand, or a search warrant at the very least, before we confront Paulson. We don't want to find ourselves on private property engaged without a warrant. We don't need the fruit of the poisonous tree to taint the ability to prosecute those responsible for your father's death. This plays out a whole lot better if we take it slow and deliver a coordinated, controlled apprehension."

Nighthawk nodded. His arms were still folded tightly across his chest, like a spring coiled tight. His forearms rippled as his fists clenched. "I understand. And you've got to remember, Sheriff, this is more important to me than anybody else in this room. I won't do anything to compromise justice being served."

The calmness in his voice seemed to put everyone else at ease, including Savage. Everybody except for Hatch. Something about his words or the way he said them gave her pause, but this was Savage's department, his unit, his people, his decision to make, and everything the man had done in their limited experience together had proven that he made good decisions, so she left him to it.

"All right then, it's settled. Post yourself up at that intersection. Keep us informed. Anything or anyone approaches, I want to hear about it immediately. We want to be there in support if and when this thing goes off the rails."

"Understood." Nighthawk didn't wait for any further clarification after receiving Savage's instructions and disappeared out the back door of the Hawk's Landing Sheriff's Office, leaving Hatch, Savage and Sinclair behind.

Littleton was still tediously gathering the details on the sworn statement being provided by Wesson.

Savage stepped away and called Clearwater at the tribal police headquarters, updating him on the case's progression.

Clearwater had just received an emailed report from the ME's office, detailing the blood toxicology findings.

"There was a large quantity of cyanide in his bloodstream," Savage said as he hung up the phone.

"Cyanide? Isn't that the stuff spies use to kill themselves if they're captured?" Sinclair asked.

"Apparently it matches with what Wesson said. Chokecherry seeds and the wilted leaves of the shrub are toxic. Any guesses as to what toxin it releases?" Savage played the gameshow host.

"Cyanide?" Sinclair muttered.

"Exactly. If eaten in enough quantity, it could kill a horse in a matter of minutes," Savage stated in a matter-of-fact manner. "Clearwater is going to shoot me the corresponding email, and we can enter it into our affidavit for our arrest warrant."

Hatch locked gazes with Savage. "Sounds like you have your smoking gun. No question now. You have yourself a homicide."

"I think with that, we have enough to push forward with the arrest warrant. I'm going to get Judge Mathis on the phone so we can walk this one through with the prosecutor."

Savage disappeared into his office and made several phone calls, returning a few minutes later.

"All right, the prosecutor is going to meet us to review the warrant when it's ready. Clearwater and I will go to Judge Mathis's office in downtown Durango. His clerks made him aware of the priority of this warrant. He's aware we have an active suspect on the loose and that we are trying to coordinate his capture."

"What about Wesson?" Sinclair asked.

"After Littleton's finished taking his statement, we should have his warrant ready as well." Savage looked at the monitor capturing Wesson's animated retelling of events to Littleton. "Wesson's not leaving."

"Well, he's going to be pissed when he finds out his voluntary statement just changed his visitor status to inmate," Hatch warned.

"Sinclair, I want you to be with Littleton when he finishes up in case there's any problems with Wesson's reaction to the news."

Sinclair nodded. Hatch had noticed her confidence had risen since their first encounter several months ago. It's funny what experience and circumstance can do to the growth and development of a law enforcement officer. Since Hatch's arrival in Hawk's Landing, the opportunity for that growth had been exponential.

"I can just hang out here," Hatch offered.

"I'd appreciate that. I'm hoping things go smoothly, but I'd love to have you there for your eyes."

"Whatever you need." Hatch smiled. There was a coyness to it, but she fought against continuing the flirtatious banter exchanged with Savage in the closed confines of his office. But as Becky went to Littleton and Savage went back into his office to begin organizing the paperwork, Hatch found herself alone in the main space of the Sheriff's Office.

"Now, it just may be some wishful thinking on my part, but am I catching something here between you and the good sheriff?" Barbara Wright whispered. She was standing close behind her.

"I'm sorry?—What?" Hatch asked, caught off guard by the unexpected question. Embarrassed Wright had noticed enough to comment.

"Oh, I don't mean to pry. But, you know, I've been on this earth for a little while, sweetheart, and woman to woman, I don't think I've ever seen two people more head over heels for each other, but equally scared to admit it."

Hatch's cheeks warmed.

"You two are about as tough as they come, facing off against danger and staring death in the face. Yet when faced with expressing your feelings, you both are all thumbs."

Hatch knew her face was red. She could feel it, the warmth of it. As perceptive as Barbara was, Hatch knew she had noticed as well. There was no point in deflecting or at least none that would be received as truth, but she tried anyway.

"Oh, come on, Barbara. There's nothing between us."

She smiled pleasantly. "Life doesn't always give us opportunities to find happiness, or for someone to share that happiness with. You're back here for many reasons, Rachel, but I think one of them happens to be the man in that other room. And I for one can't think of a better reason. He's a good person, and so are you. Both of you deserve to be happy."

"It's not what you think," Hatch said weakly. She couldn't commit any energy to the denial.

"Maybe you should be as fearless in love as you two are in battle."

The words resonated in Hatch's ears, and she knew the truth in them. With that truth came a paralyzing fear. Hatch feared the prospect of a relationship and the uncharted territory it would take her into. She'd rather be staring down the barrel of a loaded weapon.

Be brave in love. Maybe love was her new battlefield. The old Pat Benatar song "Love Is a Battlefield" suddenly cued up in her mind. The words suddenly took on new meaning. Maybe happiness was her new crusade, and, although different from any challenge she'd faced before, was something she actually had to fight for.

She looked back toward Savage as he typed furiously on the keyboard in his office, combining the detailed information from Wesson's statement with the pathologist's toxicology report forwarded from Clearwater. Savage was as tenacious as she was. It's rare in life that you find somebody who you can connect with on multiple levels. For Hatch, it had been damn near impossible, minus her one relationship with Alden Cruise, a Navy SEAL she'd met in a joint operation overseas. He was the only other man she'd ever let her guard down with and felt that deeper layer of connection.

Lost momentarily in deep thought as she watched Savage, half forgetting that Barbara was still standing nearby, Hatch's phone vibrated an incoming text message alert. She was grateful for the distraction and interruption. Hatch felt the warmth in her face dissipate and knew that the embarrassing red of her cheeks was now fading. She stared down at the message. It was from a private number. Her first thought was that it was a telemarketer until she read the message.

Watch your six, not safe for you there, the text read.

Hatch stared down at the words, trying to figure out the context. Who would text her a random message like this? Maybe it was Jed. Maybe he was trying to warn her about something. Why wouldn't Jed just call? He wasn't the type to send a text message, especially a cryptic one. She was truly baffled, even more so by the message itself.

Barbara, seeing the concern stretch across Hatch's face, asked, "Is everything okay?"

Hatch slipped her phone back in her pocket. "Yeah, sorry. It was just a strange message."

"Trust me, I know," she said with a laugh. "I get calls all the time at my house from random telemarketers. I think they think because I'm a little bit older that I'm not as savvy as I once was and that I'll fall for their little scams." She held her fists up in defiance.

"Well, then they obviously don't know you," Hatch said with a smile and wink.

Barbara seemed satisfied, smiling and returning to her desk.

Hatch took a seat in the empty cubicle space that would undoubtedly be hers should she ever choose to accept Savage's offer of employment. She waited while the warrant was drafted, and the apprehension phase of the case slowly spun into action.

Her mind drifted to Nighthawk and the hopes that he could maintain his restraint when facing his father's killer. Hatch wondered whether twenty years ago, if she had the opportunity to look into the eyes of the man who'd killed her father, if she'd been capable of holding back the desire for instant justice, even at the age of twelve. Probably not. Hatch would've tried to gnaw through the man's neck with her own teeth if given the opportunity.

She could only imagine the fury Nighthawk would release on Paulson if given the opportunity, and she prayed Savage hadn't just given it to him.

FIFTEEN

LITTLETON FINISHED COMPLETING THE STATEMENT. WESSON DICTATED HIS account of the facts and circumstances. As per policy, Littleton had documented it verbatim. Gone were the days when suspects would hand write their own statements, or witnesses for that matter. Either their writing was illegible, or they left out critical details from their oral explanation to subsequent conversion into a written statement.

The written word stood the test of time, and it was a unique backup system to anything gathered during the interview. For the officer taking the statement, the trick lay with mirroring a suspect or witness's information in their words while ensuring that the details given matched the gist and flow of the original interview. To best do that, an interviewer would listen to the entire explanation of events and then go back through and write it piece by piece, checking with the interviewee at various intervals to ensure the accuracy of what was being transcribed.

Another lesser known trick was to intentionally put a misspelled word or an incorrect phrasing into the statement. That way, when the interviewee reviewed the statement and found the error, a handwritten correction could be made and initialed by the person. It proved that they had read their own statement and done so thoroughly enough to note a correction or two.

That was an extra layer that the court appreciated, at least on the prosecutorial side of things. Beyond signing the statement at the bottom page of each one of the statement forms, it showed a lack of coercion, demonstrating the willingness and voluntariness of the statement itself. It was a way of adding an extra measure of validity.

Littleton presented the three sheets of paper containing the information provided by Wesson.

Scanning the document while standing beside Savage, Hatch saw a notation and cross-out that had been initialed in the sloppy block letter handwriting of Wesson above it. Littleton may not be one for tactics, but apparently, he could follow the administrative protocols of a police department. Maybe there was a purpose for him within the agency after all, a way to utilize him without exposing his weakness.

Savage read through the pages carefully. "Excellent job. He's buried himself with this admission. With this statement complete, we should have enough for the arrest warrant."

Savage looked at the monitor where Wesson was seated and saw him playing with the empty can of Sprite, and folding and unfolding the empty bag of chips that had been given to him during the initial part of the interview.

"What now?" Littleton asked.

"Sit tight. I'm going to compile what you've got into the warrant and get it over to the judge for review."

"What about Wesson?" Littleton asked.

"He's not going anywhere. Keep him calm until I return."

Littleton looked nervous again.

Savage looked at Littleton, "Why don't you take him another soda and see if he wants something else to eat? Keep him in there, keep him calm. I'm going to walk over the arrest warrant with this information to the judge. I'll let you know when I have it signed."

Littleton left to grab another soda from the machine.

"Just stall him," Savage said to Littleton as he walked away. "If he asks, tell him that I'm in a meeting with the tribal police and have to sign off on the statement before he can go. I'm not letting him loose only to have to chase him down again. It's bad enough we've still got his partner out there."

"Hopefully, that won't be the case for long," Hatch added.

Savage tapped the statement Littleton had just handed him. "My thoughts exactly."

A LITTLE OVER AN HOUR HAD PASSED, AND HATCH WAITED PATIENTLY IN THE Sheriff's Office. She checked in with her mother to let Daphne and Jake know that she'd be running late. When she'd originally volunteered to help Savage, she wasn't sure of the duration of her trip. As it closed in on the dinner hour, Hatch didn't want her mother or niece and nephew to worry.

It was strange for her to check in. She hadn't had to do this for as long as she could remember. No one else relied on Hatch, and therefore she didn't have that sense of personal responsibility to anything outside of whatever task she was on. She was entering into unchartered territory, where family mattered, where being away for dinner meant something. She found it strange and delightful.

Savage had just returned from his meeting at the magistrate's office with Clearwater and the judge. He held a thick manila envelope in his hand, containing the case paperwork inside. "I've got the warrant signed. Time to go deliver."

Sinclair looked at him. "What do you want us to do about Wesson?"

"His warrant's been signed as well for his open admission as an accessory to the murder of Chief Nighthawk. Book him, but make sure you're both with him when you make the announcement."

Hatch looked at the screen, the thin man still sitting in the interview room, now alone, the door no longer unlocked. He had to know what was coming, but that was the folly with criminals. They always thought they had an out. A drunk driver being given a roadside sobriety check might think that, in their inebriated state of mind, each test meant they had passed the preceding one. In fact, the officer was actually building the case against them. That's why when the cuffs go on at the end of a DUI evaluation, many times it turns into a scuffle because in that moment, the shocked drunkard suddenly realizes they had not in fact passed the tests and were about to take a trip to jail.

The same could be true for the man inside the interview room. Up until this point, he could be under the impression that his cooperative nature had somehow removed him from any wrongdoing, which couldn't be any further from the truth. Breaking the news and divulging the fact his statement had just been turned against him could have negative consequences.

Littleton popped up from his cubicle where he was watching the confined Wesson on his monitor. He had done what Savage had asked and kept Wesson there, waiting. Littleton told the criminal they were checking into a couple of things, verifying his statement, and that it would be a little bit longer until they would get him out of there.

The soda seemed to have helped for a bit, although the nervous jitter returned about five minutes before Savage arrived back at the station. Littleton kept checking the monitor, nervously watching Wesson.

"Time to put the cuffs on," Savage said, looking at Wesson.

Littleton popped up from his seat again. Hatch could see the young and awkward deputy was eager to please his boss. Without waiting for further instructions, Littleton was already heading toward the back where the interview room was.

Savage looked over. "Becky, why don't you join him? Make sure that everything goes smoothly."

Hatch watched the monitor on Littleton's desk. He should've waited for Sinclair. Always better to approach an arrest with backup present. Additional officers negated resistance. Not always, but enough times that it had been indoctrinated into most departments' standard operating procedures. A minimum of two officers were needed to tactically effect an arrest. One would be the contact while the other would provide cover.

But Littleton hadn't waited. Hatch watched as he opened the door and entered the room by himself. Through the audio on the monitor, she heard Littleton make a rookie mistake, a critical error.

Standing in the doorway, with nothing but a table separating the inexperienced officer from the seasoned criminal, Littleton announced to

Wesson that he was under arrest for his role in the murder of Chief Nighthawk.

Becky Sinclair still hadn't gotten there as Littleton moved deeper inside.

Hatch watched in horror as Wesson slammed the soda can down on the table. In one swift rage-induced movement, he crushed and twisted it. A fraction of a second later, Wesson now held two pieces of sharp, jagged aluminum as he rushed at Littleton.

Littleton jumped back, throwing a chair into the thin man's pathway as he made a desperate attempt to flee the room. The chair did little to stop the madman's progression, only momentarily hindering his wild attack.

Sinclair ran into Littleton, and the two fell backward into the hallway and out of view from the room's camera system. Wesson pounced.

Hatch was already in motion, running full speed by Savage who hadn't been watching the monitor and had no idea what was happening.

As she rounded the corner, Wesson was already on Littleton, who was now laying on top of Sinclair. Both deputies squirmed on the ground as they tried to wriggle free.

Sinclair struggled to reach for her taser but was pinned under Littleton.

Littleton was in a state of pure panic.

Hatch gave no warning, no verbal command to the can-wielding maniac. She moved at full speed, closing the last three feet as Wesson struck down at Littleton's exposed throat with the jagged end of the torn Sprite can.

Hatch thrust her right leg out, kicking the bottom of her boot hard against the side of the unsuspecting Wesson's head, just a fraction of an inch before the green and white can was impaled in Littleton's throat.

The impact launched Wesson off to the side, slamming the deranged man's head into the corner of the doorframe just above the latch with a sickening thud. For a second, Hatch thought she'd killed him.

Wesson groaned. He was dazed, but not completely out. At least he was off of Littleton, but Wesson's rage was now focused on the woman who had just stomp-kicked the side of his head. His eyes did little to hide the murderous intent. The definition of madness lay just beneath his pinpoint pupils. He sprung at her like a cat. Both cans still in his hands up high and coming toward her. But he was attacking from a low point, diving toward her midline.

Hatch stepped back enough that Wesson came up short, turning his desperate attack into a belly-flop as she struck up with her left knee, catching the man across the bridge of his nose.

She felt the crunch of bone as Wesson's head snapped back as she drove upward, shifting all of her weight behind the blow.

The cans flung out of his hands, and the thin poacher ended up with his back flat against the wall in the narrow hallway. Hatch's attack gave Littleton and Sinclair the opportunity to scramble to their feet. They now seized the shift in advantage, tackling the unconscious man to the ground.

Littleton shook uncontrollably as he tried to get his cuffs out of the pouch on his patrol belt.

With cuffs in hand, Sinclair called out, "I've got 'em! Just hold him down!"

Littleton held the man's limp wrists as Sinclair secured him, then double locked the cuffs behind Wesson's back.

They sat him up, and Sinclair checked for a pulse. "He's still alive."

Blood poured out of Wesson's face at the bridge of his nose where Hatch had delivered the devastating strike. "I didn't hit him that hard," she said with a hollow laugh before turning to face Savage, who had arrived at the party late.

"If you're ever in doubt that you're losing your edge, I think that just answered the question." After visually inspecting Hatch for damage, Savage turned his attention to Sinclair. "Littleton's going to stay here and keep an eye on Wesson. Put him in the holding cell until Sinclair returns to assist in the booking process."

Littleton's eyes went wide.

Savage leveled a gaze at the young deputy. "You good with that?"

Littleton looked away from Savage and down at shackled Wesson. He then turned back and did his best to puff his chest. "Sure thing," he said. His voice still held a quiver of trepidation.

Savage turned to Sinclair. "Becky, I'm going to have you come with me and Hatch. I just checked in with Nighthawk. He said there hasn't been movement on the road leading up to the house since his arrival. If Wesson's reaction to arrest was any indication, we're walking into a real shitstorm with Paulson."

"Is it just going to be us?" Sinclair asked.

"I've reached out to Durango and asked if they could get a small contingent of their tactical response unit to post up on standby just in case things go awry. I'd rather have them on hand than to request the aid after the fact."

"That's a good idea," Hatch said. "Makes a lot of sense."

"Clearwater and a couple of his guys are also going to meet us. We're going to move in tandem toward the target." Savage then focused his attention on Hatch. "Ready to go?"

"You mean as a consultant?"

"Of course." Savage looked at the bloody Wesson and chuckled. "Good job consulting with Wesson."

"Then I'm in." She tried to smile, but the adrenaline countered.

The three stepped out the back door into the cool spring air. The dry mountain temps were beginning to dip with the fading light of day. Savage tossed Hatch a windbreaker on the way to the Suburban. It was navy blue with the stenciled star for the Hawk's Landing Sheriff's Office over the heart. The back read Sheriff's Office in big, boldfaced yellow letters.

"You're really trying to sell me on this, huh?" she said.

He shrugged it off. "Just trying to keep you warm." He threw on a similar jacket, as did Sinclair, and the three in matching uniforms departed for the ranch that potentially held their prime suspect.

Savage keyed up the radio. "John, we're on our way to you."

Nighthawk responded in a deadpan voice. "Standing by."

SIXTEEN

Clearwater and one of his patrolmen, the squat stocky one who'd given Nighthawk the hard eyes on scene the other morning, pulled up, meeting them at the entrance. The timing had been impeccable as Savage, in his Suburban containing Sinclair and Hatch, arrived at almost the same time.

Savage stepped from the vehicle and gathered everybody into a cluster.

Deputy Nighthawk joined them.

"Listen, we have a real threat inside there." Savage paused, looking at each member of the ensemble cast present before continuing. "Denny Paulson's a dangerous man. The warrant in hand speaks to that. Keep in mind Paulson's a hunter. Wesson's been gone for hours. There's a high likelihood that Paulson's inside, which means he's had ample time to make himself well-prepared for our arrival."

"You mentioned Durango's tactical unit will be here to assist. Any idea how long until they arrive?" Clearwater asked.

"They're about thirty minutes out. It's only going to be a small contingent, and they're on orders from their chief to assist only if needed. We're going to take the initial approach. They'll stage themselves here, by our vehicles, when they arrive."

Clearwater seemed satisfied by Savage's explanation.

"Based on the information given in Wesson's interview, much of the property is booby-trapped. He didn't offer much in the way of detailing the extent of it, but we have to assume the threat is real."

"Those CFA nutjobs scare the hell out of me. Unpredictable lunatics," Clearwater hissed.

"True. That said, be prepared to encounter potential IED's. Guys like Wesson and Paulson have been preparing for something like this for a long time. Everybody must be vigilant, eyes sharp, moving slowly. Complacency is a killer."

No truer statement, Hatch thought.

"For those who haven't been formally introduced, this is Rachel Hatch. She's assisted our agency in the past on a case. I found her experience and expertise to be extremely beneficial."

"She's amazing," Sinclair offered.

"Hatch here is operating as a consultant with us for the time being. Meaning she's non-tactical and will be assisting in a non-hands-on capacity. Her role, and the reason I brought her here today, is to help us in identifying any countermeasures Paulson may have at his disposal. Hatch has extensive experience in this regard."

She felt the group's eyes upon her and offered a nod of acknowledgement.

"If anybody has an objection, now is the time to speak up," Savage said. Savage went face to face, scanning the crowd. As he locked eyes with each person in the semi-circle surrounding the front hood of his Suburban, each gave a nod of approval, the last of which came from Nighthawk.

"All right. Good. It's settled then. John, I'm going to have you lead the way with Hatch. You're going to be her shadow. She is going to be your eyes as we make the approach. The rest of us will move a few feet behind." Savage let out a sigh. "I hope we don't encounter any resistance. But hope is just a wish made by the unprepared."

Hatch had hope for a potential future with Savage. His comment made her realize she was more prepared to face Paulson's minefield than enter into a relationship.

"Everybody is vested up, right?" Savage asked.

Everybody nodded. Hatch was suddenly glad that Littleton was still back at the station. Without him there, there seemed to be less anxiety within the group.

"Once we get down to the gate, we're going the rest of the way on foot."

"How are we getting through the gate?" Clearwater asked.

"Bolt cutters. Beats ramming it," Savage said.

Hatch caught him giving her a half smile to let her know that last comment had been for her. Ramming through Jed Russell's gate had served its purpose for Hatch under the circumstances. She also knew tactics shifted based on the target. And it would be a critical mistake to crash headlong onto the property.

With the plan in motion, they drove in a caravan down the dirt road with Savage's Chevy leading the way to the ranch's gated entrance.

It was slightly ajar. The chain lock was nowhere in sight.

Hatch leaned up from the backseat, looking out the windshield for the lock. The spare ballistic vest Savage had given her released a sour smell as her body heat warmed the inside cotton liner. Although the vest carrier looked clean, Hatch knew from experience the soft Kevlar absorbed the sweat and retained the odor of its previous owner. The pungent odor dissipated the nearer she was to Savage's licorice-infused scent.

"Looks like somebody is rolling out the welcome wagon," Savage said as he turned off the engine.

"Not a good sign." Hatch stepped out of the backseat and onto the dirt road.

"Why's that?" Sinclair asked as she joined Hatch.

"Because I'm pretty sure Wesson wouldn't leave it unlocked."

"If somebody was in a hurry, they might," Savage added, joining the group. "Any guesses on who might be in a hurry to leave?"

"Exactly," Hatch said.

"Paulson?" Sinclair slowly caught on.

Nighthawk walked ahead of Clearwater and the stocky patrolman.

"John, are you sure nobody came or went while you were here?"

"I'm sure. Why?" Nighthawk crossed his arms over his chest.

"The gate's unlocked."

"I didn't drive down here. You told me to stay out by the main road."

"Don't get defensive. I'm not blaming you. There was a gap of over two hours before I had posted you here." Savage turned to the whole group. "Paulson might not be here, but regardless, we've got to make our approach under the assumption he is."

"Even if he is gone, the property poses a threat of its own," Hatch echoed Savage.

"Let's get ready to make our approach. John, I want you to use the rifle while you provide cover for Hatch when she leads us in. There's a decent amount of distance to cover before getting to the ranch."

Nighthawk returned to his vehicle and popped the trunk, returning quickly with an AR-15 Colt Commando slung at center mass with the muzzle down.

"Do you really think it's a good idea to have her lead us in on this?" Clearwater asked.

"She's the most experienced out of everybody in this group," Savage said. "If there's anybody I trust to get us safely onto this property, it's Hatch."

Savage's response silenced the group. Hatch felt uncomfortable being the center of this line of discourse. Both men were right. A civilian shouldn't be leading a felony warrant service. She was also the only person qualified to do it. The safety of everybody present revolved around her. A burden she didn't take lightly, but one she shouldered, nonetheless.

Sinclair squinted off in the distance as the group readied themselves. She then leaned a bit closer to Hatch and, in a low whisper, said, "I'm glad to have you with us. Any last-minute words of advice?"

"Be ready for anything."

Nighthawk slid up close and was armed with his Commando. A single-point sling gave the weapon mobility. He carried it at the low-ready with his right finger indexed across the trigger housing. "Good to go whenever you are," he said.

Hatch adjusted the Velcro strap, cinching it tighter before buttoning her windbreaker over it. The stink of it was now trapped inside. "Stay to my right side and trail a few steps behind me."

"Okay," Nighthawk said.

"I need you to have a clear line of sight should you need to use that thing." She eyed the assault rifle, wishing she had one of her own. "If I stop moving, you stop. Understood?"

He nodded.

"No time for idle chit chat while we move. We only speak if we see a threat."

"I'm a good shot." Nighthawk tapped the eleven-inch matte black barrel of his rifle.

"Paulson's not the only thing we're going to be watching for. If we need to tactically relocate, the only safe path is the one we've already travelled. And even then, you'll need to move with care."

"Tactically relocate? Isn't that just a fancy way of saying retreat?"

"Where I come from, there's no such thing as retreat." Hatch spoke with a nonchalant tone.

"Weren't you born and raised here in Hawk's Landing?"

"Born…yes. But I was raised on the streets of everywhere and nowhere."

"What's that supposed to mean?"

"It's something we used to say in my unit. The world's a big place, and the Army took me to places you've heard of and some you never will." Hatch looked at the focused resolve in Nighthawk's face. "You would've done well in the military."

"How do you know that?" he asked with genuine interest.

"I'm usually a good read of people."

"And you see that in me?"

Hatch nodded. There was something in the way he asked the question that made her want to circle back to this conversation at a later date. Now was not the time.

"Follow my lead," Hatch said as she stepped off toward the gate.

She approached the gate adorned with threatening warning placards. Hatch pulled on the gate and it swung outward with a loud creaking sound, slicing through the silence.

With the gate open wide, Hatch looked back and gave Savage a thumbs up. He immediately acknowledged her signal by returning the gesture. He stood approximately ten feet away with the others, minus Nighthawk, who stood off to her right and slightly behind, as she'd requested.

The first few steps on the ranch's property were the most unnerving, but the tension she felt radiated throughout her body. She knew the tingle in her damaged right arm was always present like a soft hum. But now, facing a potential minefield, it seemed to be more pronounced. Hatch knew the people's lives behind her depended on her. Just as her team had. She couldn't fail. It wasn't an option. Because here, failure meant certain death.

Every few feet, Hatch would stop and scan the surrounding area, visually inspecting every square foot of space around her. She would get low to the ground, looking at the surface from different vantage points and searching for indications of any traps.

The width of the driveway leading up to the house, which was about a quarter mile away, was wide enough an eighteen-wheeler could pass through. The surface was a hardpack of red dirt. Hatch skirted the right-side edge of the road.

Halfway between the entrance and the house, on the right-hand side of the road, she caught a glint of the setting sun reflecting from an object sticking out between a small cluster of broken rock.

Hatch stopped dead in her tracks. She squatted down, peering out. The beam of light vanished as the sun passed behind the trees. The object in the rocks became clear.

Without looking back over her shoulder, Hatch said just loud enough for Nighthawk to hear, "We've got a big problem."

SEVENTEEN

Hatch's eyes traced the protruding metallic object poking out from beneath the jagged chunks of rock covering it. The metal's smooth gray finish failed to blend into the neutral brown of the stone. Had it been painted to match the landscape, Hatch might've missed seeing it. Whoever set the trap failed to go the extra mile in camouflage, and for that, she was grateful.

She'd seen enough improvised explosive devices during her time overseas to say with certainty the metal tube was definitely one.

A steel capped end of the pipe bomb extended out. Hatch edged forward just enough to see a small black rectangular box attached to the top, most likely some type of detonator. Impossible to tell from the distance whether it was remotely activated or a wire fuse. It might even be rigged to a pressure plate.

Nighthawk had followed her instructions by maintaining his distance. Hatch called him forward with a wave of her hand.

Nighthawk appeared beside her a moment later and took a knee. His weapon was up, aiming at the front of the house. "What do you see?"

"IED. Up ahead on the right. Pile of rocks just past that shrub."

Nighthawk lowered his weapon slightly and eyed the area. "I've got it. What do we do now?"

"That's going to be Savage's call. It's his show. I'm just along for the ride."

All the patrol radios had been shut off for fear any transmission could trigger one of these homemade devices.

"Are we already in the kill zone if that thing is live and he's watching?" Nighthawk whispered.

"Depends," Hatch said. "Minimum safe distance is twenty-one feet. We're beyond that, but barely. Distance also depends on what explosive the pipe contains. We won't know that until it's disarmed."

"State Police have a bomb squad. Not sure how long it would take to get them out here. Savage would know."

"There's another option. Do you see those rocks placed around it?" Nighthawk nodded.

"It's done so to focus the blast out toward the roadway."

"How does that give us an option?" Nighthawk looked confused.

"If they rigged the road, we may be able to safely navigate around it." Hatch looked back and flagged Savage up. "It's going to be a judgment call now."

Savage closed the distance, getting a few feet away from Hatch and Nighthawk. "What have we got?"

"IED right side. It's directed toward the roadway. Might need to call in a bomb squad."

"Durango doesn't have a bomb squad. We'd have to reach out to the State. It could be at least a couple hours before they get here."

Hatch looked at Savage. "The way I see it, you have two options."

"Go ahead," Savage said.

"You can relocate back to the gate and stage the group until the bomb techs arrive."

"Why do I feel like there's an option you like better." Savage reached into his breast pocket and retrieved a handful of licorice.

"What if we go around it?" Hatch offered. "I mean, the directed blast is intended for the roadway. If we go off-road at this point and take a wide berth, we might avoid any of the IEDs."

"And you're comfortable navigating this path? How far wide do we need to go?"

"Well, I say from here, since it hasn't detonated yet, we make a beeline to the right. Get behind it, give it at least 50- to 100-foot-wide berth, and then we'll approach up the right side of it. It'll be slow going, but a heck of a lot faster than waiting for the bomb squad to come through."

"You lead, we'll follow." Savage then moved back to his original position with the rest of the group.

Hatch gave Savage a moment to relay the information to the others before moving out.

Hatch broke right, moving slow while staying low. Even though she was unarmed, she moved as if she had a firearm. Nighthawk maintained his overwatch on her right side, shielding her from the house. He was her weapon, her armed protection. They moved in tandem, with the rest of the group lagging ten feet behind.

Hatch led the group in a wide flanking maneuver up toward the house, stopping every few feet to scan the ground in front of her.

There was no sign of movement from the house as they got closer. The tension of passing the IED brought a flash of memory back to Hatch of the devastating nature of these homemade explosives.

She felt a tingle along the webbed scar tissue of her arm, a reminder of the fragility of life and the caution that must be taken when dealing with any armed adversary, especially a committed and desperate one. The killing of a police chief would've pushed any criminal to desperate measures in an effort to avoid capture. But here they were, closing in on Wesson's ranch, and there was no sign of Denny Paulson. It was silent except for the crunch of footsteps or the occasional gust of wind. Darkness began to set in, slowing her progression as light faded.

There was an eerie calm that caused the hair on the back of her neck to stand on end. Hatch feared it would be broken by gunfire and fought the urge to ask Savage for a weapon. She felt naked approaching the house without one. It went against everything she had ever learned, but she was trying this new persona, the consultant, the non-combatant. It felt awkward, like a brand-new pair of shoes that weren't yet broken in. And with each step, she felt the mental squeak of her conflict in the new role.

"I don't see any movement from inside," Savage whispered, coming alongside Hatch.

The group moved up with him, and they were now roughly thirty feet from the front door of the house.

There were several trees lining the yard between the group and the ranch house. They fanned out, finding cover behind them. Hatch and Savage ended up sharing an oversized Blue Spruce as their makeshift ballistic shield.

Savage broke the silence of the encroaching night with the commanding boom of his voice.

"Denny Paulson, this is Sheriff Dalton Savage with the Hawk's Landing Police Department! If you can hear my voice, come to the front door now!"

Silence answered.

"This is Dalton Savage with the Hawk's Landing Police Department. We have a warrant for your arrest. Come to the door. Do it now!" His voice boomed, rolling off the trees and into the surrounding emptiness of the space, like a natural megaphone.

Out here in the wilderness, there were no ambient noises like cars or trucks passing by. It was a stillness that Savage's words shook, but nothing happened. The one-level ranch house looked more like a converted double wide trailer. The construction looked shoddy at best.

"If you can hear me inside, turn on a light so I know you're in there! We're not going away, so it's better if you come out!"

Still nothing.

"Maybe he's not there," Hatch said. "Maybe he bolted as soon as Wesson left."

"Maybe you're right." Savage sounded somewhat defeated.

Nighthawk kept his AR-15 trained on the front door. "I've got no movement. Nothing in the windows."

"If you do not answer, we are coming in!" Savage shouted. "We have a warrant for your arrest! There's nowhere for you to run!" He turned to Hatch. "What do you think?"

"Hard to say. We could hold our position and call in tactical. They may be better suited to handle an entry should you decide to go in."

Savage looked around at the group with him, now scattered among the trees. Hatch could see it in the sheriff's face. He wasn't confident in their ability to pull off the safe execution of a tactical entry.

"I think you're right. We'll let Durango's tactical unit handle it."

He pulled out his cell phone.

"Ron, can you bring you and your team up? Come to the gate. I'll have somebody meet you there and guide your men in. You're going to have to go on foot. There's an IED on the roadway, so vehicles are out of the question."

Savage ended the call.

"John, I need you to retrace your steps and guide the tactical unit to our position," Savage said to Nighthawk, who was crouched low behind a nearby tree.

Without saying a word, Nighthawk broke cover and began making the trek back toward the main gate. He moved much faster now that a path had been cleared.

Hatch watched him go as the night swallowed the last embers of the day's light.

EIGHTEEN

TACTICAL ARRIVED, FOLLOWING BEHIND NIGHTHAWK. NO IEDS WENT OFF, no gunshots came from the house, no sign of life inside. Hatch was beginning to think the assessment that Denny Paulson making a run for it was the likely situation.

Ronald Connors, a fit, athletic African American looking to be in his late 30s, was muscularly built and a few inches taller than Hatch. He was the commanding officer for Durango's tactical response unit. Savage knew him from previous situations.

"You ready for us to make our approach?" Connors asked, his body stoic, his eyes focused. "We're going to make a front door entry. There's only four of us today, so I'm going to need your guys to cover the windows."

"Ready to go when you are," Savage said.

"We're going to breach and hold at the front door, try to establish communication, and then if not, we'll make entry."

"Sounds good. We've got you covered. Nighthawk's got the long gun and can provide you adequate cover while you make your approach."

Breach and hold was the new tactical protocol put in place recently for SWAT units. It was used when there wasn't an issue of exigency, such as an active killing event, and when the unit was armed with a felony apprehension warrant where there existed a potential for firearms. In this case, that was a high probability, so breaching the front or one of the entrances to a residence and holding position was the preferred method. Teams would then call the suspect out. This had become standard operating procedure for many tactical teams across the United States. The days of the dynamic entry were becoming relatively obsolete. It was deemed safer to do it this way, for both officer and suspect.

"See you on the other side," Connors said. He and his team formed up. They, too, had a ballistic shield. Another man, who was about five foot five, had equally broad shoulders, and stocky legs, picked up the shield like it was nothing and carried it on his arm, leading the team in a hunkered down modified Groucho walk behind the ballistic protection. They were in full SWAT body armor and Kevlar ballistic helmets as they made their approach to the house.

Hatch watched their tactical movements and could tell Connors had trained his men well. They moved like a well-oiled machine, like the units Hatch had been attached to in the military. Each could react, move and address threats while the others would know their partners and be able to read and react accordingly. She had a good feeling about this group. She was glad Savage had the foresight to bring them along.

Connors and his three other tactical teammates formed a single file line with the stockier of the men holding a ballistic shield in front of him. He shouldered the weight with incredible poise. Hatch had known the challenge of carrying such a shield for an extended period of time, but the beefy man was able to do it with little to no exertion.

The shield man held it out a few inches in front of him, covering the vital parts of his body, his head and his chest. Even though they were heavily armed and protected by the extensive bulletproofing provided by the Kevlar vests, the shield was designed to take high caliber rounds.

The rest of the team stacked up with Connors taking position as the number two slot behind his point man. The shield bearer brought his pistol around in front of the shield, using the ballistic visor of the shield to sight out through the canted weapon's sights.

They progressed slowly, taking each foot leading up to Wesson's ranch house with measured calculation.

The last man in the stack had an AR-15 similar to Nighthawk's. It was equipped with an EOTech sight. He provided rear security and would address any threats at long range, should they encounter one. They increased the speed of their steps as they closed in on the last few feet before reaching the porch.

With such a small tactical unit on hand, they decided they would not try to split and take a dual entry or hold an additional perimeter point. They were going to use the mass of their force on the one single entry point and adjust should the situation dictate.

Connors and his men crossed quickly up onto the porch and then fanned out, with two men in the ballistic shield posting on the left side of the door frame while the other two peeled off and took the right. The shield had served its purpose, and its holder now holstered his weapon, trusting in his partners to handle the busywork of the operation should they encounter resistance.

With the same hand that he had just held his pistol in, he reached over and gripped the doorknob. It was open.

The third man who had been carrying the ram set it aside, leaning it against the wall, freeing his hands up and making him a more active asset of the assault team.

Connors tapped the shoulder of the squat, strong man holding the shield. He pushed wide and hard with the door, swinging it open. A clang of metal on wood sounded in the quiet as a flashbang grenade was deployed. A concussive blast of blinding light and noise followed.

"Durango PD. Expose yourself with your hands up, weapons free. Do it now," the commander of the small contingent of tactical officers boomed.

Nothing. Not a sound.

Several minutes passed. The breach and hold shifted to dynamic entry.

The assault team member on the other side of the door then tossed a flash bang in. All members of the team retreated, allowing for the concussive blast and blinding light to have its effect on the main space of the ranch house before entering.

The small rectangular home shook as the flash bang initiated the team's dynamic entry. The shield man led the way into the room. The gun was back in his hand as quickly as if it had never left.

As he entered, Connors stayed tight on his heel, and the other two men filed in behind him.

Hatch could hear Connors' callout from inside the main space seconds later. "Target down! Main room! Clearing!"

Hatch felt the tension rise in her throat as she watched the men disappear into the darkness of Wesson's ranch home. She could hear them calling out as they cleared each room.

Less than a minute later, Connors called out again. "Clear! Coming out! You've got a DOA in the living room."

Savage turned and gave Hatch a surprised look. "Didn't see that coming."

"Nobody did," she said as the remaining members from Savage's Sheriff's Office and the two representatives of the tribal police department appeared from the cover of the trees to meet Connor and his men on the front porch of Wesson's house.

NINETEEN

Hatch was the last to step up onto the porch and found herself beside Connors. Even though they had cleared the house and found the body of Denny Paulson in the living room, there was still an edginess to being on the property, especially after passing the IED. How many other traps awaited them inside the house? This was definitely a scene that should be cleared before any investigation was underway. Savage apparently had the same thought.

Standing on the threshold of the door, not entering, but looking down at the body, one of Connors' men had checked the pulse and found there was none. Although it would be up to the medical response to determine death, there was no sign of life, and the body was cold to the touch.

Sticking out of the center of his chest, just left of the sternum, was the bone handle of a knife that had been plunged all the way to the hilt. From where Hatch stood, it looked as though Paulson's nose had been broken. His blood-encrusted face had darkened the stubble of his five o'clock shadow in a brownish rust-color.

"I don't want anybody in or out at this point for safety reasons and to hold the scene. Becky, I want you to start the crime scene log and hold the door. Nobody in or out. Do you understand me?"

She nodded and took out her notepad.

"Get the names of everybody on the tactical entry team who went in. And Ron, if you could, give her a detailed account of your entry tactics from what we didn't see so she can document it in the initial report of our finding. I'm going to call Littleton and have him get started on some paperwork for a search warrant. The scene is cold, and we need to search it properly. We don't want to lose any evidence here. We'll just hold the status quo for now."

Everybody was in agreement, especially Hatch. She knew from her time as a military police officer, preserving the scene was critical. When working a homicide, where exigency had been removed, it was essential to take a momentary pause. It wasn't just good practice, it was founded by legal precedent and protected by the 4th Amendment. The mere fact a dead body was present did little to change a person's right to privacy. Once all lifesaving efforts were abandoned and the scene was secured, investigators could no longer continue to search the premises until legal consent or authorization was granted. Without exigency, investigators were mandated to take a step back and get a search warrant to effectively dig out the house.

To effectively search a house, you needed a court order. The Supreme Court protected property, one of the most important rights of the country's citizens. It protected people like Wesson and Paulson, even if they didn't believe in the laws affording those protections.

Even in the wake of a homicide, a warrant would need to be obtained to go through for evidentiary purposes.

"I'm going to head back to the station and get this set up. You sure you didn't see anybody come or go while you were here, right? You didn't hear anything?" Savage turned his attention to Nighthawk, who was standing on the porch, staring blankly into the room at the dead man who had killed his father.

He barely seemed to register Savage's comment, and gave a dismissive, subtle shake of his head and mumbled, "No, nothing."

Clearwater peeked inside the open door.

Hatch had noticed something in his face when he turned. Seeing the dead had a different effect on each person. The scene might've been enough to cause him pause and to react. It wasn't every day that an officer saw another human being with a knife buried deep inside. But it wasn't his reaction to the body as much as his reaction to the knife itself.

Clearwater looked from the bone handle directly over to Nighthawk.

Nighthawk snapped out of his daze and glared at Clearwater before turning away.

Clearwater looked like he wanted to speak but didn't know how to phrase the words.

Hatch watched the odd exchange from the corner of her eye. There was something strange to it, but she couldn't quite place it.

Nighthawk stepped down the three warped steps of the poorly constructed porch and out into the grass. He now stood in the patchy grass with his back to the house.

Hatch didn't say anything. She just took in her observations and tabled them for later when she was alone with Savage so they could discuss it. But something was off. She just couldn't place the exact what. Her investigative curiosity began to itch at the back of her mind. And like any itch, it needed to be scratched.

Hatch walked over to Savage, who was quietly finishing a conversation with Connors. Savage turned to face her.

"I can't thank you enough for guiding us through," Savage said.

"Looks like your case took a strange turn," she said, deflecting the praise.

Savage already had a cheek full of licorice and was reaching for more. "Tell me about it. Crazy, right?"

Hatch thought about the non-verbal exchange she'd just observed between Nighthawk and Clearwater. She tried to put herself in Nighthawk's shoes. If she'd traveled around the world chasing her father's killer only to find him dead, before she had her vengeance, her pound of flesh, she'd have been greatly disappointed if the opportunity had been stolen from her. Maybe that's what she'd witnessed. It was wishful thinking, and Hatch knew better.

"Looks like our friend, Clint Wesson, is going to have some explaining to do back at the station," Savage said between chews. "He was probably the last person to see Paulson alive. Funny how he laid the murder at the feet of his partner, who is now dead and conveniently unable to refute any of the claims."

"Sounds like you're going to have your hands full for a bit cleaning up this mess. Any way I can get a lift back to town?" Hatch felt out of place. She'd done her job by successfully navigating the pathway to Wesson's house. Her work was done here.

"I've got to stay here for a while to get things situated. I'm going to wait for the medical examiner to arrive before I head back to the office and work on the search warrant with Littleton."

"I'll give you a ride," Nighthawk offered, standing close enough to overhear the conversation.

"Good idea. Thanks, John." Savage turned to Hatch and lowered his voice. "Thanks again for coming out here today. Better to be safe than sorry, right?"

"Always." She inhaled the candied air around him. "It's my pleasure. But I'll be the first to admit it felt a little weird making that approach empty-handed. I don't know if I would want to do that again."

Savage smiled and got a little closer. "Well, you know where the badge and gun are in my office if..."

Hatch rolled her eyes. "Let's meet up later and discuss some things. I gotta get back home. And you've got a scene to work."

During that exchange, Hatch had a vision of her future life with Dalton Savage. The problem was it didn't look right in her mind. Hatch couldn't see herself playing homemaker while her law enforcement husband was out fighting crime. Something needed to give if she planned on making this relationship work. *Be brave in love.* Hatch thought of the conversation with Barbara.

Hatch then physically shook herself, casting the thoughts from the forefront of her mind. *Did I just make a mental leap to the idea of marrying Dalton Savage? Has being home these past few days thrown me that far into a loop that I'm considering settling down for real?* As much as she fought to repress the idea of it, these thoughts continued to invade her mind.

"Call me later if you want. Otherwise let's touch base tomorrow." Hatch hated the fact she had to feign casualness.

"Coming?" Nighthawk asked as he began to walk back in the direction of the gate.

Hatch took his cue to exit. She bounded down the rickety steps and caught up to him. The two walked the path she'd cleared earlier as the crickets began their noisy song, welcoming the coming night.

TWENTY

"You showed some good tactics out there. Your movements were tight, controlled, and I liked the way you handled the AR. You weren't ex-military, so where'd you learn? Police academy doesn't usually breed that type of proficiency." Hatch was not one for small talk, but she'd realized she knew next to nothing about Hawk's Landing's newest deputy.

"No, but being raised on the reservation means I was raised to hunt. My father had trained me from an early age in the ways of my people."

"It sounds like you and I had a similar upbringing."

They continued walking, giving a wide berth to the pipe bomb she'd found. It took a quarter of the time to traverse their way back to the long driveway where Nighthawk's department-issued SUV was parked.

Hatch continued, "I don't mean to pry, but you were born and raised on the reservation, correct?"

Nighthawk nodded. "Correct."

"What made you leave?"

"Lots of reasons." His pace slowed a fraction. "I'll tell you one thing…It wasn't easy."

"Leaving never is." Hatch was also learning that returning home was sometimes more difficult. She kept that thought to herself.

"I guess the biggest reason was that I didn't want to arrest my friends and family."

Hatch understood this all too well, thinking back to Cole Jensen. Circumstance had forced her hand, causing Hatch to put a bullet in the man who'd once been her high school sweetheart.

"The reservation is big in land, but small in population. There are less than two thousand people living there. And I knew pretty much every one of them."

"That's something I never considered until I moved back home. I policed on bases around the world."

"Everywhere and nowhere, right?"

Hatch gave a soft chuckle at hearing her phrase being used by the deputy. "Correct."

"From an early age I knew I wanted to work in law enforcement. I was aware if I followed in my father's footsteps, I would end up having to police the people I knew. Some part of me felt that it was wrong. So, I looked outside the reservation, but wanted to stay close to my kin. Hawk's Landing was exactly what I was looking for."

"How did that go over?"

It was the first time she'd seen Nighthawk smile. He followed it with a soft laugh, more of a chuckle. "Not well. To say that the community didn't welcome me with open arms when I came back to work my father's death, well, that was pretty indicative of their feelings toward me. Those of us that leave the reservation are not looked highly upon. Some feel I've turned my back on my people. On my family." His smile faded like the last wisps of a racing cloud.

"Clearwater didn't seem to have too much of a problem with you."

"He's my uncle."

"I didn't realize." Hatch now rethought the exchange she witnessed between the two at seeing the dead Paulson. One lost a father, the other a brother.

"My uncle and I were close growing up. His son is only a year younger than me, and we were like brothers." Nighthawk slowed to almost a stop as they neared the main gate to Wesson's compound. "I saved his life once."

"Life debts are rarely ever paid in full," Hatch said, having been there herself.

"Very true. I guess that's why my uncle never could hold a grudge against me. Even after I left the reservation."

"What happened with his son? How'd you save him?"

"He was drowning. There's a small lake on the reservation. We used to fish it with our fathers. One day when I was fifteen, we took the canoe out. Bruce, my cousin, was screwing around dancing near the bow. He slipped and went over the side."

"He didn't know how to swim?" Hatch asked.

"It wasn't that. When he'd fallen over, he smacked his head on the wooden oar. Hit it so hard, he snapped it in two. He went under. I jumped in and pulled him out. Getting his limp body back into the boat was one of the hardest things I've ever had to do in my life. If not the hardest."

"But you did it," Hatch said, impressed.

"I did. He had a concussion and his head needed some stitches."

"Beats being dead."

"Exactly." Nighthawk was quiet for a moment. "For some reason, Bruce never treated me the same after."

"Some people can't handle being saved. It makes them feel weak. I'm sure in time, he'll realize what you did and open back up to you."

"Doesn't matter anymore anyway."

"I guess. At least your uncle is appreciative."

"Life debts, right?" Nighthawk had a vacant expression. "I guess he feels a deeper level of connection to me. Hard to hate the person who saved your son."

"True," Hatch offered.

"This is going to sound hokey, but after that moment in the lake, I knew what my life's purpose was. I always wanted to do something where I could help people in need. My father was a cop, and it felt like law enforcement would probably be the best path for me to achieve that goal. But after saving Clearwater's son, it had solidified any doubt. I was in, hook, line and sinker from that point forward in my life, and everything I did led to me wearing this badge." He proudly tapped the tin star on his chest as they walked through the open gate, exiting the property.

"Well, I can say this from my short experience working with the Sheriff's Office here, Dalton Savage is as good a cop as they come. And I know personally that he is very happy to have you in his employ."

"Thanks. I know he's trying like hell to get you to join up."

"Trying and failing," Hatch said with a laugh.

"Well, if my vote counts, I'd be happy to work alongside you."

"I appreciate that."

"How long are you planning on sticking around this time?" Nighthawk asked.

"How's forever sound?"

"I'm sure Savage will be happy to hear that."

She wanted to question him about what that meant but didn't want to open that line of conversation and expose her personal interest in the sheriff, especially to a man she hardly knew.

"Well, forever seems like a pretty good amount of time for you to figure out whatever it is you're looking for."

There was a simple wisdom in Nighthawk's comment, and she realized she'd only been home for less than two days. She didn't need to figure everything out now. There'd be time for that. Things would take their natural course. She just hoped that course led her to Savage. But as Savage said, hope was the wish of the unprepared. How right he was.

They entered Nighthawk's patrol vehicle. He made a k-turn and drove away.

Hatch felt some of the tension release after putting distance between herself and the IED-laden grounds of the ranch compound containing the knife-impaled body of Denny Paulson.

TWENTY-ONE

"How'd the scene work out yesterday?" Hatch had the phone cradled along the right side of her head, using her shoulder to keep it pressed in place while she continued to stretch, balancing on one leg like a flamingo. She pulled gently at her left ankle, stretching the quadricep muscle. The morning's run had been harder than normal.

Hatch's subconscious fear that her new attempt at life without the military, or without a cause to fight for, left her desperate to prove she hadn't lost her edge. Her mind was restless, leaving her in a fitful state. She'd woken earlier than normal in a cold sweat. The nightmares of the firefight that had left her burned and maimed had started to haunt her sleep again. She applied the only remedy she'd found effective in combating them. A hard morning run.

She took the trail that her father had taken her on many times before, the same trail where she had found his body down by the brook. She'd pushed her pace on the second leg of it, and her legs burned now as a result. That, and the fact that she hadn't fully acclimated to the altitude and dry air of the Rocky Mountains. It would take her a couple of weeks of headaches and dehydration before her body and lung capacity would adjust.

Training at high altitudes taught the body to work under oxygen-deprived exertion. The altitude caused the body to accrue more red blood cells, increasing the ability to carry more oxygen. Returning to sea level where there was more oxygen gave her a boost of endurance. Athletes had been doing this type of training for years, all done to give them an advantage on the playing field. Hatch had used this to her advantage as well, although her arena had been the battlefield.

Hatch was not training for any advantage in sporting competition. She was pushing herself to maintain battle readiness. She'd been tested twice since leaving Hawk's Landing, but in the interim since her return, and without a fight on the horizon, she'd become hyperconscious that she'd begun to slip. That the edge of mental preparedness was dulling.

That was the beautiful thing about running: You kept moving forward, and it gave you a sense of completion, regardless how far you went. This morning had been a brisk seven miles with the last three moving along at a six-minute per mile pace.

Her lungs still burned. She could taste the exertion in her mouth as she spoke into the phone. And she liked it. It felt good to hurt. Pain made her feel alive, it made her feel connected to the source of the experiences that had forged her. As much as she wished things had been different in her life, it was the gut-wrenching heartache that had made her who she was now. The past couldn't be changed, and no matter how much she wished it could be, Hatch understood its impact on the present.

"You sound a bit winded," Savage said.

"Pushed myself this morning. Did a quick seven-miler. Felt good, though. Haven't run like that in a while."

"You know, you could always just take up licorice."

She laughed, knowing that the reformed smoker had found his balance in the form of the bite-sized chewable black candy.

"No, thanks. I'd rather burn my energy off than eat it."

"Whoa, what are you saying?"

Hatch laughed. For as much as Savage consumed the candy, his body had no signs of the extra sugary calories. He was rigid, his body a rock. Hatch still held onto her memory of laying against him in the motel room several months back.

"Got any plans today?" Hatch asked.

"We're going to be following up on some of the evidence collected. The scene's been processed. We didn't finish until after one in the morning."

Hatch remembered the tedium a homicide scene required, having worked her share in CID before being brought into Task Force Banshee. She also remembered the rush that came with it when trying to solve the ultimate puzzle.

"I'm going over the reports now," Savage said. "To be honest, I've been staring at them for too long. I could use a little break this morning. Why? What did you have in mind?"

"I just wanted to see if you wanted to join me for a hike."

"This from the girl who just ran seven miles?" Savage said.

"I said hike, not run." Hatch was smiling. She wondered if Savage was too. "I'd really like to just catch up with you outside of the Sheriff's Office. Might be healthy for you to disconnect from the case for an hour or two. It's supposed to rain later, I figured now might be as good a time as any."

Savage cleared his throat.

Hatch worried she might've pushed too hard and quickly offered an out. "I know you're going to have a lot of work ahead of you. I just thought it might help get the investigative juices flowing before you dive back in. We can always do it some other time."

"No, you're right. I think if I stare at this computer screen for another second my eyes are gonna explode. With Paulson dead and Wesson in lockup, the next step will be compiling the case facts for prosecution. That aspect of the case will be time consuming, tedious and unless the evidence at the scene paints a different picture, I'm leaning toward Wesson as our doer. Even though, after our early morning interview today, he denied any knowledge of Paulson's death."

"You interviewed him today?" Hatch found herself somewhat hurt that she had not been called in to be the assist, to consult.

"I did. He was shipping off to county lockup from our holding cell, so I took another crack at him since he hadn't lawyered up yet. Figured it might be the last opportunity. The interview didn't last long. It was short-winded, and a big letdown compared to yesterday. He wasn't as cooperative as he was before."

"It happens," Hatch said.

"It does, especially after his first statement locked him into the conspiracy to commit capital murder. Maybe the night in his cell gave him time to reconsider his cooperation. Which is to be expected, but I thought I'd still have a decent enough shot of getting something else out of him, specifically with regard to Paulson."

"And you got nothing?" Hatch asked, non-accusatorially.

"Nothing as far as an admission, but I will say this. As much as I want to believe that he did it, there was something about Wesson's reaction to the news of Paulson's murder. He seemed to be genuinely shocked, as if he was caught off guard by it."

"Strange," Hatch said, more to herself.

"I didn't mention anything about how Paulson was killed in the hopes that maybe Wesson would slip up and divulge something about the bone-handled knife we found buried in the man's chest."

"Did he?"

"Nope. Just before Wesson lawyered up, he asked me how Paulson died."

Hatch understood the significance. Savage told Wesson about the murder but not the method of death. It was a smart move. The obvious being Wesson mentioning any detail that could be known only to the killer. Wesson had passed the litmus test for his claim that he didn't know anything about the murder.

The more subtle test, and the one Savage just alluded to, added weight to Wesson's claim. He asked Savage for information on how Paulson died. It spoke to Savage's skill that he also noticed. The killer wouldn't ask. The killer would already know.

Clint Wesson, who had the day before been loquacious at best at describing the circumstances leading up to the death of the Ute reservation's police chief, was all of a sudden recalcitrant, no longer speaking volumes. Either it was because he knew the dire situation he was facing in the wake of his first statement, or he really had nothing to do with his partner's death. If that were true, then this case just got a whole lot more interesting. Everything in Hatch's gut told her Wesson didn't kill Paulson.

"Well, in light of that news," Hatch said, "maybe you do need a little break. Clear your head for an hour or so. I know it helps me. When I'm looking at something for too long, things get a little blurry. When I take a step back, completely separating myself from it, that's when I get a much-needed perspective."

"I could use a little of that perspective right now," Savage sighed, adding a soft chuckle. "All right, I give up. I don't have an excuse to keep me from hiking with you. Just promise me that there's no running involved."

Hatch let go of her ankle, and her left leg descended to the floor. The tingle in her muscles was less intense, but still noticeable. "Trust me, I'm not running any more today," she said with a laugh. "But I probably need a shower before we meet up."

"Where should I meet you?"

"Here, at my house? We'll take the trail that leads out the back. I want to show you something."

"Give me an hour so I can get things organized here, then I'll be over. Tell your mom if she happens to have a pot of that coffee on, I'd be happy to take a cup off her hands."

Hatch rolled her eyes at the comment. Savage's secret love affair with Hatch's mother's morning brew was endearing.

"I'll tell her you'll be stopping by, and I'm sure she'll make you a fresh pot. See you soon."

Hatch ended the call and then headed inside to get cleaned up. She was equal parts nervous and excited at the prospect of their upcoming walk. Taking her first steps to, in Barbara's words, be brave in love.

TWENTY-TWO

Hatch hadn't taken an hour to freshen up. The great thing about exertion in a dry climate like the mountainous region of Colorado was that after sweating profusely, it took less than ten minutes for her to be completely dry. She still decided to hop in the shower to rinse off.

She'd told her mom and the kids that Savage would be stopping by. Her mom's eyes brightened at the news. Before Hatch could ask, her mother immediately set about percolating another batch of coffee. Hatch laughed to herself.

The kids were excited too. In the time when Hatch was recently away, Savage had made a point of stopping in and checking on the family from time to time. After the trauma the children had faced during an armed confrontation in the house, Savage had taken on a de facto uncle status, every once in a while surprising the kids with a small toy or gift, or just merely his presence.

According to Hatch's mother, he didn't stay long when he would visit, but he popped in enough that the kids had established a connection with him. They got excited and asked if they could come on the hike. Hatch toyed with the idea. She thought it might be nice, playing at some semblance of family. Her mind even flashed to an imaginary moment in time where she and Savage walked hand in hand while the kids scampered ahead. She shoved it from her mind. It was a leap she wasn't really ready to make.

Hatch wanted some alone time with the man. She had things she needed to discuss. Casework was one of them. She also wanted to lay everything out on the table to see if she had been right regarding the potential for a relationship between them. Hatch knew the only way to do that, to truly let her guard down and test those waters, would have to be done without the children present.

She let the children down as easy as she could. Hatch almost immediately recanted after seeing the disappointment in their eyes, more so in that of Daphne's. The hurt puppy dog look she had given Hatch had almost been effective enough to cause Hatch to concede.

Instead, Hatch leaned down and gave her niece a conciliatory kiss on her head. "Next time, I promise, little Daffodil. I just have some things I need to talk to Dalton about, and I prefer to do them by myself. You understand?"

Daphne batted her eyes in a last-ditch effort to change Hatch's resolve. Seeing that it didn't, she gave a wink. "Girl stuff, right?"

Hatch blushed and then laughed. "Right. Girl stuff."

Daphne seemed satisfied by it, and then Hatch worried. Maybe Daphne thought this was some type of moment of proposal, a six-year-old's imagination could potentially run wild. Returning from the hike, Daphne could have already formulated in her mind that she had married Savage on the walk. Hatch prepared herself to have a counterargument when they returned and hoped that she had misread the child's expression of excitement at the affirmation that girl talk was going to happen.

The dirt and rock-covered drive made a loud crunch and pop as the wheels of Savage's Suburban rolled up to a stop, making it hard to approach undetected. There was no real need for a security system on the long drive to the isolated house that was the Hatch compound, as her father had referred to it. By car, it was one way in, one way out. Another defensive strategy her father had put in place, unbeknownst to Hatch in her youth, but she realized now after her training that her father's lifestyle choice was not too dissimilar to that of the poachers. Her father had selected this location because it was a defensible position. But they found him anyway. All those precautions did little in the way of protecting him.

Jake didn't put up much of a fight about wanting to go. He had been diligent in his practice with the makiwara board since Hatch had built it. In fact, he was warming up to do just that when Savage knocked at the door.

Jake was practicing some of the formations he'd learned in karate class. The choreographed movements were filled with stances, blocks, and strikes. It was a dance of sorts, designed as a way to rehearse coordinated attack scenarios. Hatch knew that real world combat was very different from the formations of her martial training. But she was equally well aware that the foundations built in those rigid attacks and counterattacks were the core of fighting.

The more formations you train, the more complex a scenario a person could respond to. The more frequently you trained in those techniques, the more they became second nature when their use became a necessity.

She saw a drive in Jake that she had seen in herself when she'd been younger. His love of martial arts had exploded after he had effectively saved the family. His act of heroism had enabled Hatch to save herself as well. Bravery didn't pick an age. When opportunity presented to be brave, those who have it in themselves to answer the call, answer it regardless. She was pleased to see that fire burning brightly in her nephew.

Hatch's mother brushed past Hatch on the way to open the door. "I've got it dear," she said, almost floating by.

Jasmine Hatch swung the door wide. "Well, if it isn't Dalton Savage."

"Miss Hatch." He tipped his imaginary Stetson. He then looked beyond Hatch's mother, making eye contact with Hatch and gave a second tip of his invisible hat. "Miss Hatch," he said, smiling at his own joke.

Rachel's mother revealed the cup hidden behind her back. "I thought you might like a little cup before you two head out."

He took the cup in both hands and held it up to his face. He took a deep breath as steam rose up and took his first sip. "I don't know how you do it, Jasmine, but this coffee gets better every time I taste it. I think you should open your own bistro."

She laughed and stepped back into the house, giving Hatch top billing as Savage stepped closer.

Although it was early spring, the mountain air always kept things a touch cooler. Hatch had donned a loosely fitted long-sleeved shirt and some khaki cargo pants. She had on a pair of low-cut boots with just enough ankle support to keep her from twisting anything on the walk.

Savage was still in his uniform. It was designed for the rugged terrain. The button-down gray shirt and dusty jeans added to Savage's chiseled jawline and steely eyes, making him look as though the Marlboro Man had just stepped off of a billboard and into her living room. The only change she noted was that he'd traded snakeskin boots for a pair of brown hiking boots.

He sipped on the coffee as he followed Hatch deeper into the house.

"The trail you mentioned leads out of the back of your house?"

"Yep," Hatch said. "I know it well. It's something I intended on sharing with you before I left for New Mexico, but time got away from us last time. I didn't want it to slip by this time around."

"I'm looking forward to it." He gulped the coffee. He set the empty cup down in the sink. "Now that I've had my fix, I'm ready."

"I think you're going to need a twelve-step program to get you off that stuff."

Savage laughed as Hatch led him through the hallway to the back door.

"I want you to know I left my radio in the Suburban. Figured you were right about taking a break. They have my cell if they need to reach me. I want to go offline for a little bit."

Hatch held back her smile, not wanting to give away too much of her pleasure at the fact that Savage had taken their time together seriously enough to shut out the distraction of his duties for her.

Savage walked by Daphne, who was now back at the kitchen table, coloring her next masterpiece. Papers were scattered about, next to a half-eaten bowl of Froot Loops. "Hey, did you grow since I last saw you?"

She looked up at him, and he mussed her hair. She smiled, her eyes bright, her smile genuine. "Maybe I did," she said, pleased with herself.

"Maybe you should come by more often," Rachel's mom chimed in.

Savage blushed.

Hatch flashed her eyes at her mother without Savage seeing as a silent plea to stop. Hatch was suddenly a teenager all over again.

"We should probably get a start on our hike," Hatch said, before her mother could embarrass her anymore.

They set out the back.

Jake had just begun punching the makiwara board in a slow rhythmic fashion.

"What's that?" Savage asked.

"It's a makiwara board. It's designed to toughen the knuckles and perfect punching technique."

"Cool." Savage walked over to Jake and stood by like a proud father. He looked on as Jake took up a slightly modified horse stance to deliver the disciplined strikes.

Hatch was happy to see Jake was not hitting with too much force, striking just hard enough to be effective.

"Impressive stuff, Jake," Savage said.

As with Daphne, the acknowledgement by Savage brightened Jake's face, even though he tried to maintain focus on the board in front of him. Hatch could see from the subtle change in posture that Jake was pleased.

"Auntie Rachel taught me," he said, without taking his eyes off the post in front of him and delivering a strike a little harder than the last, to punctuate it. He grimaced slightly, the impact aggravating his tender knuckles that were just beginning their conditioning.

Hatch saw it. "Remember, Jake, not too hard. Not yet. There'll come a time for that. Pace yourself and build that endurance slowly so it lasts. No good if you hurt those knuckles early because then you have to start it all over again. It's a lot easier to keep it going than to restart."

In that statement, Hatch knew exactly why she had pushed herself as hard as she had this morning. She wanted to keep her edge sharp. If she never used it again, fine and great, but if the need called, she didn't want to need a reboot. Easier to keep going than to restart.

"We'll be back in a little bit," Hatch said.

They left Jake to continue his training as they set off into the wood line. Hatch led Savage as they forged ahead into a place in the woods that held the biggest part of Hatch's past.

TWENTY-THREE

As they walked, Hatch guided them to the path that led down to the brook. Hatch stopped at the boulder that, as a child, seemed enormous to her. She sat upon the rock that had become a place for her to reflect and gain perspective. At the foot of it, near the bubbling water, was the spot where she had found her father dead.

"This is where my life changed forever," Hatch said, staring down at the dirt. "I'm going to be honest with you, I don't know who I'd be without it. All I know with any sense of certainty is that who I am today started here. My father had already begun training me, readying me for a cruel world, but the lesson taught by his death did more to further that cause than any lesson he could've shared. It fast forwarded my life, turning me from child to adult in an instant."

Savage remained silent for a moment before speaking. "I can't believe what that must have been like for you. For what it's worth, if the person you became is because of it, then at least there's something positive that came from his death. I'm just sad that it was born from such a tragedy."

Hatch realized her first stop of their hike had dampened the mood. The sky seemed to be listening, too. It darkened as storm clouds rolled in. "Sorry, this trip was not designed to be all doom and gloom. It wasn't the reason I brought you here, but I couldn't pass it without mentioning what it means to me."

"I'm glad you did."

"We're going to cross the water here, at its lowest. I want to take you up the rise. There's something truly beautiful up there, and I want to show it to you."

"Can't wait."

The trek up was slower. The path became less defined, which Hatch actually liked. That meant fewer people had crossed here. It had been seldom that Hatch had crossed paths with anyone during the thousands of times she'd taken this trail over the years to sit atop the ridge and reflect.

As a child, she remembered feeling as though she were a pioneer, an explorer first discovering an unseen land. She'd remember when her father had first brought her here. She was ten years old. Closing in on the ridgeline now, she felt the same euphoric excitement. It was something she hadn't experienced in a long time, and she knew the reason. Savage was with her.

This ridge held one of Hatch's last memories she had of childhood, a real childhood, where the sense of wonder wasn't dashed by life and horrors and tragedy.

"So, you don't think Wesson did it?" Hatch asked. The thought popped into her head for some reason, and since they were alone, she figured she'd pick Savage's brain a bit.

The investigator in her could not be quenched. Being an outsider on a criminal investigation left her with a nagging desire for more, or at least the understanding of it. She now understood why there was such a fascination with true crime books and television shows. She'd always been an insider, but now, pushed to the outside, she found an aching desire for answers. It was a uniquely odd position to be on the outside looking in.

"I mean, if I had to bet on it," Savage said, "I'd say he wasn't lying. But it doesn't make sense. Wesson would have a perfect reason to kill him. Partners in crime often turn on each other. Makes the most logical sense. I figured Wesson had killed Paulson after I went to his property and before he came in to be interviewed. But I'm not so sure now."

"Fear is a great motivation for murder. It would be logical Wesson would fear Paulson turning on him. But I agree with you that his reaction sounds a bit off."

"I had some misgivings after working the scene last night. But I was still half expecting Wesson to turn State's witness against his friend and plea for leniency in exchange for full cooperation. With Paulson dead, who would be around to argue otherwise?"

"The evidence would eventually speak the truth."

"And that's why I had my doubts this morning before going in for the follow-up interview with Wesson," Savage said.

"Did you just say that you had your doubts before the interview?"

"When we processed the scene last night, Sinclair found something that raised a major red flag. Wesson's reaction to the news of Paulson's death only further added to my suspicion."

"Are you going to make me beg?" Hatch stopped walking and was staring eye to eye with Savage, whom she could see was getting a kick out of prolonging his finding. "What did Sinclair find?"

"Wesson hadn't left the gate open. The lock had been cut. We found it down in the drainage ditch."

"Great find by Sinclair," Hatch said.

"Becky's really come into her own as a deputy recently. I think a lot of that has to do with you."

"Me?"

"You're a natural leader. I know I've been pushing you to come on board, but it's not just your ability to investigate that makes you valuable. You've got an intangible quality that brings those around you up a level."

"The busted lock raises a lot of questions." Hatch couldn't help but shift the conversation away from herself. "Any leads?"

"Not yet. When I saw Paulson dead on the floor, I immediately thought we had an open and shut case with the doer already in lockup. Figured Wesson was going to lay a self-defense claim at my feet." He looked up at the ridge and then laughed to himself. "I guess nothing's ever that easy. Hell, Denny Paulson isn't even his real name."

"Changed his name because of his affiliation with the Colorado Free Americans? Or because he's wanted?"

"I took his prints on scene and ran them through AFIS. Got a hit out of

Richmond, Virginia. Denny Paulson used to be one Denny Clark. And a real piece of shit. He skipped town on a serial child rape case. He's been on the run for nearly three years."

"He's not running anymore."

"And now we can add murder to his criminal resume," Savage said.

There was a disappointment in his voice. Hatch understood. Savage couldn't deliver the justice Chief Nighthawk deserved. Clark's death had stolen the opportunity for the closure an investigation provided.

"Any idea on a possible suspect?" Hatch asked.

"Nothing yet. Wesson's property falls within Hawk's Landing jurisdiction, so that means Clark's murder is now our case to handle."

"Maybe something will come from the trace evidence recovered on scene?"

"Time will tell. The knife's going off to the lab tomorrow. I'm hopeful the deep ridges of it might have captured some DNA," Savage said.

Hatch was silent for a moment, but not because she wasn't listening. She had heard everything Savage had to say. Her mind drifted to the look exchanged between Nighthawk and Clearwater after tactical cleared the house. It made sense at that moment.

Clearwater saw something, and Nighthawk's reaction confirmed it. That subtle exchange between the two Ute men, an outcast and his uncle who owed a life debt, became all too clear.

"I'm going to say something, Dalton. It's the other reason I brought you up here. It pains me to say this, so let me say my piece before you interrupt."

Savage pulled out a couple pieces of licorice. "Go ahead. I'm all yours."

"When we were on scene at Wesson's place after the house was cleared, I saw something that I should've mentioned earlier. But to be honest, I wasn't sure what it meant until you told me about Wesson."

"What are you getting at?"

"I think you know."

Savage was silent.

"How long was Nighthawk standing guard on that road?" Hatch didn't wait for an answer. "Murder is a crime of motive and opportunity. John Nighthawk had both in spades."

"He's a good kid." Savage's gaze drifted toward the sky, and his words trailed off.

"His father was murdered in cold blood by a couple of lowlifes." She thought about her own father. Even with justice finally delivered, Hatch still felt the embers of her rage burn, unsatisfied. "What happened was enough to make the best of people go off the rails."

"Wesson and Clark probably had a long list of people willing to stick a knife in either one of their hearts. Might not have been John."

"Do you really believe that?" Hatch asked.

Savage looked down at his mud-covered boots but didn't answer. His silence was answer enough.

"I hate to ruin this hike, but it had to be said. I only know Nighthawk from our limited conversations, but by the little bit I gathered, he seems like a great guy." Her conciliatory offer only appeared to add to Savage's burden.

"I guess it would answer another one of my questions," Savage said.

"What's that?"

"All those pole cameras staggered along the property fed into a hard drive." Savage sighed and took out a couple pieces of licorice. "It was missing."

"But how would he have gotten the drop on Paulson, correction, Clark?"

"I don't know," Savage said. "I guess that's something I'll have to ask Nighthawk during his interview."

Savage slumped, leaning his weight against the trunk of a sturdy bristlecone pine.

Hatch could see the weight of this revelation was having a debilitating effect on the seasoned sheriff. She thought of her own need for vengeance and the bloody path she took to find it. Would Savage hold her in the same regard if he ever found out? What made Nighthawk's decision any different from hers?

"There's more than one way to let this thing play out," Hatch offered, approaching the topic delicately.

"What's that supposed to mean? Am I supposed to turn my back on Clark's murder?"

"Should Nighthawk hang for taking a child rapist and cop killer off the streets?"

"That's not how the world works. This isn't some hunter killer mission in a foreign country. If we don't follow the laws, things would disintegrate into anarchy." Savage pleaded his case, but there was no fight in his voice.

"You've got to do what's right for you. I'm not going to stand in your way." Hatch softened her tone. "You're a good man, Dalton."

An awkward silence fell upon them. Hatch realized her plans of taking Savage to the ridge were falling apart.

"I've got to figure exactly what I'm supposed to do with this situation." He looked at his watch. "I should probably be getting back."

"This is not exactly the hike I had in mind," Hatch said as distant thunder rumbled. Dark clouds blotted out the sun. "If you can bear with me a few more minutes, it's only a little way up from here, less than a five-minute walk."

Savage looked conflicted.

"Then let me share this little piece of me with you, maybe it'll help with the decisions you're facing."

"Just up there?" Savage asked as he started walking.

Hatch took up alongside him as they made their way to the top of the ridge.

TWENTY-FOUR

As they moved up the hill, Hatch could see that Savage was distracted. She was angry at herself. There was nothing that could be done, but she wished she had saved that conversation for the walk back.

And now any attempt to discuss anything else, like the status of where they were in rekindling a personal relationship was temporarily put on hold. It would come out of left field if Hatch were to say, "So, Dalton, where do you and I stand on things?" Which is what she had intended. But best laid plans sometimes fell apart.

She worked to recompose her thoughts, to stay focused on the other reason she had brought him here. Hatch wondered if it would have as much meaning and impact for him now that he was thinking about Nighthawk and whatever potential implications that knife held.

They reached the top of the ridge.

It was as if Mother Nature had carved out a bench from a boulder. Centered in a clearing of trees, just a few feet from the edge, was a large flat rock. She admired her hilltop sanctuary as a beam of sunlight broke through the hazy, overcast sky when they crested the top of the ridge.

"My father told me that the stone bench had been built just for us. My sister was never into the outdoors. This spot was something that belonged to me and my dad." She thought of some of the moments she shared with her father at this very spot.

As a little girl, Hatch remembered her father telling her that this piece of the world had been carved out for him and his family. "I knew even at ten years old that it was fanciful at best, playing on the imagination. But because my father had said it, I pushed reason aside and allowed myself to believe it."

She sat on the stone, leaving space for Savage to join her. She patted the flat cool surface of the rock and looked at him.

The tension was still in his face. She could see his mind was elsewhere, but he placated Hatch and took a seat beside her.

"I was never really close with my father," Savage said. "Hearing you talk makes me realize what I missed by not having a father like yours. As a kid, I used to pretend dads like yours existed. For the longest time, I didn't think it was possible. Mine was either drunk or in jail."

Hatch had never heard Savage speak of his father, and now she knew why. She should have picked up on some of it as much as she had gone on about needing to find justice for her own father. Savage had never offered any similar stories in return. In hindsight, she realized he probably didn't have any.

"So, why'd you bring me here, Hatch?" His focus on her seemed to return.

She thought about talking about the status of a potential relationship between them but held back. Sitting with him now, even in the open fresh air and her nostrils tasting a bit of the licorice that always seemed to encircle him, she didn't have the nerve. So, she danced around it.

"I came back to Hawk's Landing in the hopes of trying to find myself… again. It hasn't been an easy adjustment. But today on my run, I came here. I sat right here and spent some time thinking about my dad. I thought about a conversation he and I had when he'd first sat me on this rock at age ten. It was here, sitting right where I am now, that he had told me that life was bigger than any one person. He told me that we're here to do right on a bigger scale and that the individual actions of one person can make a difference."

Hatch rubbed the rock's surface as a drop of rain struck her hand.

She continued, "I didn't understand it back then, but it was here where he first shared the code for how he lived his life. He told me we're all given a special set of gifts, and how we use them determines who we are. And the people who use them for wrong need to be punished. Those who are too weak and don't have the strength to fight need to be protected."

Savage gave her his full attention.

"My dad had said to me that he was a protector, but he sought people who did wrong to others. And then he punished them. It's what I live by. Coming back here made me realize that no matter what I do, that code handed down to me by my father is still in my bloodstream. I could never outrun it."

"Maybe you shouldn't have to," Savage offered.

"I guess what I've been trying to say is that I've been really trying to figure out a way to truly settle back here in Hawk's Landing. I've been thinking a lot about your offer, and maybe working with you at the Sheriff's Office is the best way that I can balance it all now. Where I can help those who need it, punish those responsible. In all that, I'm hoping to find something I've been missing for a very long time."

"What's that?" Savage asked.

"A sense of family."

He nodded, his hand drifting near the pocket that held the licorice. Hatch could tell the direction the conversation was heading in was making him nervous.

"I'm sorry. I don't know why I brought you here. It just felt like I needed to share that piece of me with you. I needed you to understand where I'm at right now in my head. I know I'm not easy to handle. I know that about myself. I know I come off a little bit rough."

Savage laughed. "No! Who told you that?"

And then suddenly, maybe it was his smile, maybe it was the emotional connection this bench had for Hatch, but she suddenly felt a burst of confidence.

Be brave in love.

"I came back here to Hawk's Landing for my family, for my niece and nephew, for my mother." Hatch paused, willing herself to let down her guard and say the words in her head aloud. "But I also came back here for you."

Her words seemed to linger in the thin mountain air.

Did I just say that? She actually had to ask herself if she had thought the words or if they had come out of her mouth. She frantically attempted to read Savage's face for any acknowledgment of her words. And then with the reddening of his cheeks, Hatch had her confirmation that the message was received.

He let out a sigh. "Oh, thank you for finally being brave enough to say something. Barbara's been in my ear ever since I told her you were coming back to town."

Hatch moved a fraction of an inch closer.

"Hatch, I'm no good at this stuff. But I want you to know that I've thought about you every single minute since you've been gone. I don't know what happened to you while you were away. Something tells me that I probably shouldn't know or want to know. Whatever you did enabled you to come back home. I never thought that would happen. But ever since I saw you walk through the doors of the Sheriff's Office, I've been praying every night that you'd never leave again." Savage broke into a boyish grin. "Why do you think I asked you to work with me, to be a consultant? I needed to have you around me. I'm all left feet when it comes to the dance that is dating. And I'm sorry for that. I'm better with a gun than my heart, I guess."

"You and me both," Hatch said. "Hanging up my guns made me realize that I had to focus on that other piece. The heart." She reached over, her hand sliding over his.

Savage twisted his body, squaring his shoulders to her. He reached out with his left hand and pulled Hatch closer. His fingers, with gentle firmness, gripped her scarred, mangled arm. Hatch leaned in close, licorice penetrating her nostrils.

Her lips neared his when she stopped cold. "Don't move."

Savage's eyes resonated with shock, followed by embarrassment as he released his grip.

"I'm sorry. I misread this," he stammered. Savage shifted back from Hatch.

"Shh. Don't move," she said. "Rattlesnake, by your left ankle."

Savage froze.

"Stay steady. Maybe it'll move along. Just give it a second."

Savage then began sliding his right hand down his side. His movements were incrementally slow, almost sloth-like.

Hatch realized he was going for his duty weapon, suddenly wishing she had one of her own.

"I'm not going to be able to take the shot without moving," Savage said. "I'm going to hand you my gun."

The two moved in slow motion, trying not to disturb the coiled rattler nearby.

"It's mating season. That means where there's one, there's usually another," Hatch whispered. "You see any others behind me?"

He shook his head slowly.

His thumb was now on the holster. It was a level two retention holster, meaning he had to push down on the hood and then rock it forward before being able to pull the weapon free.

Hatch edged her right hand closer to her lap and turned it palm up, giving Savage a place to put the gun once he had it out.

"Take it slow."

The click of the plastic hood as he pressed down caused the rattler to shift. The distinctive rattle cut the silence.

"Easy, easy," Hatch said through steady breaths.

He pulled the gun free.

Hatch felt the nylon-based polymer of the Glock's frame touch the center of her open palm.

Savage suddenly yelled in pain and fell off the back of the stone bench as Hatch fired two quick shots.

The snake's head exploded from the second round's impact. Hatch then visually scanned the ground for any other rattlers. Not seeing one, she immediately skirted around the flattened boulder.

Savage was holding his left leg above the ankle, near the bottom of his calf muscle. "It got me."

"We've got to get you to a hospital. It's a long walk back to the house," Hatch pulled out a folding knife clipped to the inside of her back pocket.

She took a knee beside Savage's injured leg and flipped open the three-inch blade with a flick of her thumb.

"Are you going to cut the holes wider and suck out the poison?" he asked, looking down at the sharp edge of the blade.

"That's an old wives' tale," Hatch said.

"Then what's the knife for?"

"I need to loosen your pant leg. Alleviating pressure as the leg swells is really the only thing we can do right now until we get you to a medical facility with an antivenom."

She gripped the bottom of Savage's jeans. Hatch then cut along the outer seam, creating a flap that extended up to his knee. She then repeated the process on the inseam.

"The clock is ticking. We've got a lot of uneven ground to cover before getting back to the house. I'm going to call ahead for an ambulance." She pulled out her cell phone. "Damn it."

"What?" He pulled a handkerchief from his back pocket and wiped at the blood dripping from the two puncture wounds.

"No cell signal."

Hatch then grabbed a nearby stick. It was about six inches long with a one-inch diameter. She then took the handkerchief from Savage and wrapped and tied it off just below the knee. Hatch then slipped the stick on the inside of the knot. She began twisting, cinching the knot tighter until Savage winced in pain. "It's not a true tourniquet, but it'll slow the blood flow enough, to hopefully stop some of the poison from spreading."

Savage groaned as he examined her handy work.

"Can you stand?" she asked.

Savage answered by performing the task and pushing himself to his feet. He was unsteady, and Hatch helped by sliding herself under his left shoulder and acting as a crutch. The Glock was still in her hand, her finger indexed along the cool steel of the slide.

"Might as well keep this out in case we run into more of our woodland critters," Hatch said.

"You said you've got no signal. Let me try mine." Savage dug in his pocket and pulled his phone out. His brow furrowed. "Strange. Me neither."

"We've got to get back to the house," Hatch said. "You keep trying to get a signal while we move."

Savage nodded, and they began their three-legged race down the uneven territory, slipping and sliding on some of the scree and talus rocks that lined the path.

His left leg was swelling rapidly, and Hatch could see he was in a tremendous amount of pain. Halfway down, nearing the brook where Hatch's father had died, Savage lost his footing altogether. In doing so he threw himself off balance and fell, taking Hatch with him.

She tried to catch herself just before striking the ground. Savage caught the brunt of her weight as the two fell into a dense network of bushes in the foliage alongside the trail.

Just as a gunshot rang out.

Hatch looked at the gun in her hand, half-thinking she'd somehow accidentally discharged the weapon during the fall.

Savage was looking at his gun in Hatch's hand and must've been thinking the same thing.

"Not me," she said.

Hatch scanned the world around her. Then she saw it. Looking up to a nearby tree, where they were just standing before Savage toppled them both, Hatch saw the fresh hole in the trunk. A bullet hole was clear as day, right at the height of where Rachel Hatch's head had been located only moments before.

Her mind, doing a million different evaluations in a matter of split seconds, looked at the wood, the hole, the direction, the sound from the impact.

One thing was certain. This was no accident. Somebody was on the hunt. And they were the prey.

TWENTY-FIVE

Her mind raced to determine the direction of the threat. Hatch scanned the dense wood line until she saw what she was looking for. It took her a couple of painstaking seconds until she pinpointed it on the alternate side of the ravine. The glint of a scope, barely perceptible, flickered momentarily against the dark landscape. Had she not been looking, Hatch probably would never have noticed. But whoever was out there had made a mistake. They'd missed.

Hatch grabbed Savage. Remaining low to the ground in a half crawl, she dragged him by his shirt behind the base of the large pine tree that had just taken the round.

"We've got a real problem."

"What the hell was that?" Savage asked, looking wild-eyed at Hatch.

"That wasn't an accident." *Who the hell is trying to kill us?* Hatch thought about the text message she had received from the private number. *Watch your six, not safe for you there.*

In that split second, near the spot where her father was shot dead, she knew just exactly who was on the other side of that tree line. And who was coming for her.

Talon Executive Services had found her. She'd disregarded the warnings at every pass. Her father couldn't run from his past in these mountains and apparently neither could she.

"Not really the time for a long-winded explanation, so let's just say in my absence and in my search for my father's murderer, I may have kicked the proverbial hornet's nest. Now they've come to collect their pound of flesh."

Strange as it was, Hatch was calmer in this moment than she had been on the ridge expressing her feelings to Savage only moments ago. She was the calm in the storm. And the storm brewing in the clouds above was nothing to the one taking place on the mountainside below.

"Hell of a first kiss," Savage said.

"We still haven't gotten there yet." Hatch gave him a wink.

"I guess that gives me a reason to survive this."

"I know this place, but we can't go back yet. I can't bring these people back to the house. I can't bring this upon my family. I have to keep them safe. We have to keep the fight here for now."

Savage looked down at his calf and then at the Glock in her hand. "I'm only going to slow you down."

Hatch didn't argue. "Stay down and out of sight. I'll be right back."

"That Glock isn't going to be of much use against a long gun."

"Hopefully they make the same miscalculation you just did," Hatch said.

Hatch took a moment behind the cover of the tree to formulate her plan of attack as she scanned the hillside for her best course of action. It didn't take long for her to find what she was looking for. She just hoped it was just crazy enough to work. *Hope is the wish of the unprepared.* Savage's words. The thing was, Hatch had been preparing for this her whole life.

She coiled herself up like the rattler who had just ravaged Savage's leg and prepared for her opportunity to strike.

TWENTY-SIX

Hatch, eyes sharp, took two quick breaths. Her heart rate steadied. She'd be exposed for a few seconds before being able to tuck behind the rise of uneven rock and boulders up ahead to her left. If she could make it through the unprotected twenty-foot gap without getting shot, she had a chance at flanking the position of the person who had just fired at her.

Everything now seemed amplified: her hearing, her focus. She thought if she concentrated hard enough, she could hear the flap of a butterfly. It felt like something out of a David Carradine Kung Fu Saturday afternoon special. She knew why her battle senses were so elevated. This was her home turf. She knew this land better than anybody, regardless of their skill. This mountainside was as comfortable to her as her own skin.

Hatch reconciled her moment's hesitation. If she died here on this mountain in proximity to where her father was killed, then so be it. Then she felt the fire of her rage brighten into its full glory again. She felt herself in total control. And it felt good.

Hatch exploded from behind the tree, her head down, her body as low as possible while maintaining the dead sprint she was in. *One one-thousand, two one-thousand, and down.*

She heard the zip of the bullet as it passed behind her head. A millisecond later, she slid behind the cover of a fallen tree. The uprooted giant gave a cluster of roots to tuck behind. She had played here as a child with her sister. This had been their stomping ground. She knew every inch of the uneven terrain as well as she knew the scars on her arm and the disjointed tattoo underneath.

They'd be lining up their next shot, trying to predict where she'd pop out next. She hoped her movement had frozen any forward progression of the sniper team. If they had sent a full kill squad, then her chances of survival were near zero. But if they had been dumb enough to send two men, trained or not, to take her out, then they should have sent better people and not have missed.

She had a swath of rock and tree that was now providing her total cover and concealment as she moved at breakneck speeds. She neared the ridge where she and Savage had just sat. It would be her next point of exposure.

Hatch used the anger and rage to push her forward. Her legs still burned from the morning's exertion, but she put the discomfort out of her mind. It was nothing compared to what threats lie ahead.

A few more steps and she found herself at the edge of an outcropping of trees. In the distance, approximately fifteen feet away, was the stone bench. Hatch needed to break free from the cover of the last tree and make it to the drop-off.

What Hatch didn't get to tell Savage because of the snake bite was that on that day, at age ten, when her father had first brought her here and given her the speech, etching her life's code into her very DNA, he followed his lesson with something he called *the test*.

Hatch's father had told her how easy it was for people to speak about doing something, but to act on it was what separated a bystander from a hero.

Hatch remembered the seriousness in her father's normally kind eyes. She remembered fearing what lay behind those eyes. She knew he would never hurt her, but she saw in that moment how dangerous a man her father was. Hatch now knew she had the same look. And on that day, nearly two and a half decades ago, the test was anything but simple.

Her father had brought her to the edge of the ridge a few feet from the bench. He asked her, "What are you most afraid of?"

She remembered looking at him and wondering why he asked because he already knew her biggest fear. "Heights."

"Then it's time to act. You're going to be afraid of a lot of things, Rachel," she remembered hearing him say. "There's a lot of things to be afraid of, but the bravest people feel their fear, recognize it, acknowledge it, and then they confront it. Today, you're going to show me whether you're going to be a bystander or a hero in life. Today, you're going to show me if you're going to be able to act on the code I shared with you."

Standing so close to the edge, her stomach dropped, and her head felt light and her knees buckled. At that point, her father let go of her hand and stepped back. "Rachel, I want you to go down. Climb down the ridge."

"But Dad." She tried to find a plea worthy of his understanding, the right words that would stop him from sending her over the edge of the high ridge.

"Don't worry. I've been preparing for this day for quite a while. I set up a cargo net. It's bolted to the other side of the ridge. All you have to do is get over the lip and grab it and climb down to a narrow landing twenty feet below. Once down, you can walk back up and around the other side. It's easy to get back up, but you've first got to climb down."

Hatch remembered the feeling, wanting to prove herself worthy, wanting to make her father proud, and wanting to make the insufferable knot in her stomach go away. She remembered the dizzying feeling as she took little quarter steps toward the ridge's edge.

When she got close enough, she dropped to her knees, taking the last foot's distance on all fours like a dog.

"I don't care how you get over that ridge and onto that cargo net. I only care that you do it." Her father's encouragement bolstered her bravery.

Ten-year-old Hatch edged forward, and then, laying her belly flat on the dirt, she dragged herself over the rock cliff.

She remembered the feeling of relief when she found the ribbed coil of the cargo net her father had anchored to the stone face. The whole experience was surreal.

Hatch had been impressed as a child that her father had taken the time to pick this spot and go through the trouble of setting up this net, this challenge, just for her. She appreciated it even more now as an adult, having the benefit of hindsight. Her father loved her so much that he had put this much thought into preparing her for the world.

And now, facing an armed opponent and the potential life and death struggle that was already underway, her dad's training formed a direct corollary from his past lesson to its present application. It was also integral to her current plan for survival.

Hatch hoped that in the years since she'd last climbed the net that the weather conditions hadn't deteriorated it so badly that it wouldn't sustain her weight. But she had no choice. If she didn't keep moving, if she didn't outflank and outmaneuver the shooter, then they were already as good as dead.

She blew out a lungful of air, pushing the memory of her childhood away, with the last thought being her father's look of approval.

Hatch ran, exposing herself to the gunman's aim once again. She moved quickly but made sure she zigged and zagged every few steps to make herself more difficult to track. She knew the spotter would have already caught the movement and that the sniper would be working the weapon around. They'd most likely be in a fluid shooting position now that she was already on the move. She knew this because it's what she would've done.

The timing had to be perfect.

She sprinted at the bench. She knew if the gunman were bringing the weapon up to bear on her, he would assume she'd be going for the cover of the stone bench. She was banking on it.

As the shot rang out, Hatch made her move. In the deafening wake of the gunshot, she changed directions, twisting her body in dramatic fashion as she fell to the ground and rolled off the edge of the ridgetop.

She hoped the timing of her fall coincided close enough to the gunshot. There was only one way to tell, but she'd have to remedy her current situation first.

Hatch was hanging by her fingertips. The frayed rope of the cargo net had held, but the twisted way in which it caught her weight had nearly pulled her arm out of the socket. Searing pain pulsed down her damaged right arm. She was losing her grip.

She was momentarily suspended above the landing below. She remembered looking down as a child and feeling terrified. Now she barely registered the height. As a kid, the drop seemed to go on forever, but now as a grown woman, she felt she could make the drop without really injuring herself. It was a risk she didn't want to take, though.

She could feel the Glock tucked into the small of her back. Her feet found the rungs of the cargo net. Gaining purchase and re-centering herself on the wobbly old netting, Hatch worked herself down to the landing below.

Hatch followed the outcropping of rock which acted as a natural stairway that led around to the other side of the ridge and to her objective. She hoped this move would cause them to lower their guard.

She moved quickly up and around, flanking the position the shooter had just fired from. Glock in hand, Hatch hoped her move had just leveled the playing field because it was her turn to go on the offensive.

TWENTY-SEVEN

Hatch came up the rise. It was a lot easier than her descent down on the cargo net. Her right shoulder burned wildly. It tingled all the way down to her fingertips. If she hadn't dislocated, she certainly strained some ligaments. All those worries would have to be put out of her mind until she dealt with the problem at hand. Although she didn't get a clear view at the people firing at her, she knew from experience that any marksman sent to eliminate a threat like her would undoubtedly be operating as a team, both sniper and spotter. Just like Amalleto and Wenk had done when they'd killed her father. Both men were now dead. She hoped to provide the same end to the men now hunting her.

She crept up the rise and tucked in behind a split tree trunk that had been gashed open by a bolt of lightning and had long since rotted and died. From her vantage point of cover and concealment, she exposed a minimal amount of her forehead and face. Hatch scanned the terrain for the killers. Her gamble had paid off, and her ruse appeared to have worked.

Her fall off the cliff timed with the gunshot had the intended effect. They weren't moving over to the ridge to examine or look for her body. They were already moving on to the next known threat, Savage. They were quiet, barely disturbing the brush as they stalked forward through the uneven terrain.

The sniper now had a long bolt-action rifle slung across his back. The two men had opted for handguns. The smaller weapons made the landscape easier to navigate, enabling them to stay balanced as they moved.

She looked over at the large base of the tree where she had left Savage. He wasn't visually exposed, but she knew he was there. He'd never see them coming. It wouldn't matter if he did. She had his gun.

Hatch brought the weapon up and stepped out from cover.

The two contract killers were ahead of her now by about thirty feet, moving in a dense line of trees. She didn't have a clear shot. She kept the weapon at the low ready and pressed forward, using the trees to maintain cover.

As she closed the distance, Hatch was surefooted. She stepped heel to toe, rocking to the outside of her foot, using the edge of her boot to roll down on the ground beneath to minimize her noise. She was as silent as a whisper and was moving quicker than the two men who must've just arrived at Hawk's Landing.

The men who'd made the critical mistake of coming to her home and trying to kill her.

She bottled the rage. Controlled it. Honed its energy as she pushed forward. The killers crossed the overgrown footpath that she and Savage had used to ascend to the ridge top. They were now less than ten feet away from where Savage lay.

They paused a few feet from the tree, both men looking at each other as they used hand signals to silently formulate their ad hoc plan of attack.

Hatch raised her weapon.

The sniper who had fired two shots at her and missed stepped wide around the base of the tree, bringing his handgun up to bear on the supine Savage.

The gun kicked in her hand twice. She didn't register the sound of its deafening roar. As soon as the second round left the barrel of the Glock, she shifted her point of aim to the spotter. Out of the corner of her eye, she watched as the sniper toppled backwards, slamming to a stop against an outcropped boulder alongside the trail.

The spotter was already in motion, spinning toward Hatch as she fired. His training and experience kicked in. He was on the move. He fired wildly, laying down a barrage of bullets in her direction.

His rounds struck a nearby tree. His aim was off. He was using defensive fire. Caught off guard, he was trying to find a position to defend himself from her ambush. The hunter had become the hunted.

He was good, but Hatch was better. He dove toward the trail, tucking himself into a roll as he hit the ground before popping back up.

It was a solid move, one that Hatch had used before to her advantage in combat. Moving in quick erratic directions made it difficult for a shooter to regain target. Dynamic movements were the best way to shake off a gunman's aim.

But Hatch knew this. She'd anticipated this. And just as they had tried to lead her with the shot on the ridge top, she did the same. She had the tactical advantage being at a slight rise and firing down.

She fired a three-round burst, locking onto the spotter. He was a small and wiry man. And when the rounds struck, she saw his wide, dark eyes register in horror that he'd been hit.

He twisted wildly and collapsed to the ground. Hatch waited a moment. Neither man moved. Hatch approached the spotter first. He lay closest.

"Dalton, it's me," she called out. "Hang in there."

He made a whimpering sound and crawled into view from around the base of the tree. His face was already pale white and sweat drenched his forehead. The venom was beginning to work its black magic. She needed to get him to a hospital quickly, but she couldn't do that if she was dead. Tactics dictated survival.

The sniper had gone down first and hard. He hadn't moved since. She assumed her shot group had been effective. The spotter was on the move when she had shot though. He was still alive, crawling away.

It was an odd tactic from a seasoned operator until she realized the reason why. One of her gunshots must have struck his hand, which lay blood-covered down by his right side, leaving a trail in the dirt like a slug. He was using his left arm to pull himself forward and toward the gun he had dropped when he was hit. He wasn't trying to get away. He wanted his weapon. He wanted to end this.

Hatch had the same idea.

She darted forward, breaking cover and closing the distance. Her long legs made quick work of the rugged terrain.

Her speed increased with the path's decline. She came up hard behind him, stomping her foot down on his wounded arm and freezing the man in place as his left hand reached out for the butt of the gun. It was only inches away.

He winced and let out a strange yelp as her boot pressed hard into his wounded hand. The spotter was laying on his belly and was unable to fully turn, but he twisted his head enough to make eye contact with Hatch. There was no fear in his eyes, only rage. She understood its source.

The spotter was in bad shape. He spat a mouthful of blood onto the dirt trail. One of the rounds she'd fired had nicked his neck, and he was bleeding profusely.

Hatch analyzed the wound and knew it was grave. A mortal wound that left the man little time in this world. Hatch figured she would capitalize on that.

The fight wasn't completely out of him. He swung his left arm down toward a knife strapped to his thigh, a last-ditch effort by a trained warrior. Going down without a fight was not an option.

She kicked him hard in the throat, knocking the last bit of effort out of the spotter. She stepped back, distance rendering the knife moot. He was out of options as he let out a gurgled curse.

Looking down the Trijicon front sight, Hatch centered it on the man's forehead, just between his eyes. She had him dead to rights.

He must have realized it because he stopped moving. It was either that or the amount of blood lost was taking its toll.

"How many?" she asked.

He smiled, his teeth blood covered. He spat, and it smeared off to the side of his lips. He looked like a deranged clown who'd been caught in the rain.

"You're already dead," he sputtered the words, barely audible. He was choking on his own blood.

SMOKE SIGNAL

"Seems like you've got that part all wrong." Hatch remained still. The only movement came from the front sight as it oscillated across the man's forehead. "I'll ask you again. How many more?"

The spotter's face became a grayish white as the blood continued its exodus. He said nothing.

"There are kids down in that house. If you have any amount of decency left in you, then you'll tell me what is coming."

Something about the mention of children seemed to soften the hate in the man's eyes.

Hatch seethed with anger. "I know what you're doing. I know who you work for. The assholes who employ you killed my father twenty years ago. You're not taking me too. And nobody's touching those kids. I don't know what they told you about me or why I'm your mark, but I guarantee you it's all lies."

Still nothing from the spotter. He was fading fast.

"You don't have long until you bleed out. And there's nothing I can do about that. People like you and me sometimes end up in the crosshairs. But those children in that house are innocent. What you do with the time left matters! They're six and eight, for God's sake! They don't deserve to die!"

She could see from his eyes that he agreed. He coughed wildly like a flooded engine sputtering to start. He spat again, clearing his mouth of the blood rapidly filling it. A tendril of sanguine spit connected from his cheek to the dirt ground where he lay, twisted and dying. "There's another team. Four men. They're off a ways in the woods. We didn't know about the kids, but there's no stopping them. Nobody goes back on an order in this group."

"My father did," Hatch said, looking down at him. She watched the life flicker in his eyes, fading, like the wick of a candle nearly burning out. "Not all orders have to be followed." She thought of her father. Down at the bottom of this trail was where the consequences for his disregard of an order had left him dead.

"They'll never stop," he said, "not until you're dead." He spoke through deep gurgled gasps. Hatch had heard the sound too many times in her life.

She knew what it meant. She watched as the last bit of life drained out on the ground around him. His body went limp.

Hatch held her point of aim a few seconds longer, ensuring that this wasn't some last-ditch ruse to draw her in. Satisfied, and with time running out, she closed in and pressed hard against his blood-covered neck. Finding no pulse, she quickly searched his body. She removed two spare magazines for the SIG 226, laying inches from where his left hand had reached. She took the weapon and magazines, stuffing the gun into her waistline and the spare mags into her cargo pocket.

She moved over to the sniper's body. He still hadn't moved from where he had fallen into a crumpled mess. She edged up close, keeping the gun trained on him and dropping a knee into his chest as she searched for a pulse. Nothing. He was dead.

She quickly took the rifle, unslinging it from his back. She then took the spare pistol from his dead hand. His finger was still on the trigger. Hatch's head shot had stopped him before he could take the shot on Savage.

Hatch added his spare magazines to her collection. The rifle lay next to her as she added the two SIGs to her rapidly increasing arsenal. Counting the bullets inside each gun, she had a total of six magazines.

Hatch left the dead men and went to Savage. He was nearly as pale as the spotter, though his eyes were still sharp.

She lifted one of the flaps on Savage's cut pant leg. The area around the two-pronged bite of the rattler had swollen to the size of a grapefruit and appeared to be growing. Puss-colored blood oozed from the wound.

Had the situation not been so dire and the threat still looming, she might've made a joke about how he looked like Bruce Banner in mid-transformation to The Hulk. No time for that with the rattler's venom taking hold. The swelling was the body's way of pushing out some of the poison.

"I hope they've got an antidote on hand," Savage mumbled.

Hatch knew the hospital would have some in stock, but she knew the best way to get the right anti-venom would be to identify the specific type of rattler that committed the offense.

"Hang on," she said.

Hatch darted back up the hill without waiting for a response. She grabbed the carcass of the dead rattler and threw it over her shoulder like a bandolier. It was long. Hatch guessed it to be nearly four feet. Recovering the cargo, she ran back down to Savage.

"Figured it's a lot easier for me to bring the snake into the hospital and get you the right antivenom quicker." The decapitated snake swung freely across her chest.

She returned Savage's Glock back to his holster and hoisted him up.

"We've got to move! Time is running out, and there's more of them out there somewhere."

"Who the hell are these people?"

Hatch balanced Savage's weight, becoming a human crutch. She kept one of the Sig Sauer pistols in her hand while leaving the spare stowed in the small of her back. Savage balanced on her right side while they began making the unsteady descent down to the brook below.

"It's the same people who killed my father. Well, same company at least."

His face scrunched as he tried to comprehend this. "What? Why?"

"I found the people responsible." Hatch paused. She wondered if Savage would understand her implication. "They're a company that doesn't like loose ends. And they're not going to stop until I'm dead."

"Well, then they're not going to stop because I'm not letting you die today."

Hatch liked that he wanted to protect her, but he was wholly unprepared for the threat in his current condition. "I need to get back to the house and get you to a hospital, but we can't do any of that until we deal with the problem at hand. Those two aren't the only ones here."

"There are more?"

"Four. If I'm to believe the spotter's dying declaration. Which I do." Hatch looked out in all directions. "They're probably going to start here when they realize what happened, then they're going to come for us. That means Daphne, Jake, and my mom are in real danger."

Saying the names of her niece and nephew aloud caused Hatch to move faster, while still managing to carry Savage's weight. The tall, rigid lawman was dense with muscle, and she felt that now as she shouldered his weight.

They moved down the hillside and across the brook where her father had been killed. Every passing second was one closer to the threat that now faced her family.

Hatch broke from the wood line with Savage at her side. The three-legged race against time took on a near sprinter's pace as the back of her house came into view. Jake was nowhere in sight. The makiwara board stood alone as lightning struck in the distance immediately followed by a deafening crack of thunder.

They rushed through the back door of the house as the storm closed in. Accompanying it, somewhere out in the woods surrounding her home, was a team of highly trained killers.

TWENTY-EIGHT

HATCH BARGED THROUGH THE BACK DOOR. HER MOTHER WAS HANGING UP the phone as they walked in. Jasmine Hatch was the epitome of horror at seeing Savage and Hatch.

"My God, Rachel, what's happening?"

"The people who killed Dad are here now. Here for me."

Hatch's mother broke into tears and had a giddy, almost laugh-like quality to her cry. She'd come immediately undone and was rapidly approaching the hysterical. This was too much for the ex-hippie, who'd lived through a similar experience twenty-plus years ago.

Hatch could see her mother needed to be given a task and purpose, distracting her from the impending threat and making her useful in whatever stand they intended to take.

"Who did you call?" Hatch asked.

"The police. I told them I heard gunshots, that you and Savage were on the mountain. They said they were sending everybody."

Hatch thought about that statement. Everybody in the Hawk's Landing Sheriff's Office meant two more people would be coming. Three, if Nighthawk wasn't on the run. It still didn't put them in much better shape when facing off against four highly trained killers.

"I need you to take Jake and Daphne to the basement. Do you understand me?"

Jake bowed his chest up at hearing this. "I can help, Auntie Rachel." He eyed the gun in her hand.

She walked over and kissed him on the forehead. "You are so brave, Jake, and I know you want to help, but this time it's too dangerous. The best way you can help me is by protecting your sister and grandmother. Get them in the basement, keep them safe."

Hatch addressed her mother, who was still crying. "Mom, don't open that door for anybody unless it's me or Savage. Do you understand me?"

She nodded while wiping at the tears streaking her face.

Taking his job seriously, Jake immediately went over to Daphne, who looked completely terrified. He gave her a hug and whispered something in her ear before taking her by the hand and leading her into the basement.

Daphne followed Jake while looking back at Hatch with a wide-eyed stare.

"It's okay, my little daffodil. Nothing's going to happen to you."

With the kids gone, Hatch once again turned her attention to her mother. "Mom, I need you to stay calm for the children. You need to hold it together down there. Do you understand me?"

Jasmine Hatch wiped her face on her sleeve, collected herself as best she could, and nodded.

"Take this," Hatch said, handing her mother a Sig P226.

Jasmine Hatch shook her head from side to side and put her hands up, deflecting the weapon. The ex-hippie was wholly against such violent tools.

"Mom, I need you to take this. It's a measure of last defense, and I pray you do not need it, but you cannot let them hurt the kids. Do you understand me?"

She nodded and reluctantly put out her hand.

"All you have to do is point and shoot."

"There's no safety button?"

"Not on this model. Don't point it at anything you don't intend to kill."

"I hope it doesn't come to that." Jasmine Hatch's voice quivered in sync with her body. She then disappeared down the stairs to the basement.

Hatch shut the door behind her mother. She then shoved the kitchen table over against the basement door, barricading it as Savage collapsed to the ground.

TWENTY-NINE

With her mother, niece and nephew secured in the basement, Hatch used her cell phone and dialed the Hawk's Landing Sheriff's Office dispatch, better known as Barbara Wright. She got a strange busy signal and looked down. The call didn't go through. She still had no signal for her cell. Savage groaned as he stood and steadied himself against the kitchen counter, near his beloved pot of coffee.

Hatch put her cell phone away and cursed under her breath.

"What is it?" Savage said, his voice strained. The poison in his system caused vascular constriction and seemed to be choking the rugged lawman's voice.

"My mother said she had just got off the phone with your office, but my cell still isn't working," she said. "They're jamming the cell signals. Thank God for my mom's resistance to technology."

Hatch picked up the phone from the kitchen wall. The cord of the landline dangled loosely as she listened to the dial tone. The landline was still intact. Hatch hit redial. This time, Barbara's sweet voice came through after the first ring.

"Hawk's Landing Sheriff's Office. Barbara Wright speaking. How may I help you?"

"Barbara? It's Hatch."

"Rachel, my dear? What's wrong? Your mom just called. Are you okay?"

"No. Listen carefully. Dalton's been bit by a rattler. He's going to need medics, but they're going to have to stage for now. I've got four armed men somewhere out there in the wood line outside my house. Two more are dead. These are trained ex-military special operators. Whoever you have responding this way, I want you to have them stage out on the main road. I don't want them trying to confront these men. Call Connors over at Durango PD. Have him mobilize his tactical unit. We're going to need a full tactical response here immediately."

"My goodness," she said, out of breath. "Are you okay?"

"I'm fine. Just do it."

"What are you going to do?" The voice on the other end was unsteady. Wright was nervous. And it was obvious by her tone.

"I'm going to do what I do best." Hatch ended the call and looked over at Savage.

"You're not flying solo on this one," he said. He stretched out his shaky hand.

Hatch tossed the dead snake on the floor and unshouldered the Ruger bolt action rifle. She ejected the magazine and counted seven rounds. With one in the barrel that gave her eight total of the .22 caliber magnum rounds.

"Listen, Dalton. I know you want in on this fight, but I'm telling you, you're not up to it, and with each passing minute, that venom is going to take more of a hold on you."

"I'm not just going to sit here and let you run off to die without me helping." Each word came between ragged breaths.

He wasn't doing well. She could see that. But sometimes you could push through the discomfort.

"I'm not planning on dying." Hatch looked over at the kitchen table shoved against the basement door. "Guard the door. Do not move. Do you understand me? Do not move from that door. You hold it. At all costs."

He gulped audibly, his ability to swallow was becoming more difficult. Savage let go of the counter that was supporting his weight and wobbled uneasily over to where Hatch had directed. He propped himself up now against the table, using it for support. "I'm not going anywhere, and if they want to get down to that basement, they're going to have to go through me first."

If Hatch had any doubts about her feelings for this man, in that split second, they were all but erased. He was the truest kind of hero, willing to sacrifice himself, unwavering in his commitment to her family. If it was possible to love somebody in the short time that she'd gotten to know him, then that's what she felt. Love for the man slowly succumbing to the venom of the snake, but willing to fight nonetheless. She gave him one last look before leaving the kitchen area.

"You stay alive, Rachel Hatch," he said with a gasp. "You still owe me that kiss."

"I'm going to head upstairs. I'll have a better vantage point from the upper rooms. I'll fall back here if I'm compromised." With the SIG 226 tucked in her waistband and the extra magazines in her cargo pocket, Hatch left Savage and quickly darted up the stairs.

She shut all the lights off. Although it was nearing midday, the surrounding high trees cast the house in a dark shadow made darker by the storm clouds in the gray sky. The last tendrils of light were absorbed in the thick overcast clouds and coated the house in relative darkness. Hatch didn't want any of the light inside to backlight her as she moved about.

Thunder erupted in the distance, and rain began to fall, slow at first, growing steadier and louder with each passing second as the droplets pelted against the windows of the house in the sudden downpour.

Hatch had been trained by some of the best. She used the upper windows as a vantage point, entering each room on all fours, only peering up from the center of the room and staying far enough away so the glass would obscure her from sight. She didn't want to give them a target.

Hatch looked out from her mother's room and then through the converted study that was now Hatch's bedroom again. Seeing nothing, she moved on.

It was in Daphne's room that she spotted the first glimmer of movement in the tree line, a single man. He was in dark olive drab overalls with a digital camouflage pattern. He moved deftly and quickly through the dark woods. She only caught a glimpse of him in the open before he disappeared again. She saw the direction he was moving in and began to track.

The dying man said four men were coming. He could have lied. There could be twelve or two for all she knew. Or maybe, just maybe, in those moments when he was facing death, he had seen the need for truth. A last act of contrition. His own dying penance given. If he'd been truthful, she could count her enemies as they fell and keep a running tally.

Then she heard a sound breaking the white noise of the rain against the roof. It was a pop followed by the shatter of glass. It came from downstairs. It was followed by another. Then another. They were gunshots.

Were they aiming at Savage? Were they firing randomly into the house?

Hatch watched for the one target that she'd had a visual on. She waited, looking where he had disappeared behind a thick network of bushes by a cluster of trees.

Another pop and shatter of glass. Hatch waited.

Then the man down below broke cover and stood. He raised up with a six-round multi-launcher. She now understood what the pops of glass were. They weren't firing at Savage. They had no target. They were breaking the glass, making it easier for them to deploy whatever munitions they had. They were going to try to draw her out.

The *thump, thump, thump* sounded as the man below fired three canisters in through a lower window.

Hatch seated the butt of the Ruger into the pocket of her shoulder, taking aim as the man stood for a moment too long, evaluating the effectiveness of his projectiles.

She fired from the center of the room out through the glass toward the man below.

His head snapped back. The momentum threw his body in an awkward and unplanned backflip, twisting him midair. He flattened on the ground, face down, unmoving.

The gas tickled her throat and eyes as she heard Savage coughing wildly from below. If the snake bite hadn't incapacitated Savage's ability to fend off an attacker, whatever gas it was, most likely CS tear gas, would greatly exacerbate his ability to confront any threat.

There were still three more assailants to contend with.

She moved back from Daphne's window, crossed down the hallway and made her way back toward her mother's room at the front of the house. The glass in the room she had just been in was shattered. It was followed by a thud and clang of another canister striking the floor. This time, however, she didn't smell gas.

When the canister erupted, she saw smoke. Smoke and flames billowed out of the room where her niece slept. Whoever had taken that shot was now using phosphorus munitions. The incendiary device burned out of control. The hallway was already catching fire as Hatch ran down the stairs.

When Hatch's father selected this house, he did it to protect his family. Hatch was well aware of the reasons why he'd gone through so much trouble. With the house burning she remembered what her father had told her when she was young. There had been a nasty lightening storm when Hatch was eight. She ran into her parent's bedroom when a bright flash outside lit up her room.

As she lay tucked between her parent's warm bodies, her father had tried to console her. He explained that when he refurbished the mountain house, he had added some fire protections. At the time she thought he was just overly safety cautious. But now she understood his mindset and level of preparedness.

The next morning, Hatch's father had taken her into the attic to show her what he meant. He had added an extra layer of fireproofing into the walls and had encased the pipes. It meant little to her at the time aside from putting her fears to rest.

Now it made all the sense in the world. Hatch's father explained that even with the extra precautions it would only provide a temporary window of time. Hydrocarbons were used in many household items which is a solid form of gasoline. They burn fast and release deadly gasses. A recipe for disaster.

Hatch's father told her that best case scenario gave thirty minutes before the house would become fully engulfed. Hatch subtracted fifteen minutes from the equation based on the munitions used to ignite the fire.

Her family's survival hinged on her ability to eliminate the threat before time ran out.

Her mental clock started to tick.

After grabbing a sheet from the hallway closet, she made a makeshift turban and mask. She looked like a bedsheet ninja. She took the stairs two at a time. The lower floor was a cloudy sea of CS gas, and it burned at her eyes. She rubbed at them and stayed low as the smoke began to form a dark cloud along the ceiling.

She'd deployed this type of CS gas on several standoffs during her time as a military police officer. Hatch had been exposed to several doses of the tear gas during a variety of training evolutions. She was accustomed to the sting and burn and knew that she could fight through it if she had to.

During one standoff, they had gassed the suspect's house for several hours. They eventually made entry, only to find that he had somehow absorbed the pain of it without giving up. They found him tucked inside an attic space with his face wrapped in his t-shirt. Although in severe discomfort, he still put up one hell of a fight. Hatch learned a lot about self-preservation, survival, and the ability to tolerate pain in a real-world environment, something that would be unacceptable or uncomfortable in a training simulation. This was no training environment.

Hatch made her way over to the kitchen and grabbed an oven mitt. Covering her face, she went around the room, collecting the canisters that were still dispensing the gas and threw them back out the windows.

Savage choked on the air around him and looked miserable in his discomfort.

Hatch grabbed a hand towel hanging from the stove handle and soaked it with water from the kitchen faucet. She ran to him. "Put this over your face and eyes. Cover them."

"What the hell is going on, Hatch?"

"We're in trouble," she said. "Just hang tight. Get below the table. Stay low. They're going to be coming. They'll know they can't wait. Time is ticking. They can't leave me alive, and the house is on fire. Fifteen minutes until we're cooked."

Hatch watched as Savage's bloodshot eyes went wide. His brain was playing the catch-up that anybody in his position would be, trying to figure out how to overcome a circumstance like this. Hatch, on the other hand, had been baptized in fire. She'd been in as bad, if not worse, circumstances, and she was still here to tell the tale. The only thing Savage would see in her eyes was resolve.

In that moment of chaos, she thought to herself, if she were them, how would she clear this obstacle? How would she cover the death of so many people? Now that they were exposed, and they had failed in whatever their plan was out in the woods, how could they kill a family and a sheriff and walk away from it? They must have a cleanup crew to police up after them, but what would be the cover? How would they...?

And then it came to her.

"They're going to blow the house."

THIRTY

"What?" Savage said, his eyes widening even further, if that was possible.

"They're going to burn it down. They'll rewrite the history of this moment. After we're dead, they'll fix it. But a fire? A fire destroys a lot in the way of evidence. If we try to run out there, they'll cut us down."

Savage said, "And I can't run, not now. I can barely feel my left leg. I'd just slow you down."

"Our propane tank. That's what they're going to hit. It's on the back side of the house. I've got to go." Hatch began moving.

"Wait," Savage said weakly.

She disregarded his plea. She knew that any seconds wasted and any further deliberations were going to give opportunity to the three men remaining outside.

Thirteen minutes until the fire consumed everyone inside. Everyone who mattered in Hatch's life.

Her instincts had been right. As she closed in on the back door, she saw one of the camouflaged men moving toward the oversized propane tank at the back-left corner of the house. Opposite was the makiwara board she had just built for Jake.

He carried the rifle at the low-ready and brought it up to bear as he scanned for threats. The man didn't see her and knelt down by the tank. Hatch watched as he pulled something from a pack on his back and placed it against the large cylindrical metal encasement that housed enough propane to blow the house and burn everything inside in a matter of seconds.

She took aim, focusing on the man's chest, the biggest target. It was one she would have to spend less accuracy trying to nail. She fingered the trigger and began to pull as several shots rang out, and the window she was behind disintegrated before her eyes.

Hatch was pelted with glass. She fired the rifle just before diving to the ground.

She scurried across the broken glass as it cut into her forearms and knees, scampering in a modified low crawl, moving around to the kitchen.

There were two in the back. She wasn't sure if she had dropped the one by the propane tank but wanted to be close to the basement in case things erupted. She wasn't going to let her family and Savage burn to death. If that meant fighting her way out with them behind her, then she was damn well going to do it.

Nothing. No explosion. She took momentary solace in the fact that maybe her round had found its mark, but that still left the second man out there. She moved herself around to the back bathroom. There was a small circular portal-sized window just above Hatch's eye level. She wouldn't be able to position herself with the rifle, so she set it aside and withdrew the SIG.

Standing on her tippy toes, she peered out. There on the grass by the propane tank lay one of the soldiers who'd come to kill her. His arms sprawled out wide like a child making snow angels. The device he placed against the tank was still there. The man who had fired at her, who had nearly killed Hatch, was now low crawling around the back side of the propane tank. She saw his boot disappear behind it just as she had peered out the window.

Ten minutes left. Each passing second seemed to fly by faster than its predecessor.

She pressed the muzzle of the SIG against the glass of the decorative portal window. She knew that making contact with the glass would distort the first shot, but it would make additional rounds that she fired accurate and true.

She aimed to where the dead man was, and then worked her angle and point of aim back to the device that he had laid against the propane tank.

Less than a minute later, her assumption was proven correct. He was working his way back to finish setting up the bomb or looking for its detonator.

Hatch waited. Seconds later, the gunman's face appeared in view.

As he reached over to the dead man, Hatch fired. A succession of rounds erupted from the P226. She kept both eyes open, sighting down the front sight post at her target, engaging through the small portal while balancing herself on her tippy toes. Hard shot at best. Near impossible for an amateur. But Hatch was a great shot. And she was no amateur.

She fired six rounds and watched as the man, whose face had barely appeared in view, disappeared into a plume of red. He lay with his dead arm outstretched near the man who had placed the explosive device.

In the silence that followed, Hatch continued to survey the two downed men for any signs of life. No movement from either.

The fire roared wildly out of control as the second floor became engulfed. Hatch could hear the crackle and pops of things exploding under the oppressive heat. Each sound served as a reminder, like the ticking of a clock, that the countdown had begun. It wouldn't be long before the house that she had grown up in, built primarily by her father's hands, would be turned to ash and soot, and everybody inside buried with it. Unless she could find the final shooter and get her family out of there.

Eight minutes on the clock.

She was still focused on watching the back. The biggest threat right now came from the propane and the potential explosion waiting to be ignited. She didn't know how far the man who had planted the bomb had gotten, and she didn't know what type of detonator was rigged to it. She'd hoped he hadn't gotten far enough to activate it, and knew that if he had, it was already too late. The fact that the house hadn't exploded, that the propane tank still remained intact, told her it wasn't set to activate. She knew she needed to go out and remove it, but to do so would be a death wish.

There was still no sign of the last gunman.

She waited at the back of the house for what felt like an eternity as two more precious minutes ticked by. Hatch trusted Savage could cover the middle where the kitchen was, but the front was left exposed.

Then she heard it. A loud bang from the front door. She recognized its sound. The wood framed door splintered as the last man standing breached the front door.

The last gunman was here, and Hatch had picked the wrong side of the house.

Hatch dropped low. She crawled across the floor. Bits of broken glass buried deep in her shins and forearms as she made her way out toward the kitchen. She ignored the cutting pain as she pressed forward toward the coming threat, toward the last member of the Talon Executive Services' kill team assigned to eliminate her.

As she crossed the mud room and into the main space of the kitchen, she came up into a low crouch and raised her weapon in front of her. The last man passed across her line of sight for a split second. He was moving too quickly for her to get a shot as he crossed the hallway into the living room.

In his wake, she heard the clang of metal on the wood floor. Hatch was already in motion seconds before she was blinded by the flashbang's detonation only a few feet ahead of her current position. Hatch had deployed flashbangs on numerous entries in her past life. She'd also sat in the shoot house training rooms where she'd honed her skills, experiencing firsthand the devastation of the bang's effectiveness. Her focused effort used to track her target had left her unprepared to shield herself from the blast.

The blinding light and the deafening noise that came with it was designed to put an enemy at a temporary disadvantage, to eliminate their basic senses of sight and sound, and to give seconds of vital time to gain the upper hand. Hatch was now victim to its disorientation.

She was blind. Sparks filled her vision, and her ears rang. It would set her back several critical seconds in her hunt. Hatch tried to compensate, having seen him dart to the right and into the living room that led into the kitchen, which meant it led to her.

Savage was crumpled under the table, fighting for consciousness as the snake's venom took hold.

Hatch, desperate for her vision to return, blinked rapidly. She blindly fired twice with the Sig in the direction he'd run. After delivering the burst of gunfire, she dropped to the ground and started crawling toward Savage.

Hatch then changed position again, rolling sideways and bringing herself over to a pantry abutting the refrigerator that separated the kitchen from the open living/dining room.

She pulled the refrigerator door wide, trying to give herself additional cover. She knew it wouldn't be enough to stop a round but might slow it enough to give her a fighting chance.

Bullets pelted the heavy stainless-steel door, puncturing it.

Hatch sprawled back. She breathed heavily, her vision still spotty, but clearing. Now or never, she told herself. *Heroes don't stand idle, they act.* Her father's words provided comfort as she prepared to face off with her killer.

With only five minutes left on her mental countdown, she slid out from behind cover, back flat on the floor, and aimed up toward the threat.

The gunman was already taking aim when Hatch got a clear visual of him. She had lost. In combat, action trumped reaction. He'd beaten her to the punch.

Time seemed to stand still as the shot rang out.

THIRTY-ONE

Hatch looked up to where the gunman had been, only to find the stoic face of John Nighthawk, a wisp of smoke exiting from the muzzle of his department-issued Glock.

"Nighthawk?" Hatch asked, as if in a dream. The ringing in her ears was still pronounced, but not so much that she couldn't hear anymore. Her vision was nearly fully restored, although there were little sparkles that fluttered past her eyes as she scanned the young deputy, who lowered his pistol and gave a half-smile.

"You okay? I saw your smoke signal. I figured I'd come and help."

"Smoke signal?" And then it dawned on her as something crashed from the second floor. *The fire.* "Where's everybody else?"

"They're still down on the main road holding position. After I saw the smoke rising up above the trees and heard the gunshots, I knew I couldn't wait for tactical." He spoke quietly. There was a humbleness in his delivery. "I had Sinclair and Littleton stay back with the ambulance. I know SWAT's on their way, but who knows how long that could be? I couldn't just let you die here."

Savage groaned and then slid further down and was now lying flat on his back. His eyelids flickered as sweat poured from his brow. With the wet hand towel she'd given him covering his face, he looked deranged.

Hatch knew the venom was doing its damage, attacking the vital organs. Time was slipping away. Getting him to the hospital was her next priority.

"Call the ambulance. Get them up here now."

Both of them holstered their weapons and reached down to Savage. In a team effort, they brought the Sheriff to his feet.

Smoke was starting to infiltrate the first floor of the Hatch house, mixing with the remnants of the CS gas, creating a caustic environment.

Savage perked up slightly as though the movement had awakened him, if only temporarily.

She looked at Savage and the barricade that he was now propped up against. Here he was, succumbing to the venom of the rattler while sitting in a burning house, surrounded by four dead contract killers. Her family was still hiding in the basement below, undoubtedly cowering in fear.

Hatch knew in that moment that the people she loved most in the world would never be safe with her alive.

Then she looked at Nighthawk, the deputy who had most likely killed Denny Clark. If not for him, she'd have been killed by this last threat. He saved her life and a life debt was owed.

A life debt went deeper than any law written by man. Life debts could only be repaid with life. If Nighthawk hadn't broken rank and protocol to come to her aid, Hatch, Savage, and the rest of her family would be dead. Her niece and nephew would've burned alive in this house.

"No time to mince words," she said to Nighthawk. "I can't leave, and neither can you."

He looked confused. "I don't understand."

"No time for lies. I know the knife buried in Denny Clark's chest came at your hand."

Nighthawk took a step back.

"I would've done the same thing," Hatch said. "Hell, I did. It just took me twenty years to find the person responsible."

Savage looked back and forth through hazy, cloudy eyes at both people standing before him.

"You saved my life," Hatch said to Nighthawk, "And now I'm going to save yours."

"I don't understand," Nighthawk said softly.

"Give me your clothes," she said.

"What?"

"Just do it." Hatch left no question in her voice.

"Dalton." She gently slapped the man's cheek, rousing him. He was slipping again. "Are you with me?"

His eyes lacked focus, but he nodded his head. "I am."

"This doesn't work without you. I need you on this. John Nighthawk and I die here, today."

"But..." Savage started to speak.

Hatch just shook her head. She was saddened to speak the words, but they needed to be said. "They'll never be safe as long as they think I'm alive, and we'll never be able to be anything if I'm always looking over my shoulder." Hatch looked at Nighthawk. "I wouldn't even be having this conversation with you right now if it wasn't for him. If Nighthawk hadn't stepped in like he did, I'd be dead. We all would be."

Savage gave an approving nod in the direction of Nighthawk and then broke into a wild coughing fit.

"He needs to be a ghost, too. And I have a plan to make it all go away. To give everybody a fighting chance at life."

"What kind of life would you have if you run?" Savage asked.

"I don't know, but it'd be one in which I knew that Daphne, Jake, and my mother were safe. It would be a world where you're still alive. Because the other future is one filled with death and fear. I can't give that to them or you. I know what that feels like, and I refuse to allow those kids downstairs to live that life."

Nighthawk was standing in his boxer briefs and white undershirt and socks. Hatch then looked at the last contract man on the ground with a bullet hole nestled in the side of his head, the one that Nighthawk had placed there.

"He looks to be about your size, right?" Hatch said.

Nighthawk obviously already understood what was happening and began undressing the dead man. The exchange of clothing took a matter of minutes.

The smoke and fire began rolling down the stairwell in waves from the upper floor.

"Time for you to go," Hatch said to Nighthawk. "And John, thank you."

Nighthawk looked to his sheriff for final approval. Savage outstretched his hand weakly, and the two men shook.

"I'm sorry," Nighthawk said.

"Me, too," Savage said.

The exchange complete, Savage gave a nod of his head and a tip of his imaginary Stetson as Nighthawk disappeared out the back door wearing a dead man's green camouflage overalls.

Hatch watched him go for a brief second. He moved deftly as he sprinted and disappeared into the woods. She turned her attention back to Savage.

"Let's move this table." She was all business now. The hard part was yet to come. She opened the door and called down the stairs. "Mom. It's me. It's safe."

She heard a squeal from Daphne as she barreled up the stairs ahead of everyone. She flung herself into Hatch, wrapping her arms tight around her waist. Hatch reciprocated, engulfing the girl holding her as tight as she could, breathing in every scent of her, trying to freeze the moment, hoping she could hold her forever.

Jake was right behind and joined in the hug as they balanced atop the stairwell. The children were wearing clunky Vietnam era M-17 gas masks, shrouding most of their faces.

"We only have a minute, and I need to talk to you all about something. You may not understand it now, but hopefully in time you will. And when you do, I hope you find it in your heart to forgive me. We literally have seconds to make this work, seconds to change the future, the course of it at least. But to do it means I have to do something that pains me more than anything I can remember." She felt the scar tissue on her arm. The damage and her memory of the pain paled in comparison to the ache in her heart.

Both kids, still in her embrace, now looked up at her. For the first time since Hatch could remember, her eyes moistened. As the tears streamed down her face, it mixed with the CS in the air and burned. But Hatch knew these tears would sting regardless because of the source of their pain.

Her mom looked at her in dismay, and it saddened her to see it. Hatch would never have the opportunity to give her mother the life she had hoped, the relationship she desperately deserved and needed. The kids would lose Hatch all together after already losing so much.

The pain of this moment was nearly unbearable, but Hatch fought through the hurt, knowing it was the only way. The other option was death guaranteed, and she could not bring that upon them for all of the selfish needs she felt right now.

"These are the people who killed my dad," she said, looking down. Then she made eye contact with her mom. "I got the one who killed my father, but they are coming for me now. They will always be coming for me. I am a liability. I am the voice that could destroy them, and they know this. They won't stop until I'm dead. That means you are in danger every second that I stay here, every second that I'm alive."

"What? What are you saying, Rachel?" her mother stammered, the words coming out in choked gasps, a combination of the toxic air and desperation.

"I can't leave this house. I have to die in here, or at least they have to believe I'm dead. Otherwise, it's a lifetime of looking over your shoulder, it's a lifetime of pain. I will not do that to you. I love you all too much for that to happen."

She turned and looked behind her at Dalton Savage when she said that last piece. She wanted him to know he was included in this.

Daphne didn't speak. She made a whimper and then buried her head into Hatch's lap, pulling her tight at the waist in a six-year-old's version of a death grip.

Jake looked hurt and angry. "No," he said as a tear fell. He tried to pull away, but Hatch grabbed him by the hand. Her thumb caressed the red, soon-to-be calloused knuckles of the young boy, approaching manhood earlier than anyone should.

"I'm proud of you, Jake. I am so proud of you." He fell into Rachel, nearly knocking her over and sobbed loudly. Hatch had never heard him cry before. She never wanted to again.

Hatch's mother joined the hug. They held each other as Hatch whispered in her mother's ear, "I love you, Mom. I'm so sorry for the pain I've caused you. I'm so sorry for the pain I'm causing you now. It was never your fault."

Her mother broke like a dam holding back a reservoir. In Jasmine Hatch's case, it was twenty years of pain that had been bottled up inside. Hatch's words released her from the shackles of guilt. The embrace, although Hatch never wanted it to end, needed to. Time was running out.

"Stay low to the ground." Hatch took off the sheet that was wrapped around her and put it over her mother and niece and nephew, shrouding them from the smoke.

She then turned and went over to Dalton and handed him the dead snake. "You're going to need this when you get to the hospital." She paused, clearing her throat. "You have no idea how sorry I am for the way things turned out."

He shook his head. He didn't have words.

"Do you know what you need to do?"

"I think so," he said.

"I'm a twin, right? You've already done an autopsy. You've got photos from the morgue. You can make this look good. You can write the report and say I was found in the woods later, died of smoke inhalation, or however you want to make it fit the bill. But whatever you do, they have to believe it. If not, you'll all still be in just as much danger."

"I can do it," he said.

She looked back at her family under the cover of the sheet. "Will you ...?"

"I'll keep watch and take care of them. I'll look out for them as if they were my own family."

"Thank you," Hatch said, her voice almost a low hiss, a whisper. This moment in time had zapped her of all energy.

Then Savage did something that surprised her completely. He pulled her close and kissed her hard. She tasted the licorice. He released her and then hobbled himself over to Hatch's mother, who aided in taking some of his weight off his injured leg.

He shielded the children from the heat on the stairwell as they moved out toward the front door.

Hatch waited and watched them go. Her vision of them leaving was clouded by the tears in her eyes.

As they disappeared out the front. A torrential rain doused them, washing away the acrid smoke as they made their way out toward Savage's Suburban, still parked in the driveway.

They looked back, but the one that held Hatch's gaze the longest was Daphne. The littlest member of the Hatch family never looked away. The Suburban roared down the driveway, disappearing from sight.

Hatch retreated out the back in the same way Nighthawk had left as the fire lit the dark sky.

THIRTY-TWO

Clearwater plated the sirloin, using tongs to take it straight from the pan to his plate. He grabbed a beer from the fridge and took a seat in the quiet of his small kitchen. The only light came from the fixture on the ceiling. He popped the top to the beer can and took a sip, setting it down beside the plate. Twisting a bit of sea salt and pepper on top, Clearwater picked up his fork and knife and prepared to cut when he said, "You're going to make me eat alone?"

He took a bite and chewed slowly. "There's a steak on the stove. I cooked an extra one for you."

John Nighthawk stepped from the darkness of the hallway and entered the kitchen.

"Did you think I didn't notice you were there?"

Nighthawk said nothing. He went to the stove and grabbed the steak. There was a familiar comfort to the room, having spent much of his childhood into adulthood surrounded by the walls of this home. Clearwater was, after all, his only blood uncle. He had always looked out for him. Nighthawk skipped the fridge, bypassing the cold beer inside, and took a seat across from the older man.

Clearwater slid a brown shoebox across the table.

Nighthawk looked at it suspiciously.

"Open her up."

He did, momentarily setting the steak aside. Nighthawk peered in and saw the bone handled knife that he'd buried into the chest of the man who'd murdered his father. There it was, in a shoe box on his uncle's dining room table.

Clearwater looked at him. He could feel his stare upon him. "He always said he wanted you to have it. Your father loved you. And although it hurt him when you left the reservation, he knew you had your reasons."

Nighthawk took the knife in hand, feeling the ridges of shaped bone. He remembered when his father had made it.

"Your dad was with you that night in the sweat lodge. When you came out and told him your plans to cut your own path, that you'd seen your way. He told me you saw the wolf. He knew at that moment you'd leave to find your own pack. There can be only one alpha. It's why he carved that handle. He'd always intended to give it to you."

Nighthawk took the blade, the finely forged edge glinted in the kitchen light. He traced his finger over the wolf carved into it. Nobody had noticed it that day when he and Savage had worked the scene of his father's death. When Savage had given him time to pay his respects, Nighthawk had seen the blade sheathed along the belt line on his father's backside. He didn't know why at the time, but he took it.

Maybe it had been a desperate act to hold onto a piece of his father. But now he knew the reason. The knife was meant for him. It seemed fitting he used something forged by his father's hand to exact the justice his father deserved. It was in his hand again. He eyed it carefully, appreciating every ridge and nook that his father had carved. He set it down beside his plate and looked at Clearwater.

"How'd you get it?"

"That was a gift from our friend, the sheriff, over at Hawk's Landing," Clearwater said. "Nobody's going to be looking for you now. You can stay with me for a while if you want. Nobody will say anything around here. You know how it is."

Nighthawk nodded. He did, and he knew they wouldn't. "But my dad was right. I've got to cut my own path."

"I figured you might say that," Clearwater said. "Look in the box again."

There was a small manila envelope folded in half at the bottom of the box. He opened it. Inside was a stack of cash, a passport, a driver's license and a birth certificate. He looked over at Clearwater, who was smiling.

"I can be pretty resourceful when the time calls for it, and this one definitely warranted my best efforts. You have a chance to start a new life now, free and clear. But never forget where you came from."

"I won't," Nighthawk said softly. "Thank you—for everything."

"Where do you think you'll go from here?"

Nighthawk shrugged. "Everywhere and nowhere seems like a pretty good place to start."

THIRTY-THREE

It had been a couple days since Hatch had left. Jasmine sat at the kitchen table and stared out the window. She saw a mail truck roll up the driveway. Everything that approached the house in the last few days had made her nervous. Sheriff Savage had stopped by quite regularly since her daughter's departure, checking in on both the kids and her.

The house had survived thanks to her husband's foresight. The fire department had arrived in time to save the second floor. The attack left the house scarred along the right side, not unlike her daughter's arm.

The scent of Jasmine's coffee battled the stink of the fire.

The truck pulled to a stop, and she saw the deliveryman approach with a small package in his hand, just larger than a shoe box. The doorbell rang and Jasmine jumped.

She waited until he drove away before getting up from her seat and going to the door to see what had arrived.

She was shocked when she saw the sender's address had been postmarked from Mombasa, Kenya. And it was addressed to Rachel Hatch.

Jasmine brought the box inside, set it on the table where she was sipping at her coffee. She opened it. Inside, she saw a tightly wrapped tin. Removing the wrapping, she opened the lid of the container.

A floral bouquet of the scented tea leaves greeted her nose. She'd never smelt anything like it. It was wonderful. There was a small card underneath at the bottom of the box. Jasmine retrieved it.

It read:

Ms. Hatch, I hope that this tea finds you well, that you are able to find the peace and happiness you deserve. I hope that upon your return home, you are able to shed your burdens and share in your family's love. Wishing you well on whatever path your newfound peace leads you on. Your friend, Khari

THIRTY-FOUR

Hatch sat in the diner. It was crowded, but she was invisible. She slouched down just a bit so that even her height didn't seem impressive. As she blended with her surroundings, Hatch sipped at her coffee and fought back her urge to spit it back into the cup. Only a few days of drinking her mother's amazing blend had made this a poor attempt and a sad excuse for a substitution. She now better understood Savage's addiction to it.

Even though it was lunchtime, she had ordered the breakfast platter, and her side of pancakes had just been delivered. As she unfolded the newspaper, news of the fire in Hawk's Landing had made page six of the Denver Post. Hatch read it as though it was a frontpage story, because for her it was. It described how a botched home invasion had ended in tragedy.

The article read:

The Hatch family of Hawk's Landing faced tragedy three days ago when a brazen home invasion occurred at their mountain home in broad daylight. Several armed gunmen attempted to forcibly enter the home. Responding to a panicked cry for help, Hawk's Landing Sheriff's Office deputies responded to render aid. Sheriff Deputy John Nighthawk, the newest member of the depart-

ment, died on scene as a result of a single gunshot wound to the head. Sheriff Dalton Savage was also injured during the course of events.

Deputy Nighthawk was killed in the line of duty while rushing to aid and protect the Hatch family. Rachel Hatch, age 35, died in the fire. Cause of death is ruled asphyxiation due to smoke inhalation.

The two children in the home, whose names had been redacted from this article to protect their innocence, were unharmed, as was Hatch's mother, Jasmine Hatch. A closed casket service is being held for Hatch on Tuesday. The body of Deputy Nighthawk has been cremated and his ashes scattered upon the Southern Ute Reservation where he was raised.

There are no details regarding the suspects involved in this case, as they remain unidentified at this time. Sheriff Dalton Savage gave a brief statement regarding the circumstances revolving around this home invasion. His statement was given while he was being treated for a rattlesnake bite at an area hospital.

"It is a tragic loss of life, and at this point in the investigation, it remains completely unclear as to who these people were who targeted the Hatch family. We're looking into several leads at this time, but as of right now, it looks as though this might be connected to the murder of Southern Ute Police Chief William "Billy" Nighthawk. Hatch was assisting in the investigation. The suspects in the murder have strong ties to the Colorado Free Americans' extremist movement, which has a hatred of law enforcement."

Sheriff Savage went on to say, "Deputy Nighthawk exemplified the best of us here at the Sheriff's Office. We are at a loss with his passing." He had this to say about Rachel Hatch, "She was an asset to our agency in the times we needed her assistance. I hope she finds the peace in death that she could never find in life. I will miss her every day."

SHE FOLDED THE PAPER.

Hatch knew without a doubt that the Talon Executive Services' hierarchy would be watching the story closely. She hoped that the efforts made would be good enough to cover her tracks for good, and more importantly, to keep the people she loved safe.

Hatch bit into her pancakes, chewing slowly as the butter and syrup flavor profile tingled her taste buds. Her phone vibrated. She looked at the incoming text message.

Glad you made it out okay, it read.

She looked up, scanning the diner, her left hand moving to the Sig at her back. The phone vibrated again.

Ready to meet?

Hatch stared down at the phone. "Yes," she typed.

Come to where the moon kisses the sea, it said.

She immediately knew who was on the other end of that line, the person who'd given her warning of the impending threat against her.

It was the first decent feeling she'd had since leaving her family behind.

With a mouth full of pancakes, she knew where she was heading next.

Read on for a sneak peek at Firewalk (Rachel Hatch Book Five), or order your copy now:
https://www.amazon.com/dp/B08H2HRKVT

Join the LT Ryan reader family & receive a free copy of the Rachel Hatch story, *Fractured*. Click the link below to get started:
https://ltryan.com/rachel-hatch-newsletter-signup-1

GET YOUR VERY OWN RACHEL HATCH MERCHANDISE TODAY! CLICK THE LINK below to find coffee mugs, t-shirts, and even signed copies of your favorite L.T. Ryan thrillers! https://ltryan.ink/EvG_

THE RACHEL HATCH SERIES

Drift

Downburst

Fever Burn

Smoke Signal

Firewalk

Whitewater

Aftershock

Whirlwind

Tsunami

Fastrope

Sidewinder (Coming Soon)

RACHEL HATCH SHORT STORIES

Fractured

Proving Ground

The Gauntlet

Join the LT Ryan reader family & receive a free copy of the Rachel Hatch story, Fractured. Click the link below to get started:

https://ltryan.com/rachel-hatch-newsletter-signup-1

Love Hatch? Noble? Maddie? Cassie? Get your very own Rachel Hatch merchandise today! Click the link below to find coffee mugs, t-shirts, and even signed copies of your favorite L.T. Ryan thrillers! https://ltryan.ink/EvG_

FIREWALK
RACHEL HATCH BOOK FIVE

by L.T. Ryan & Brian Shea

Copyright © 2020 by L.T. Ryan, Liquid Mind Media, LLC, & Brian Christopher Shea. All rights reserved. No part of this publication may be copied, reproduced in any format, by any means, electronic or otherwise, without prior consent from the copyright owner and publisher of this book. This is a work of fiction. All characters, names, places and events are the product of the author's imagination or used fictitiously.

FIREWALK CHAPTER 1

Her red hair was almost ablaze as the late afternoon sun filtered through her long, wavy curls. Exposed by a loose-fitting tank top, her pale skin complemented the red tones of her hair. She looked like a porcelain doll on display. She downed the last bit of her drink and laughed at something the woman with her had said. The men in the dark Toyota 4Runner watching her did not.

"It's a long drive. Might need to sample the goods before we get there. She's a fine piece of—" Trevor started, a thin smile began etching across his face.

"Don't even think about it. You were lucky the last time. If they ever found out you touched the last girl, you and I wouldn't be sittin' here," Alejandro said, shifting in the driver's seat to face his cohort.

Trevor Fairmount, undaunted by the warning, stared out of the tinted windshield of the car, licking his lips hungrily and rubbing the bristles of his patchy beard.

Alejandro swatted the ponytailed head of his partner, shocking him out of thought.

"What the hell was that for?" He looked at Alejandro with anger.

"To snap you out of whatever stupid fantasy you're running through your sick mind," the driver said, his gaze lacking frivolity. "You touch this one and you won't have to worry about Mr. Carmen's muscle. I'll put a bullet through your thick skull my damn self."

"Don't act like you're so high and mighty. What about that girl from Tulsa?" Trevor's face drew up into a sneer. "Because if I remember right, it was your idea to—"

"Shut up!" Alejandro turned away. The leather seat squeaked loudly in the silence that followed. "She was different, a throwaway."

Trevor shrugged, showing zero empathy. "They all seem the same to me."

"That's why you're still on the snatch-and-grab team."

"Uh, so are you, dipshit."

Alejandro gripped the steering wheel with enough force that his knuckles whitened. He wanted to smack the back of his partner's head again. Or, better yet, drive his fist into Trevor's bony face. He knew his anger was not caused by his partner's snide comment itself, but the truth behind it. He wanted to be done with this part of the job. Sure, his employer paid well, but he saw himself as more. He wanted to be done making these "runs".

For Alejandro Dominguez, this job was a chance for him to revamp his life. The two-time convicted felon had little chance of finding meaningful work. He tried, and he failed. But he had a particular skill that made him an asset to the organization. He was a good wheelman; that is why they recruited him.

He was bright; at least when he compared himself to his partner with whom he'd been paired for the last year.

He despised Trevor, but there was little he could do about their partnership. It wasn't like he could go to HR and request a change. They were at the bottom tier of a much larger organization, but Alejandro aimed to prove himself worthy of a promotion. As long as he avoided messing with the merchandise and delivered consistently enough, he could potentially move his way up to middle management and leave this despicable work to somebody else.

However, Alejandro was under no illusion that his partner would ever rise above his status, especially with the way he was ogling the redheaded teen at the bar. He was determined to make sure that Trevor's hands remained to himself during their long ride to the border.

"What's with you lately, man? You're actin' all the sudden like your shit don't stink. You know you're not better than me, you two-time loser."

I am better than you...dipshit, he thought to himself. But he knew that was not the case. He had been justifying his mistake a thousand different ways.

He hated the fact that Trevor had the nerve to bring up the castaway girl. It was a mistake. He'd been off his game that day. His girlfriend just broke up with him and he was enraged. He took his frustration out on the inebriated girl they had been tasked with transporting. Putting it out of his mind afterward, he made desperate attempts to bend the truth of its atrocity to make sense of what he'd done. He was angry at himself for showing weakness and giving into his primal urges. Seeing the young, nearly unconscious girl in the backseat of the car compelled him to give in to Trevor's whimsy. Until now, they never spoke of it. The fact Trevor felt the need to bring it up made him a liability. Something he'd need to remedy.

Although he had been caught and thrown in Maricopa County's prison system for a botched bank robbery, his decision to not talk about his felony caught the eye of his current employer.

Mr. Carmen whom Alejandro had met once, when he was first brought onboard liked him for two very important reasons. He could drive a car like no one else and he could keep his mouth shut. In the underworld, these traits made him a rare commodity.

In the year he had provided his skills to the organization, he earned enough to upgrade his lifestyle. Alejandro recently moved out of the rundown efficiency apartment in the Maryvale subdivision of Phoenix. Prison did not leave him with much after his release, but he now owned a condo. He also bought himself a nice, new ride. However, he never used this personal car for work purposes.

The organization rotated the vehicles used for these types of transports. The license plates were legit, but no owners could be traced or verified. The company took care of all the logistics. All he had to do was drive.

And keep Trevor's hands off the merchandise. The latter was proving to be increasingly difficult.

His job was simple: Make the pickup, make the delivery, and don't get caught anywhere in between. Simple rules in theory, but in practice, these rules were harder to follow than he expected. Since Alejandro had been added to the team, they never had to trade out drivers, and on this, he prided himself. He came in as a driver one year ago, after they went through six drivers in less than three months prior to his arrival. It was never openly talked about, but he assumed the drivers who had been "let go" did not go on to other careers. It was rumored that these other drivers were dead. In the criminal world, rumors usually carried as much weight as truth, maybe more.

Alejandro Dominguez was not a killer. He had never fired a gun. In the underworld, not having pulled the trigger is a sign of weakness. So, whenever the topic appeared up in conversation, he never gave a direct answer. He quickly learned to be aloof enough to never deny or confirm. By leaving it open, people came to the assumption that part of his criminal record involved murder. In a short period of time, Alejandro's imaginary body count grew with Trevor's imagination, and Trevor's big mouth spread the rumors among the lower tier of the organization, giving Alejandro a certain status among them.

He never talked about his past so found it funny when his fictional backstory filled in. He also never corrected anyone. Thus, as Trevor guessed about Alejandro's life prior to working for the organization, his fantasies of Alejandro as a cold-blooded killer became more vivid.

Alejandro secretly liked this power he had over his partner. While Trevor had openly admitted that he'd never killed anybody, touching girls was something his resume was filled with. Despite his one-time slip-up, Alejandro despised Trevor for his insatiable appetite for these young girls. Alejandro was committed to stopping his partner from having a taste of the newest recruit. He was not sure how to go about it.

Both men were armed, as was the protocol. But the way their snatch-and-grab system was set up, the guns were rarely-if ever-used as a method of intimidation. And they certainly did not have to strong-arm these prized targets. They had other ways of enabling an ease of transport when the time was right.

He watched carefully as the dark-skinned brunette laughed and ordered another round of drinks. Alejandro knew her only as Cassandra. She had been hired by the organization multiple times in the past at various locations. He always enjoyed watching her work. She was by far the most attractive woman in the bar. He hoped to meet her outside of the parameters of work someday. He figured since she was involved, she would not judge him for his part in this criminal enterprise. He sipped his iced coffee and fantasized about a relationship with the full-lipped, dark-skinned Cassandra.

It was always the third drink. Cassandra looked back from the bar to the patio table, where she and the redhead had spent the last hour. Alejandro knew one of the many ruses that Cassandra would have used to get this girl to stay. Her favorite was playing the role of star talent acquisitions agent. She once ran through her repertoire for Alejandro when he asked her how she did it. He was amazed at the ease with which she could coax these girls into submission.

She said it was simple. She understood the girls' needs and told them what they wanted to hear. Her star recruitment facade worked on many levels. What young teenage girl did not want to see themselves in a TV commercial or movie? Cassandra preyed on this.

She would approach her target and introduce herself, providing a fake business card. She padded her resume by rattling off big-name directors and actors she had worked with in the past. The name dropping was always done in a casual manner to maximize authenticity. After gaining their trust, she would say something to the effect of, "But the real talent... the real trick? It's just being yourself. The only way I'll know if you really have what it takes goes beyond beauty. I have to see the real you. Would you be willing to have a couple drinks and discuss some opportunities?" This line, or a variant thereof, usually worked like a charm.

Only once, about six months ago, Cassandra tried the line only to have it fail. This was a prime target. A client made a special request, offering a sizable down payment. Because Cassandra's charms were useless on this girl, Alejandro and Trevor had to come in as the muscle. It was the riskiest snatch-and-grab yet. It left him feeling exposed and was something he never wanted to do again.

It was easier when they were compliant, even if it was chemically induced, and that is what he was waiting for. He saw Cassandra make her move, only noticing because he knew what to watch for.

It was quick, a sleight of hand. As she leaned over to pay for the drinks, she dropped a crushed Rohypnol into one of them. The benzodiazepine dosage was high enough to incapacitate the girl within several minutes of ingestion. To onlookers, she would appear intoxicated. It would limit her resistance and she would be more mentally malleable.

She walked back to the high table on the bar's patio where the two had been talking for the hour. Cassandra handed the young redhead her third hard liquor drink, a Long Island iced tea. This drink was Cassandra's choice for the "young talent," she was "recruiting," Because it masked the taste from the powder.

The drug also had an anterograde amnesia effect on its users. Once in the unsuspecting victim's system it would render an inability to create new memories after amnesia set in. Basically, the drug created a chemically-induced blackout. This was why it had become known as a "date rape" drug because it had the potential to erase any sexual trauma after ingestion. It would take longer for the Rohypnol to have its ultimate intended effect. There was also a dash of crushed Ambien to add an extra punch. By the time it kicked in, it would both wipe her memory and put her down for a long nap, which usually made for an easy commute.

Cassandra liked it because her face would be erased from their memory. Trevor liked it because it opened an opportunity for him to take advantage. Alejandro liked it because it made for a relatively docile passenger for the long drive.

As intoxication took hold, Cassandra's charm really kicked in. She laid it on thick and told the redheaded girl about the money and the parties of all the famous people she'd helped. Then, as the young woman consumed her third and final drink of the early afternoon, Cassandra offered to take her to meet a big-time director. She would leave it on the table as a once-in-a-lifetime opportunity, take it or leave it.

The girl laughed at something Cassandra said as she set the tainted drink in front of her. She consumed her third drink quicker than the first two. The buzz obviously setting in, her young body was not used to the high potency of the drink.

He watched the girl with the fire-red hair slide back in her chair ever so slightly. Her cheeks blushed and her eyes watered. She began fanning her face. The excitement at the prospect of meeting whatever director or producer seemed to delight the girl beyond words. She almost leapt from her seat with excitement.

Cassandra stood and ushered the girl towards the back of the patio area to the sidewalk. Cassandra moved quickly, but not so much so that the intoxicated teen could not keep up.

Alejandro noticed that the teen was starting to sway a bit as the effects of the alcohol and drugs became apparent.

The girl stopped for a moment and steadied herself, leaning against the wall. For a moment, she looked as though she was going to vomit. This would have been bad because if her body rejected the drug, she might have quickly came back to consciousness, and that would complicate things. Alejandro did not like complications, especially when the unpredictable Trevor was sitting next to him.

Cassandra put a gentle hand on the redheaded teen's porcelain shoulder and asked her if she was okay. The girl nodded and they proceeded around the corner and out of sight.

Alejandro started the ignition and the engine purred. He slipped the Toyota into drive and coasted around the corner.

Cassandra pulled out a cell phone and gave her final performance. She pretended to be on the phone with someone important. After hanging up, she told the nearly incapacitated teen that her driver was on his way, and they would be taken to some well-known director's house for a private meeting. Cassandra's talent for selling the false dream of this girl's first shot at being a star was nothing short of Oscar-worthy.

Alejandro pulled alongside the curb beyond where anybody from the bar could see. The teen leaned forward, teetering unsteadily, as she peered into the windows of the Toyota 4Runner's heavy tints.

Cassandra's voice could be heard now, as she said, "Hey, sweetie. Look, our ride's just arrived." Her voice, smooth as velvet, rolled over her thick, full lips. She opened the door to the backseat. The young girl looked at the two men inside. She froze and looked back at Cassandra, whose eyes were still warm and inviting. Even with the alcohol and drugs beginning to work their magic, fear spread over the girl's face.

"Don't worry, dear. They work for me, you'll see. They're true professionals. Now, slide on in."

The redhead hesitated for only a second longer before she did as she was told, and slid across the rear black leather bench seat of the 4Runner. She was now comfortably positioned behind Trevor Fairmount. Her body slumped as she fought desperately with her uncooperative mind in an effort to keep her head up.

Alejandro watched her in the rear-view mirror but did not turn to face her. He always found it better that these girls never looked directly into his eyes. It was unsettling, knowing what came next. Plus, the thought of being identified later always kept him on edge. Through the mirror's reflection, he watched as the teen's head bobbed up and down loosely, like a bobblehead on the front dash of an 18-wheeler. The drugs and alcohol were fighting a winning battle, only moments before the girl would slip away into unconsciousness.

Cassandra looked at the girl one last time. "Oh, dang it. I forgot something back in the restaurant. Give me a quick second, hon. I'll be right back." She added, "Guys, keep the car running. I'll be right back." Alejandro felt Cassandra had overacted her part, but it didn't matter due to the girl's inebriated state. She nodded at Cassandra, and tried to speak, but the words were slurred into an incomprehensible series of sounds. The only discernable word in her sentence was "wait."

Cassandra closed the door and purposefully walked away.

Alejandro pressed the automatic lock on the driver's side armrest. The child locks were activated, as were the windows.

The girl's eyes widened slightly, offering the last bit of resistance as Trevor turned in his seat to face her. In less than twenty seconds, she was handcuffed and gagged. She slumped to the side. Her head came to rest against the rear passenger door.

As her eyes rolled into the back of her head, Alejandro drove toward the next waypoint in the girl's journey.

FIREWALK CHAPTER 2

Hatch looked at the gas gauge of her rental gray Ford Focus hatchback. The gas level indicator had just crossed the boundary of the quarter tank range. She never liked to let any vehicle get below that. Old habits die hard. She never let herself be in a position where she ran out of fuel. It happened to her once overseas. The experience left her cautious. A ten-mile trek with a full combat loadout in a combat environment would ingrain that habit in anyone. In that case, the gas gauge had been damaged. Regardless, ever since then , she never let a vehicle go much beyond the quarter tank mark.

She had been in Arizona for the past several hours of her drive, having just merged from the 303 with I-10 for a quick dogleg around the western outermost edge of Phoenix. She took exit 114 and followed the signs directing her to a Gas-N-Sip station at the corner of Miller Street, across from a Charlie's Chicken restaurant. The billboard in the lot advertised fresh, hot chicken available 24/7. Hatch thought it funny, that somebody at 3 or 4 a.m. would need chicken. I guess it made sense. This area was a major route for truckers, their circadian rhythm off by the all-night driving. A 3 a.m. chicken snack would be lunchtime for them.

Hatch, when working patrol in her early years as a military police officer, had worked the midnight shift. For the first two years as a new enlistee, she'd been assigned to nights. Early on, she found the adjustment tough, but once she had grown accustomed, she found it equally tough to shift back to the more normalized hours of the day shift.

She pulled to a stop at pump number four. There was only one other pump in use, a large dark-colored SUV parked on the other side at pump three. She noticed the driver was seated inside with the engine running. She was barely able to discern any facial features through the heavy tints of the glass. The driver did not seem to notice or care about Hatch's arrival at the Gas-N-Sip.

She headed toward the gas station's mart, as she preferred to prepay for her gas in cash. Less chance of a trail.

Ever since leaving Hawk's Landing for the last time, she was extra cautious about her movements. Before departing, she structured her bank account so that her money was now filtered through her mother's checking account. Her mother was listed as the beneficiary, and would be receiving a portion, fifty-five percent, of Hatch's military retirement for the remainder of her life. Although it was a dip in income from what Hatch received when she was "alive," it was more than enough when coupled with the payout of her two-hundred fifty grand life insurance policy. Having the money in her mother's account provided Hatch with a steady flow of income until she could find her way in the new world, her new world.

She figured based on the size of the car's tank, $25 should be enough to fill up for the next couple hundred miles until she got closer to her destination, Coronado, California. The Gas-N-Sip was almost at the exact halfway point between Hawk's Landing and Coronado.

The fact that she was hovering between a past life-now dead and buried-and an uncertain future was not lost on her. She had a long list of questions for her former boyfriend, Alden Cruise, the first being, how was he able to give her an advance warning before the hunter-killer team from Talent Executive Services had made her a target?

He'd sent her the message: *Come to where the moon kisses the sea.*

It was a refence to their first date. He'd taken her to Naval Amphibious Base, across the way from where BUD/s, Basic Underwater Demolition/SEAL training, took place. They sat out by the bay and talked for

FIREWALK CHAPTER 2

hours. The moon seemed cartoonishly big as it hovered above the bay's dark, calm water. She had verbalized it as saying, "It was as if the moon was kissing the sea." It was a good memory, untainted by time.

To the hired guns at Talon Executive Services, she was dead. Hopefully, the story and evidence trail created by Savage would keep them believing she was dead. Hatch took several precautions since leaving Hawk's Landing to make sure that if they conducted any residual follow-up, all roads would lead to nowhere. She took very drastic measures to fake her own death and thus further protect her mother, niece and nephew, and Dalton Savage from any fallout. She knew she would be looking over her shoulder for the rest of her life. But at least maybe, she gave her family the chance of not having to do the same.

As she crossed the sunbaked asphalt toward the store, the entrance door opened. She was close enough to feel a shift in the oppressively hot air as the overworked air conditioner inside ebbed.

A man and teenage girl exited. The duo didn't seem to match. The man was scraggly. He was thin, with a thick goatee. His gaunt face was punctuated with two beady eyes. There was a wildness in his eyes like that of a feral cat. The girl, on the other hand, looked to be seventeen, no more than eighteen. Her bleached blonde hair and sun-kissed skin contrasted with the white collared shirt and short plaid school dress. There was a maroon and gold emblem embroidered above her left breast, and a gold pin on her collar caught the sun's light.

The girl made eye contact with Hatch but only for a brief second. Hatch caught something, but she wasn't quite sure what it was exactly. She did notice the man walking beside her tighten his grip around her elbow ever so slightly as Hatch approached. It was a barely imperceptible tension in the goateed man's hand. But Hatch noticed.

As they passed, the girl's eyes cast downward.

Hatch felt herself wondering about the girl, looking for deeper meaning in the eye contact that they had made. Hatch was suddenly in a mental battle with herself as she tried to make sense of what she had seen in the girl's eyes. The grab, the man with her, the driver idling in the awaiting SUV. Everything felt off. But then Hatch stopped herself cold.

Hatch told herself to stop looking at everything as a giant threat. It was

237

so hard to dismiss her perceptions, after the fifteen years of military service. Maybe the world wasn't some big scary place. Maybe not everybody was a threat. Maybe not everybody a victim. Was everything she looked at now tainted by years of heartache and tragedy?

She gave a lot of thought to her understanding of the world away from the battlefield. She never took the time to see the normalcy of life, or at least a normal that others could understand. Circumstances had dictated a different course, and it was obvious to her and anyone who knew her why her perception might be jaded.

Regardless, seeing the girl had raised the question: Was she in trouble? Hatch struggled with herself for the answer. As a person who took pride in making split-second life-and-death decisions, she was suddenly at odds with herself.

Hatch looked for a plausible excuse as to why the girl may have looked scared or slightly downtrodden. Why did the man escorting her shuffle her along more quickly when he saw Hatch? Maybe it was his niece? Maybe he was overprotective? The girl did look a little woozy, a little off-center. She might've gotten car sick and they had pulled off at this rest stop not only to fill up, but to allow the girl an opportunity to use the bathroom. Her interpretation of the goateed man's grip on her elbow might have been his effort in of merely supporting her unsteady gait. She looked peaked.

The goateed man had not held the door for Hatch as she approached. He was moving swiftly across the parking lot back toward the idling SUV. Hatch caught the door just before it closed, pulling it wide again. As she entered the air-conditioned interior of the gas station, she looked back at the girl one more time.

The girl looked at Hatch, too. Her eyes flashed again. Hatch recognized it. This time there was no doubt in her mind. The fog of her momentary internal debate lifted. It was fear. Even in the clouded malaise that the girl seemed to be under, her eyes remained defiant.

As the door closed, Hatch saw the girl's hand flick something out onto the ground. The goateed man hadn't noticed as he quickly slipped into the passenger seat, the vehicle pulling away.

FIREWALK CHAPTER 3

Hatch stood for a moment and watched the vehicle go, holding the door ajar and feeling the air conditioning cool her warm skin. It did not speed away in any attention-drawing fashion, but she felt an urgency to the depart.

Before letting the door shut on her, she turned and quickly walked to where the girl had been moments before. The SUV was now out of sight. It slipped into traffic and was rapidly disappearing down the road, back towards the interstate.

She scanned the ground where she saw the girl drop something at the last moment. With the sun overhead in the cloudless sky, she saw a golden glimmer alongside the cracked curbing of the raised concrete island of the pump. There beside a crushed cigarette butt, was a shiny gold pin. The one she'd seen on the girl's collar. She picked it up and examined it in her hand. The sun had already warmed the metal. It was roughly about the size of her thumb nail and was in the shape of a shield. The words Academic Achievement were scrolled across the top, and in its center a golden genie's lamp. She turned the pin over. On the back was an H and A. Hatch wasn't sure the meaning. Maybe H A was a monogram? The girl's initials?

The girl had taken the effort to remove the pin from her collar and drop it after the eye contact she had made with Hatch. It was a message to Hatch and she knew it; she just did not know what it meant.

She turned and ran back to the gas station convenience store. As she moved through the threshold of the air-conditioned space, a chime rang when her legs crossed the infrared door sensor set at the entrance way.

A floppy-haired kid, no older than twenty-one, looked at Hatch with worried caution as he came in from the back door of the store. Just before the employee exit closed, Hatch caught a glimpse of a car pulling away. The gas attendant had a wad of cash bunched up in his front pocket.

He eyed Hatch and she him. She knew what she had just witnessed. The clerk had just sold some drugs out of the back of the store. A pretty good front for a dealer, using the back entrance of a highway gas station to sell. Cops would not notice a car pulling up at a gas station and leaving.

But Hatch noticed. It was the $20 bill sticking out of the corner of his pocket that confirmed the exchange had been made, and the clerk had been the seller. What he sold, she didn't know. Maybe weed, but she didn't smell the distinctly fragrant scent of cannabis. Likely, it was something harder, meth, or maybe cocaine. From the look of the attendant, she guessed it was meth.

She asked him with a sense of urgency, "I need to see a recording from your surveillance cameras. You have a system above the pumps, yes?"

"What's it to you? What are you, a cop or somethin'?" The attitude stretched across his face, his oily skin in that phase of pubescent growth, prior to manhood. Probably contributed to by a poor diet. Whatever drugs he was selling, and most likely using, also contributed to its ruddiness.

"It doesn't matter who I am. I need to see that videotape, now."

"Lady, if you're not the cops, then you got no business tellin' me what to do, 'cause I ain't gonna do it."

Hatch stopped for a second. He had a point. She wasn't law enforcement, but she had been. She knew the lingo. Maybe that's what he picked up from her when she'd first walked in. It wasn't long before the clerk wearing the nametag labeled Jimmy S. seemed to quickly discern that she was, in fact, not actively employed with any law enforcement agency. Her last opportunity for that had disappeared in Hawk's Landing.

Had she been a cop, the badge would have already been on display and would have mitigated any further resistance from the creep. He must have assumed this as well and was now firming his resistance.

"Let's go over this again. I need to see the videotapes of that pump. The one where the SUV just took off from."

"Pump three?" He said with a question mark smirk.

"Yes. Pump number three."

"I'm going to need to see your badge or something, if you--"

"I didn't say I was law enforcement, but I will tell you this: if I don't see that footage in the next thirty seconds, I will call the police," she stated firmly, with a smirk. "And trust me, they're also going to want to see that recording. They will also want a full statement from you and me. And I may be inclined to mention that I watched you come in from the back of your store with a wad of cash, having completed a drug transaction."

"Hey lady, I didn't--" he tried to interrupt.

Hatch dismissed this feeble attempt. "I guarantee you if they bring a canine here…" She let the threat hang in the air. Jimmy made a subconscious glance to a lockbox behind the counter, giving away to her the location of his stash. "Trust me, they're going to find your stash and take your money. You'll lose your job, and you'll be arrested. Or you can turn around, take me to the office or wherever you keep your video surveillance, and pull up the footage of the SUV. It's your choice."

"I don't have to do anything you tell me," he said, defiantly folding his arms. He tucked the exposed cash deeper into his pocket, staring at Hatch with attempted intimidation. It did not work. Hatch smiled back, unnerving the boy further.

"Listen, there's another way this can go down, without phone calls. I could walk back there and pull the tape myself, but I prefer your cooperation."

Jimmy looked towards a closed door near the rear of the store, and then back at Hatch, as if he thought he could stop her from going there.

"You can't do that, lady."

"Or what? You'll call the police? I already told you that was option one. And if you try to stop me, well then, I'm sure I could find another option.

241

But that one is going to leave you hurt. Look, life is full of choices, and I'd say this one matters. So, choose wisely."

She was wearing a short sleeve shirt. Her time in Africa had taught her not to feel the shame of the scars. Hatch was still learning to be comfortable in her own skin. Jimmy now seemed to take notice of the scar tissue trailing down her arm and intertwining with the tattoo there. He was taking Hatch in as if for the first time. And if Hatch's perception was correct, she saw him quiver. The rough exterior of the boy who was attempting to intimidate, fell away completely.

"I don't want any trouble, lady."

"Neither do I. All I want is to see the video."

He was quiet. She could tell he was worn down by the exchange. He must have run the options she provided. None of them registered as ideal, but he would undoubtably seek to find the path of least resistance. Getting beat up by a female or getting turned over to the cops was not high on his priority list.

"Fine, I'll show you the damned tape. But then you get the hell out of my store. Got it?" he asked, trying to offer a backend resistance.

"Absolutely. That is, after you put $25 in pump number four for me."

He looked flustered and angry, but then resigned himself. She laid the cash on the counter. Jimmy moved behind the register and pushed a button, activating the pump.

"Okay. Now the video," she said.

He walked back out from behind the counter and led Hatch toward the closed door with the sign "Manager," affixed to it.

"You know, I could get fired for this," he said, as he opened the door.

"I'm pretty sure you should already be fired," Hatch said.

He entered without any further resistance and plopped himself noisily into the poorly maintained office chair. The curved backing of the black chair was held together by silver duct tape. Three of the four rollers worked as he scooted forward with a loud squeak of the fourth. After a few strokes on the keyboard, he activated the camera system over pump number four. Using a dial knob, he rewound the taped surveillance to the point where the SUV pulled up to a stop.

"Stop there," Hatch said. She watched for a moment. "I need a pen and a piece of paper."

He rummaged the desk's disorganized top and found both. She jotted down the license plate, make and model. "All right, run it."

He ran the tape as Hatch watched carefully. The driver got out and worked the pump. The passenger remained in the seat for a moment, then exited. He unlatched the girl from the back. *She couldn't even undo her seatbelt*, Hatch thought. *What the hell did they give her?* Whatever was wrong with the girl, she was clearly incapacitated.

Hatch watched her as the goateed man guided her into the store. Right before the door opened, he whispered something in her ear. Undoubtedly, it was a threat of some sort.

"Did they buy anything?"

The kid shook his head. "Just the gas. Those two went into the back. She had to use the bathroom."

"He went with her to the bathroom?" Hatch interrupted.

"No. He stood outside though, like he was guarding her. Pretty girl like that, I guess you got to protect 'em." Jimmy offered his musings, to which Hatch paid no attention.

"Did they say anything? Did you hear her talk? Did she try to communicate with you?"

"Not that I noticed," The clerk shrugged.

"And then what?"

"They left. You came in. That's about it."

"Have you seen them in here before? Have you ever seen her? The goateed man? The man at the pump?"

He shook his head. "Never seen them before in my life."

She looked at him before taking one last look at the occupants of the SUV. She took out her flip phone and snapped a photograph of both men and the girl.

"I hope for your sake you never *see me* again," Hatch said to herself, but realized Jimmy must have thought the comment was meant for him. She offered no explanation to make him think the contrary.

She walked out into the sun, filled her tank, and drove off in the same direction as the SUV.

FIREWALK CHAPTER 3

ORDER FIREWALK NOW:
https://www.amazon.com/dp/B08H2HRKVT

Join the LT Ryan reader family & receive a free copy of the Rachel Hatch story, *Fractured*. Click the link below to get started:
https://ltryan.com/rachel-hatch-newsletter-signup-1

ALSO BY L.T. RYAN

Find All of L.T. Ryan's Books on Amazon Today!

The Jack Noble Series

The Recruit (free)

The First Deception (Prequel 1)

Noble Beginnings

A Deadly Distance

Ripple Effect (Bear Logan)

Thin Line

Noble Intentions

When Dead in Greece

Noble Retribution

Noble Betrayal

Never Go Home

Beyond Betrayal (Clarissa Abbot)

Noble Judgment

Never Cry Mercy

Deadline

End Game

Noble Ultimatum

Noble Legend

Noble Revenge

Never Look Back (Coming Soon)

Bear Logan Series

Ripple Effect

Blowback

Take Down

Deep State

Bear & Mandy Logan Series

Close to Home

Under the Surface

The Last Stop

Over the Edge

Between the Lies (Coming Soon)

Rachel Hatch Series

Drift

Downburst

Fever Burn

Smoke Signal

Firewalk

Whitewater

Aftershock

Whirlwind

Tsunami

Fastrope

Sidewinder (Coming Soon)

Mitch Tanner Series

The Depth of Darkness

Into The Darkness

Deliver Us From Darkness

Cassie Quinn Series

Path of Bones

Whisper of Bones

Symphony of Bones

Etched in Shadow

Concealed in Shadow

Betrayed in Shadow

Born from Ashes

Blake Brier Series

Unmasked

Unleashed

Uncharted

Drawpoint

Contrail

Detachment

Clear

Quarry (Coming Soon)

Dalton Savage Series

Savage Grounds

Scorched Earth

Cold Sky

The Frost Killer (Coming Soon)

Maddie Castle Series

The Handler

Tracking Justice

Hunting Grounds (Coming Soon)

Affliction Z Series

Affliction Z: Patient Zero

Affliction Z: Abandoned Hope

Affliction Z: Descended in Blood

Affliction Z : Fractured Part 1

Affliction Z: Fractured Part 2 (Fall 2021)

Love Hatch? Noble? Maddie? Cassie? Get your very own L.T. Ryan merchandise today! Click the link below to find coffee mugs, t-shirts, and even signed copies of your favorite thrillers! https://ltryan.ink/EvG_

Receive a free copy of The Recruit. Visit:

https://ltryan.com/jack-noble-newsletter-signup-1

ABOUT THE AUTHOR

L.T. Ryan is a *USA Today* and international bestselling author. The new age of publishing offered L.T. the opportunity to blend his passions for creating, marketing, and technology to reach audiences with his popular Jack Noble series.

Living in central Virginia with his wife, the youngest of his three daughters, and their three dogs, L.T. enjoys staring out his window at the trees and mountains while he should be writing, as well as reading, hiking, running, and playing with gadgets. See what he's up to at http://ltryan.com.

Social Medial Links:
- Facebook (L.T. Ryan): https://www.facebook.com/LTRyanAuthor
- Facebook (Jack Noble Page): https://www.facebook.com/JackNobleBooks/
- Twitter: https://twitter.com/LTRyanWrites
- Goodreads: http://www.goodreads.com/author/show/6151659.L_T_Ryan